Resurrecting Dylan

Book 2 From the Brothers In All Series

By

Gina Rose

Editors: Sybrina Durant, Rose Zoch and Brian Cross

Resurrecting Dylan

Copyrighted 2014

Paperback ISBN-13: 978-0-9906537-2-1,
ISBN-10: 0-9906537-2-2
Ebook ISBN-13: 978-0-9906537-3-8,
ISBN-10: 0-9906537-3-0
Paperback ISBN-13: 978-1501017988,
ISBN-10: 1501017985

BISAC Codes:

FIC027000   FICTION / Romance / General

FIC027070   FICTION / Romance / Historical / Regency

Contact Sybrina@sybrina.com.

Prologue

1812
Richmond, Virginia
The Office of Hubert Fletcher,
Solicitor of Law

"Well, Miss Melville, that about settles it," Mr.
Fletcher, her father's solicitor said.

Claire looked at him with tears welled in her
eyes and nodded her head in agreement.

"Your ship will leave port with the evening
tide, so if you have no further questions, I will
escort you there," he added.

Her father was gone now; her home had been
sold and all of the slaves had been freed. All of her
father's assets had been liquidated, and the proceeds
sent to the Bank of London to be used as her dowry,
per her father's will. She was to go and live in
London now, with a man she had never met before
in her life, the Marquess of Wentworth, who would
be her guardian until she reached the age of twenty-
one or married, whichever came first. She had no
inclination to marry, and she certainly had no desire
to move to London, but she would be utterly
penniless if she did not.

Her father had not taken into consideration that
she had a life here, one that she had worked hard to
achieve, before consigning her away to a life of
marital bondage across the Atlantic. She wanted to
be an authoress and had worked very hard toward
that end, having only just recently sold her very first
manuscript to a publisher in New York for three

fifty cent pieces. Sure, it wasn't much, but it was a start, and now she was being forced to give it all up and move away where she was expected to find a husband.

Her father had stipulated in his will that she wouldn't get so much as a Tiffin penny if she didn't marry by the age of twenty-one, thereby forcing her to comply to his wishes. He put that addendum in his will when she had refused to marry Barnaby Holcomb two years before, whom her father had personally selected. Why couldn't he have understood that she simply wasn't cut out for marriage? A husband, particularly an Englishman, wouldn't want his wife to earn a living of her own. She learned this the hard way when Barnaby, an Englishman, put his foot down on the issue just two days before their wedding. He told her that no wife of his would embarrass him by behaving in such a manner and that he absolutely forbid her to continue to pursue it. They had a very big row over it, and he had gotten so angry that he stormed out of her father's house.

Needless to say, that had been the end of their betrothal as she would not stand to be stifled in such a way. She was an American, and she had been raised by her mother to believe that anything was possible, even for a woman. Her father had punished her severely of course, but she did not let that dissuade her from what she felt was her true purpose in life. Why should she be forced into subservience to a man when she was perfectly capable of earning her own living? Her father never approved of her ideas, but she had stood firm and defied him and continued to pursue her dream to the point of her own detriment, it now seemed.

Father has had the last word on the matter, postmortem though it was, and she would have to comply or live in abject poverty. She knew she could never do that. She had been raised on a plantation for goodness sakes, where she had personal maids and slaves to tend to her every need or whim, with new clothes, shoes, and baubles whenever the fancy struck her. She knew that she had been spoiled, but there was nothing she could do about it now. She had to have money, particularly if she wanted to continue writing. Parchment and ink were expensive and so was food and shelter.

No, she would simply have to comply or at least give the impression that she was until she could find a way out of this tangle. She would have to figure out a way to gain the use of her dowry without the added burden of a husband. She was a clever girl, and if she applied herself to the problem she was bound to come up with something. Perhaps she could continue with her writing and sell her manuscripts to London publishers and make enough money to support herself. She would figure out a way somehow, but in the meantime, she was at the mercy of her father's final wishes.

"Thank you Mr. Fletcher, you have been most helpful," she said standing up.

Mr. Fletcher offered her his arm and led her to the door. She stepped out into the afternoon sun and took one last longing look at her beloved town. She would probably never see her country again, and the knowledge of it angered her. As he led her to his carriage, she promised herself that whatever lay ahead for her across the Atlantic, the defeat of her dreams was simply not an option.

Chapter One

1812
Mayfair London
The Marquess of Wentworth's home

Dylan Crenshaw, the Earl of Sumersleigh had been summoned by his grandfather to his dying father's home for what, he knew not. He had not seen his father or his grandfather in many months and presently he was in no condition to see anyone. He was in his cups again as he so often was now, and he hadn't bathed or shaved in nearly two weeks, which had become another foul custom of late. This was how life had been for him since that awful night when the girl had been killed a little over a year ago.

Wishy ... sweet, irresistible Wishy had put herself in his path and refused to be denied, causing him to compromise two of his long held principles. The first principle being that he would not dally with a servant, and the other that he would only have sex with virgins. He had become obsessed with the fear of contracting the disease that had killed his brother two years before and determined that only sex with virgins could guarantee that he would not suffer the same fate. He hadn't wanted to take advantage of the young girl, even though she had been so completely willing to give herself to him. Even though he had initially believed she was an innocent and would meet his specifications, he had tried to do the honorable thing and deny the lust that he felt for her. He was an earl and she but a ladies maid, and he felt that it was bad form to indulge his urges with the servant class as he was to one day become a duke and needed to behave with honor.

In his belief that she was an innocent, he shunned her attempts to seduce him by telling her, in very crude terms, exactly what he would do to her if she did not go back to her bed as he had commanded her several times. He told her that he would use her and abandon her after she became fat with his babe and that she would most likely end up a whore in her desperation to feed his unwanted bastard. She had run from him after the things he said, just as he had hoped she would, but, instead of going back to the safety of her room at the Gray Horse Inn, she had fled into the night, and he was forced to give chase where he later found her crying in the stables.

He had felt guilty for what he had said to her and wanted to apologize, but she was upset and they quarreled. After the argument, she resumed her relentless pursuit with a renewed determination, convincing him that she might not be so innocent after all but, instead, a very skilled and cunning light-skirt who had set her sights on him for a little sport. He had been so attracted to her, and it had been so long since he had lain with a woman that he could no longer ignore her advances when she stripped naked before him and began a very artful seduction. In a terrible moment of weakness, he succumbed to her ploys, ravaging her with a brute savagery that quite stunned them both.

It was then that he heard her cries of pain as he

angrily ripped through the barrier of her innocence. Then, the ugly truth of what he had actually done shone bright to mock him and everything he had previously stood for. He was then angered anew and told her that he wouldn't marry her and that she had miscalculated if she thought to trap him into it. He told her to get dressed then stormed out of the stables because he couldn't bear to look upon her another moment. While waiting for her to finish dressing, he had wrestled with his conscience, deciding that maybe he could marry her after all and that it would really be the only honorable thing to do after what he had done. He had decided that on the following morning, he would ask her to marry him, but he never got the chance as she died moments after their tryst.

They had been set upon by a couple of ruffians who had been hired by Diana Habersham in an attempt to kidnap Alyssa, her cousin, to keep her from marrying her fiancé, Gabriel Hawkins, the Duke of Windhaven. The ruffians accosted them just outside the stables, knocking him unconscious and then sending Wishy inside to tell Alyssa that her friend had come with a message. She did as she was bid as they had no doubt used the threat of more violence against him, and she had cared enough to try and protect him from further harm. Wishy panicked when they grabbed Alyssa and tried to save her, but she was savagely bludgeoned upon the back of her head, killing her instantly. When Dylan came to and realized that she had been killed, he lost all sense of reasoning, killing the two men while they lay helplessly on the ground after having been rendered unconscious by Gabriel.

Gabriel had met Alyssa in a brothel where she was auctioning her virginity so she could get money to escape her own fiancé, Alistair, who was also Diana's half-brother. Since Gabriel and Dylan were best friends, he had been traveling with them to Gretna Green where Gabriel and Alyssa were to elope, and that was how he had initially encountered Wishy. Gabriel had assigned her to Alyssa as a ladies' maid, and the four of them had stopped at the inn for the night after a long grueling day upon the Great North Road. Dylan wouldn't even have been with them at all, had it not been for the fact that he had met Alistair at the brothel the night of the auction and saw the madness in his eyes and felt that his friend needed to be protected.

Alistair showed up at the brothel with Bow Street in tow, searching frantically for the woman who had been auctioned. He had heard about a woman matching her description, calling herself Audrey Flowers and felt certain that it was Alyssa. Dylan, who sat alone in the card room when he had been approached by Alistair, knew without a shadow of a doubt that she was indeed the woman he sought and decided to intervene. He didn't want any harm to come to his friend or the woman so he misdirected the man, convincing him that she couldn't possibly be the woman he sought, sending him harmlessly away.

Dylan himself had tried very hard but lost the bid for Alyssa that night to the Duke of Yarbrough, but Gabriel, who was a bitter rival of the duke was determined that Yarbrough would not have her as his cruelty was well known. Therefore, he challenged him to a game of twenty-one and won the girl for himself along with twenty thousand pounds.

"Look at what you've become!" his grandfather's voice brought him out of his reverie.

True, Dylan was a mess, but he didn't care. He only wanted to find out what the old man wanted so he could go back to his home where he could wallow in his self-loathing with only his Scotch to keep him company. He shrugged his shoulders in answer, which seemed to further infuriate the old duke. The two men were in his father's library, and he was slouched across the sofa, his grandfather was standing across from him with his rear-end resting upon his father's desk. He had been avoiding a moment such as this for the last year and found that he was becoming more agitated by the minute.

"What has come over you man?" he demanded.

"I'm tired," Dylan answered simply.

"What have you to be tired from? All you do is lie about and drink yourself into a slovenly stupor, day in and day out. Maybe you're tired of that; have you ever consider that?" his grandfather railed at him.

No, he hadn't considered that; it was his intention to drink himself to death so he could put an end to his miserable existence. He was too cowardly to put a pistol to his head and actually pull the trigger to expedite the problem, so instead, he opted to simply waste away.

"I see nothing wrong with the way I choose to spend my spare time," Dylan lamely replied.

The Duke of Blackstone was still a formidable man even at his advanced age of nine and seventy. He was tall and robust for a man of his years, and his silver eyes could leave even the king himself trembling when they were fixed upon him as they were fixed upon Dylan now. Dylan wasn't trembling though; the old man didn't scare him. His grandfather loved him with all of his heart; after all, he had practically raised him. His own father had been struck down eighteen years before in a terrible riding accident that left him paralyzed from the waist down. In the last two years, his father's health had begun to deteriorate, and in the last few months it had begun a rapid decline leaving him quite addled and helpless. He could no longer do even the most simple of tasks for himself and required round the clock attendance by a team of caregivers.

"How can you say that you see nothing wrong with it? Can't you see that you are dying man; is that what you are trying to accomplish?" the old man asked with a sparkle of tears in his eyes.

Dylan refused to answer this as there seemed to be no point in doing so. His clever grandfather had figured things out quite accurately and was determined to save his worthless hide, if only from himself.

"Answer me!" he barked.

"Have you called me here to tell me how worthless I am, or is there actually a point to all of this?" he found himself asking.

He hadn't meant to be so rude, but he was irritated now, and he wanted to go home.

"Aye, there is a point to this. Your father is dying, and you will soon be my only heir. I need you to clean yourself up and start acting as a man of your station should. My God, man, you reek, and I hardly recognize you under all that hair," he told him scornfully.

"You know I never wanted this," he said with bitterness dripping from his voice.

"That is entirely beside the point. What one wants and what one actually gets is not always a matter of choice," he said with stern authority.

Dylan's older brother, David, should have been in this position, but the two siblings had been such wastrels that his brother had contracted the pox from a life of debauchery and died. Dylan had initially counted himself fortunate that he too had not contracted the malady, but lately he had begun to wish that he had died in his place. When his brother died, he took stock of his life and changed his whole outlook, modifying his life and his behavior patterns accordingly, and in so doing had ultimately caused the death of a beautiful young woman.

Had he not been engaged in a battle of wills with his own repressed cock, she would never have fled the taproom of the inn after he so callously ridiculed her, and she would still be alive today. He hadn't even been able to keep her safe while wearing two loaded pistols because he had been caught unawares while dwelling on what he had done to the chit. Subsequently, he had sworn off women altogether and made a concentrated effort to destroy his own life. He didn't deserve to live freely, frolicking with light-skirts or even whores, and he certainly didn't deserve a woman's virtue. He was a scoundrel of the worst order, and he didn't want to ruin any more lives by contaminating them with his association.

Three lives were lost because of him; why should he be entitled to breathe, let alone become a blasted duke with all the privileges that went with it? No, the world would be best served if he simply ceased to exist. Perhaps he should just put a pistol to his head and be done with it. He had tried many times, would never pull the trigger but maybe he should. Surely there was a distant cousin somewhere that would be deserving of the title? His grandfather continued to glare at him as he sat there contemplating suicide. *The old man knows what I'm thinking*, he realized. He made no attempt to compose himself as he wanted the duke to see him for what he really was; a worthless sack of shite.

"I have a task that I need you to perform," he said finally.

"How might a worthless wretch like me, serve such a fine example of humanity as you?" he snarled.

His grandfather took a steadying breath and turned to remove a letter from the desk behind him. He quickly looked it over then tossed it back behind him. He leveled his gaze on Dylan, with a tightening of his jaw before speaking.

"Your father had a friend, Captain Andreas Melville of the Royal Navy, who moved to the

American colonies when he retired from service. He has recently died of a malady of the heart and has left behind a daughter who is eight and ten and has become your father's ward," he told him.

"She is presently in route to England to live with your father until she reaches her majority, and as you know, your father is too ill to take on the responsibility, so I m entrusting the matter to you," he added.

Dylan's mind snapped to attention, and he was suddenly incredulous. Why was the old man doing this to him?

"Why can't you take her in?" he demanded.

"I am an old man, Dylan, and could die at any moment. The girl will need to find a husband and will need to be escorted to balls and parties in order to do so. An old man like myself, simply cannot keep up with such a rigorous schedule. That is why you must take charge of the matter. You are young and virile, and you will be able to see to it that she is well-protected and doesn't end up in the hands of a fortune-hunting blackguard," he explained.

Dylan didn't like the sound of this one little bit. He was hardly in condition to be responsible for his own well-being, let alone a girl of eight and ten.

"Her name is Claire Melville, and she is due to arrive within the next fortnight. I will assign your Aunt Adeline to be her chaperone so that she may live in your home without causing a scandal," he continued.

"Have you gone mad?" Dylan barked out at the old man.

His grandfather stood firm and ignored the insult, glaring at him in return. He could see that the old man was dead serious and that he fully intended his dictate to be followed.

"No, no, no she cannot stay with me; it is out of the question," he said jumping to his feet.

He started pacing frantically back and forth with his mind reeling to figure out a way to extract himself from this situation. There was no way he could have this chit in his home; it was not to be born.

"As I said, she will be staying with you Dylan, and I will brook no refusals on your part. You must step up and take this matter in hand and find the girl a proper husband. She has a very substantial dowry, and from what the solicitor said in the letter, she is very comely as well. You should have little trouble securing a husband for her in what I'm sure, will be a very expedient manner," he insisted with steel in his spine.

He had made the decision, and Dylan's feelings on the matter didn't factor in whatsoever. Well, that was fine with him; he would take the chit and marry her off to the first bugger to show any interest in her, and if he had to sweeten the pot with his own fortune, so be it. He stopped his pacing and looked at his grandfather with his blue eyes hard as ice. His grandfather stared back with his own mercurial glare, and Dylan knew that he was being manipulated by a master.

"I'm glad to see that you have accepted the task like a man. Go home and wallow in your misery if you like, but you better have yourself cleaned up and presentable within a fortnight. I will summon you again when the girl has arrived," he said with calm assurances.

So that was that; he had been defeated by his grandfather without putting up so much as a coherent argument. This was insanity and would likely be the tipping point that would send him headlong to his doom. Didn't the old man know what he was really doing to him? Maybe he did; maybe he thought that by giving him this diversion he could somehow save him from his course of self-destruction. Nothing could save him now; he was already dead.

Chapter Two

Thirteen days later

Claire hated London already; it was cold and raining, and the stench from the streets was utterly ghastly. The carriage rolled through the city, and the rocking motion mixed with the smells made for a nauseous combination, and she felt sure that she was about to lose her breakfast. The man that the marquess had sent to retrieve her was rude, surly and treated her as though he thought she were some kind of a peasant from the backwoods rather than the fine lady she had been raised to be. He would be a handsome man if he didn't look so angry and annoyed, she mused.

He was tall with broad shoulders and had piercing blue eyes. He had long black hair that he kept haphazardly pulled behind his head with a black ribbon, allowing loose strands to escape about his face as though he hadn't had time to fix it properly before being sent to retrieve her. His clothing was disheveled, and he smelled as though he hadn't bathed in weeks, maybe even longer. He had introduced himself as the Earl of Sumersleigh with a begrudging tone that implied that she was beneath his notice let alone good enough to ride in a carriage with him. The man acted as though he absolutely loathed her, and she couldn't fathom the cause for such treatment.

The old lady seemed nice enough, she supposed but she could hardly understand a word she uttered with her strange accent and slurring speech. She reeked of spirits, and it was only ten o'clock in the morning. How on earth could she justify imbibing so early in the day? What was wrong with these people, and were all Londoners so strange? If so, she was certainly in for a miserable time.

Her stomach turned, causing her to gag as they turned down a particularly smelly road. She threw her hand to her mouth in an attempt to hold back her gorge, but it had risen so fast that she was quite unable to prevent the horrible thing that happened next. In reflex to her rising gorge, she flung her head forward and vomited all over her skirt … and the earl's boots. She was barely aware of the sound of revulsion that the earl made as she was still in the throes of the gut-wrenching heaves of her dilemma. Even when she was sure that her stomach was completely empty, she continued to gag and cough, causing her eyes to water profusely from the strain. The carriage came to an abrupt stop, and the earl quickly jumped out shouting a string of oaths such as she had never heard, abandoning her with the old lady to the horrors of her malady. She didn't care; she was still heaving uncontrollably and had little thought for anything else.

The next thing she knew, the carriage lurched forward and they were making a mad dash at breakneck speed through the streets of London, presumably to reach their intended destination with all possible haste. The old lady mumbled incoherently and looked at her as though she were daft before offering her a handkerchief. Like that would be of any real help! She needed to be stripped down to her altogether and dunked in a river; what on earth would a handkerchief be good for? She took the cursed thing from the silly old bat and wiped her eyes then her mouth. She offered it back to the woman, but she shook her head furiously, muttering more gibberish, so she just held onto it. What a revolting development; so much for her grand entrance into England.

During the long crossing of the Atlantic, she had resigned herself to her situation and vowed that she would make the best of it, coming here with all the dignity and grace that she had been taught, but what did she do instead? She vomited all over an earl; the very first one she had the misfortune to meet. She hoped that she would never have to see the cranky man again after such an embarrassing ordeal, but somehow she didn't think she would be so lucky. He must be a close friend of the marquess; why else would he have come?

*****

They were off to a wonderful start; the chit cast up her accounts all over his boots. Lovely! It was just as well that she did because he had been having a hard time keeping his eyes to himself. It was less than he deserved for his lecherous thoughts. The solicitor had been correct; she was indeed a comely piece of baggage with golden tresses and eyes a shade of green that he had never seen before. They were a strange dark shade with specs of gold flecked within the iris that he personally found quite mesmerizing.

Her décolletage had been far too revealing,

allowing a glorious display of her more than generous endowments which were bouncing to and fro with the motion of the carriage. At one point, he thought that she would pop right out of her gown, and the thought prompted an erection for the first time in over a year. He wouldn't exactly call her beautiful in the fashionable norm, but she did have a certain look about her that drew the eye making one want to reach out to explore her assets. She had plenty of curves for exploration; that was indisputable, and with her come-hither lips she would make a very fine bed warmer for some lucky bloke.

Her jaw line was rather square with high cheek bones which were oddly complemented by an up-tilted nose that was sprayed with freckles but other than that she was really quite striking. He shouldn't have trouble finding her a husband; in fact, he was quite sure he would have to beat the contenders back with a very large stick once they saw her large breasts. The sooner he could get her out of his life the better; perhaps he should take her to a modiste and have her make up a bunch of frocks to emphasize the chit's voluptuous bosom just as that one had. It would surely be a motivating element for a potential groom, and perhaps they wouldn't even care about the freckles. He personally didn't mind freckles, but most men of the ton would. Ladies spent fortunes on products to make them fade, and many refused to go out in the sun at all if they were predisposed to have them.

She evidently had no qualms about spending time in

the sun because she was covered with the things. Even her lovely bosom had been sprinkled with freckles and it made him wonder if her … STOP! He shook his head in disgust; this was going to be a bigger problem than he realized. He was already having lustful thoughts about the wench. Maybe if she had cast her accounts up on his lap he wouldn't be having such thoughts; as it was now, he was still uncomfortably aroused. He should dump her on his grandfather's doorstep, vomit and all, with his refusal to spend another moment in her presence. The woman was a menace to what little peace of mind he had left.

Of course he couldn't do that; he would simply have to suffer through. He would just have to put her in the care of Aunt Adeline and make himself as scarce as possible until such times that he was required to escort her to the marriage mart. When he was done with this cursed mission he had been given, he would put an end once and for all to his worthless life, but for now he had a duty to fulfill. The old duke was counting on him and he wouldn't let him down. Dylan looked skyward and let the rain pelt his face as he sat atop the carriage beside the driver. Fortunately, the rain had cleaned his boots fairly well, but they would be ruined nonetheless. He didn't care really as he had several pairs, and since it had been raining today, he had selected an older pair. He barely had time to get himself dressed when the summons came from his grandfather this morning demanding that he arrive with all haste. He managed to get a half-decent shave and scrub his teeth, but he still hadn't bathed.

His grandfather was quite coarse with him when he showed up in such a haphazard state, but his back was against the wall, forcing him to take Dylan as he was in order to have the chit retrieved from the port on time. He instructed him to take the girl straight to his own home, saying that he would join them later for luncheon. He told Dylan that he had better come to the table freshly bathed or there would be dire consequences. Dylan didn't want to have luncheon with either of them, especially the girl, but he knew that he couldn't wriggle out of it.

Perhaps the chit was too sick to dine; that would serve his purposes quite nicely. His grandfather surely couldn't hold him responsible for the girl's condition ... the girl's condition? Could she be with child? That would certainly explain the haste in which she was to secure a husband, her very large bosom and the nausea in the carriage this morning. Great! He was saddled with an unwed pregnant woman whom he was expected to trick some poor unsuspecting slob into marrying. He sighed deeply and pulled his coat about his neck in an effort to stave off the cold.

*****

Claire had never been treated so shabbily in her entire life; she simply couldn't believe the situation she now found herself in. When they arrived at their destination, she had been quickly whisked away to a bedroom then told to strip down and await the attendance of a maid. The earl had barked out the order to the crotchety old butler before storming off, grumbling another foul string of oaths in his wake to God knows where. The butler, Mr. Simmons, she believed that was his name, took one look at her and made a sound of revulsion before shooing her forward in the direction of the stairs with one hand while he held his nose with the other. He trailed several feet behind her until they reached the landing; then he rushed ahead of her, quickly throwing open the bedroom door where he practically shoved her in while barking his command that she strip down. It was most humiliating, but she supposed that she really did reek and was in desperate need of a maid's attention.

Moments later the maid had arrived, but she still hadn't undressed as she didn't like the idea of standing naked in a strange room inside a strange house with strange people who seemed so completely hateful. She felt vulnerable enough as it was and adding nudity to it would be completely overwhelming. The maid looked at her, clucking her tongue before rushing up to her, spinning her around by the shoulders as if she were a rag-doll to undo the buttons on her gown.

"There ye go love! Step out of that gown, and I'll 'ave it sent to be cleaned," she told her.

Claire did as she was told with a degree of relief as the maid at least seemed friendly. She didn't have nearly as much trouble understanding the maid as she had the old woman in the carriage and was quite relieved. She was a plump, middle-aged woman with stark red hair and friendly blue eyes, she seemed very efficient.

"Now love, go and stand be'ind the privacy screen and I'll a've the tub and 'ot water brought in. Yer trunk is already 'ere, outside the door so I'll 'ave that brought in as well,"

"Thank you so much Miss … I'm sorry, I didn't catch your name," Claire said.

The woman giggled and said, "My name is Lucy, and I've been sent from the old duke's residence to take care of ye until ye find a 'usband," she told her.

"Who is the old duke?" Claire asked a little perplexed.

"Why, the old duke is the earl's grandfather," she said.

"Are they friends of the marquess?" she asked, still very confused.

"The marquess?" Lucy asked, now looking just as perplexed as she was.

"The Marquess of Wentworth," she clarified.

"Oh, that'd be the old duke's son," she explained.

Something wasn't making sense here, and Claire felt more confused than ever. She would never figure out all of these titles or who was who.

"I am the Marquess of Wentworth's ward, and I have been sent here from America by my father's will until I reach the age of twenty-one or I marry, whichever comes first," she told her in an attempt to extract more information from the friendly maid.

"Oh love, 'asn't anyone told ye?" she asked.

"Told me what?"

"The marquess is dyin' and the old duke 'as

given ye over to the earl in 'is stead," she told her with sympathy in her voice.

"What?" she demanded.

"Per'aps I've said too much," Lucy said with a nervous look in her eyes.

"Are you telling me that I am now the ward of that hateful man that I arrived here with?" she persisted.

"If you be talkin' 'bout the earl, then aye. 'E's the son of the marquess and this be 'is 'ome," she told her.

Claire's mind was spinning with all that she had just been told. She had been given over to that hateful man instead of her father's friend, and he was now responsible for her; this was too terrible to believe.

"Come love, go stand be'ind the screen now afore ye catch yer death," Lucy told her.

Claire let herself be led over there without a fuss as she was in a state of shock. How could this be happening to her? A moment later she could hear the hustle and bustle of activity as the servants fixed her bath. She realized that she was trembling, though not from a chill. She was scared; more frightened than she had ever been in her entire life. She felt as though she were in the midst of some strange nightmare from which she couldn't wake, she was quickly falling into despair. Her father wouldn't have sent her to such a fate had he known that the marquess was dying. Perhaps she could write to her solicitor and petition to have herself emancipated in lieu of these developments. The thought cheered her, but she quickly despaired again as it would take months to hear back from her solicitor, which meant that she would have to endure this madness for that long before she learned if it were even possible.

She was jerked out of her fretting and nearly jumped out of her skin when Lucy popped her head around the screen.

"Come love, let's strip off the rest of those garments and get ye in a nice 'ot bath. Everything will be better after ye've 'ad a bath and put on fresh clothes," she said with sunshine dripping from her lips.

Claire stepped out from behind the privacy screen and allowed Lucy to finish undressing her, after which she quickly hopped in the tub sinking down into the warm water. It really did feel divine, but the pleasure of it was tempered with the knowledge that she was stuck in this terrible situation with no way out. Lucy went right to work scrubbing her body and working up a good lather. She took the pins out of her hair and commenced to scrub her head too. It felt nice to be tended to once again after so many weeks on the ship where she shared a small cabin with another woman and basically had to fend for herself.

She was quickly lost in thought, trying to seek a resolution to her problem, when it occurred to her that perhaps she could speak to a London solicitor to achieve her ends. Yes, that's what she would do; she would seek out a solicitor tomorrow and see what could be done. Maybe she could enlist the aid of the cranky earl as he clearly was just as unhappy with the situation as she was; why, he should jump at the chance to be rid of her. The thought cheered her, and she eagerly looked forward to speaking with him as soon as possible about the matter.

Chapter Three

Claire was led to the drawing room by Lucy so she could await luncheon. She was told that the duke was here so she hoped that she could get some information out of him to better explain the situation she now found herself in. She wasn't at all happy with the idea that she could be shifted from pillar to post without so much as being asked her opinion of it. From what she had seen so far, these English were rather rude, and if it weren't for Lucy, she would cast the whole lot of them into the rubbish bin.

When she entered the drawing room, she was greeted by an old man who was presumably the duke, and of course, the old woman from the carriage; perhaps she was his wife. They were all smiles when they saw her, causing her to stumble and nearly fall. She hadn't been expecting anything even remotely similar to kindness, and she was quite surprised by it.

"Ah, there you are my dear; please come in and let us have a look at you," the man said with a wide grin and a twinkle in his eye.

She cautiously approached, quickly looking around, and was relieved that the cranky earl wasn't here; she could do quite fine without seeing him for the moment. When she stood before the man she curtsied, and he clapped his hands in approval.

"Yes indeed, you are delightful, just as my dear sister told me you were," he said beaming.

His dear sister; was that who the old woman was? Now that she took a closer look she could see the resemblance.

"Allow me to introduce myself; I am Tristan Crenshaw, Duke of Blackstone, and this is my sister Adeline Crenshaw," he told her.

"How do you do?" she said bobbing her head in greeting.

"We are top of the clouds my dear, and very happy to have you here, I might add," he said jovially.

"It has been quite an adventure getting here, I must say," Claire allowed.

"Yes, the Atlantic crossing is always an adventure. I hope you were spared any mishaps; please have a seat," he said, indicating that she should take the spot on the sofa beside his sister.

Claire took her seat beside Adeline, and the duke then took his seat across from them, looking at her expectantly, prompting her to remember that he had actually invited discussion about her journey.

"It was quite remarkable as we went through a couple of rather nasty gales. At one point, I was sure the ship would be tossed upside down, and I would have to swim the rest of the way here," she told them.

The duke laughed, and Adeline clapped her hands in appreciation of her banter. She could feel the tension leaving her shoulders now and was actually starting to enjoy herself.

"I'm delighted that you didn't have to exert yourself so, as I'm sure it would have been exhausting," he said playfully.

Adeline giggled then mumbled something incoherently. Apparently she was putting her two cents in on the issue. It would take some getting used to before she could train her ears to understand the poor old thing. Claire smiled and decided that she liked these two people very much.

"I'm glad that you got here when you did as I believe our two countries are on the verge of war. Things are not looking too good, and you will be much safer here than there," he told her on a more somber note.

"Yes, the captain was concerned that we could have been accosted by a British ship, but we had no trouble on that score," she assured him.

"That is excellent indeed. Well, now that we have gotten the greetings behind us, let us move on. I'm sure you must have some questions about how you came to be with my grandson rather than his father, so allow me to fill you in on what has occurred," he told her.

"Your father sent word to us several months ago that he was ill, and he wanted to be sure that my son was still inclined to receive you, should there be a need. He, of course, sent word back that he was, but sadly, very shortly thereafter, he had a decline in his own health that has rendered him … nearly void.

"I had no idea at the time, of course, that he had exchanged correspondence with your father, making preparations for your impending arrival, or I would have contacted him to alert him of the developments here."

"We received word of your arrival a fortnight ago and needless to say that it was too late to send word to inform your solicitor of the situation. So, as head of the family I have taken it upon myself to appoint my grandson, your legal guardian, and my sister Adeline will be chaperone until such time as you find a husband or turn one and twenty,"

He drew breath to continue, but Claire held her finger up to stop him.

"About that … I would like to see what can be done to have myself emancipated and be able to claim my dowry without having to marry," she told him.

The duke's eyes widened, and he looked at her as though she were speaking a foreign language.

"My dear, I don't know if such a thing is possible," he told her after he gained his composure.

"It may not be, but I should like to speak to a solicitor about it as I really don't like the idea of having to have a guardian, nor do I want to be married. I am an authoress you see, and I have no desire to give that up because a husband might not allow it," she barreled on.

The duke smiled sadly at her, nodding his head that he understood her desires, but the words that followed were not exactly what she would have expected.

"I was hoping that I could intrigue you to marry my grandson, but I can see now that the idea is futile," he said solemnly.

Claire was speechless; why on earth would he have hoped such a thing. The man was a barbarian, and she would never agree to marry one such as him.

"I'm sorry sir, but your grandson has been quite rude to me, and I simply would have no interest in him," she told him as kindly as she could.

"He has not been himself for quite some time, I'm afraid. He is usually quite pleasant, but for the last year he has been brooding his life away, and I am getting desperate to find a way to pull him out of it. After his father dies, which sadly will be sooner rather than later, he will be my one and only heir."

"I had hoped that you might be the answer; forgive me for my irrational hopes. Tis why I sent you to him in the first place; of course, he has no knowledge of it, so just put it out of your mind dear, and it will be as though we never discussed it," he told her.

"I don't think he is very happy at all by my presence sir, so perhaps I should go to your home," she suggested with a twinge of hope in her tone.

"Forgive me dear, but I would prefer that you stay here regardless as you still may be able to pull him out of his depression. Whether you would consider him for marriage or not, perhaps you could befriend him and in so doing inspire him to want to live again," he said with tears in his eyes.

The duke looked so genuinely sad that she felt a little guilty now for having rejected the idea so completely. But then again, she was a stranger to them and was being rather presumptuous to assume that she would be able to make a difference one way or the other. This whole situation was very strange, actually.

"Perhaps we can see how it goes for a week or two, but I can tell you now sir that I believe he hates me. There was an incident in the carriage that I'm sure will forever taint his opinion of me," she said with a blush.

"Aye, my sister told me of it. It is quite regrettable, but I still believe that a woman as lovely as you might just be the thing my grandson needs to wake up and rejoin the world."

Adeline mumbled something and the duke agreed with her. Of course, Claire didn't catch a word of it.

"My sister said that two weeks should be plenty of time to tell if he is improving and that if things do not improve, you can come and live with her; I have agreed," he said translating the exchange.

Claire was stunned that the old woman had actually said all that and that he even understood her. But the idea sounded feasible to her; she could give up a couple of weeks to the cause of aiding a man with his depression, she supposed. She was a Christian after all, perhaps this was the whole purpose for her being here; a calling of sorts. Of course, if she played her cards right, she might actually get what she wanted out of this situation; her freedom and her dowry.

"If I agree to this, will you help me with my emancipation and obtaining my dowry?" she asked.

The duke looked at her with a strange look in his eyes that lasted for a couple of seconds before his mouth twisted into a mischievous grin. She wasn't at all sure that was a good thing, but his words were pleasing, nonetheless.

"Absolutely my dear, but let us make it four weeks; shall we?" he suggested.

"You drive a hard bargain sir, but I will give you four weeks if freedom and my money await me on the other side," she told him.

"Excellent!" he said.

"Of course, you are not to speak a word of this to anyone or the deal is off," he shrewdly added.

"Of course," she agreed.

Just then the drawing room door opened, and a very handsome gentleman entered.

"Ah Dylan, I see you have decided to join us after all," the duke said.

Dylan grumbled as he advanced into the room, taking up position at the fireplace mantle which allowed her a better view of the man. It was then that she realized that Dylan was in fact, the cranky earl. He must have had a bath and fixed his hair because she hardly recognized him as the same man. He was still cranky of course, but he looked and smelled ten times better. He was dressed in tan trousers with a dark blue superfine waistcoat, and his cravat was an absolute work of art; the man was absolutely breathtaking. His eyes were so blue, like the sky on a cloudless day in springtime, and his facial features must have been chiseled by God himself, in the image of Adonis.

Her heart skipped a beat when he trained his eyes on her for a brief moment allowing her to see the tortured man that he really was. He looked so angry as though the world and everything in it completely disgusted him. Or maybe it was something else. Maybe he hated himself; maybe that's why he acted the way he did. Something terrible must have happened to the poor man to make him so miserable. She could see now that she had been set a very difficult task, but if this were the price for freedom then she would give it her all. In a month's time, she would be free to live as she chose and would have enough money to pursue her dreams too. She looked back at the duke to see that he was studying her closely. She felt a little nervous from his inspection but managed a trembling smile. He answered her with a nod of approval and then the moment was broken when the butler announced that luncheon was served.

*****

Luncheon was going along rather sedately until Dylan decided he'd had enough of the pretenses. His grandfather was fawning over the chit like she was some kind of gift from God, and even Aunt Adeline seemed besotted with her. Was everyone here blind but him? Could they not see that she was a trollop? Why just look at the way she was dressed for crying out loud; her bosom was practically falling out of that gown. He sighed with absolute disgust and threw his napkin on the table. Everyone turned their attention to him then as though he were imposing on them somehow. It was his house; they were the ones imposing on him.

"Shall we talk about the wedding?" he said.

"What wedding?" the duke asked.

"Hers," he practically spat the word.

"I believe we have to find her a husband first,"

his grandfather quipped.

"Yes, yes and it would seem that we may be on a much tighter schedule than we first thought," he said smugly.

"I'm not sure I follow you," his grandfather said, genuinely perplexed.

"Just look at that gown! I'm sure that it has not escaped your notice that she is rather … shall we say … wanton and that just this morning she was overcome with nausea for which Aunt Adeline can attest. Clearly the chit has a bun in the oven, and we need to make haste in our choice of unsuspecting victim for our parson's trap," he said with barely contained hostility.

The duke turned red and started coughing; Adeline started grumbling incoherently and Claire … well, she gasped then stood up so quickly that she toppled over her chair. She strode with calm, cool calculation around the table and upon reaching him she reared back and punched him squarely in the nose, sending him toppling over backwards onto the floor.

"How dare you say such a thing about me sir! I did not get sick because I am breeding sir; I got sick because you and the rest of this cursed place stank to high heaven, and I simply couldn't abide the stench another moment," she shouted as she stood over him waggling her finger in his face.

He quickly sat up, checking to see if his nose was bleeding, and much to his relief, it wasn't. He stood up then and towered over her and was sorely tempted to wring her impudent little neck.

"I'm sure I only speak the truth," was his crass

retort.

She kicked him in the shin then, and when he bent over to rub the spot, she grabbed him by the ears and rammed his face into her knee before slapping him in the back of his head for good measure.

"I tell you again sir that I am not breeding, and if you say so again I will cut out your tongue and feed it to you for lunch," she barked.

He straightened up from the stinging assault, wincing when he saw the look of fire shooting from her unusual eyes. He had made a mistake and insulted the woman's integrity; he could see that now, but he would be damned before he apologized to the brazen chit.

"The term is 'my lord'," he said with a snarl.

"What?" she demanded furiously.

Her eyes were blinking rapidly as if she couldn't understand his words, and the picture she made was quite comical. Had the situation been different he would be doubled over with laughter, but he could tell that wouldn't be wise as she looked ready for a fight.

"You are to call me 'my lord' and you are to call my grandfather 'your grace'," he told her sarcastically.

The woman growled … she actually growled, and the strain of the sound caused her to turn a deep shade of red as she stood there with her hands balled into tight little fists. She was clearly incensed and working herself up to give him another thrashing, so he backed up to put some distance between him and the deranged hellcat from the colonies.

"There is only one Lord and you sir are nowhere near such perfection. I will call no man lord, and if you don't like it, you can kiss my ..."

"That is quite enough," a female voice commanded.

The chit had clearly been shocked by Aunt Adeline's intervention when she snapped her head around to look at her in complete surprise. She darted her eyes back and forth between Aunt Adeline and his grandfather then finally settled her dagger-laced gaze back on him. Her face and her lovely bosom were flushed with rosy blush, and her eyes were shimmering with unshed tears of anger; she was really quite remarkable. She was quite beautiful standing there all riled up and reminded him of Boudicca, ready to do battle for her principles; the only thing missing to complete the picture was a sword and shield. He shook off the unwanted thoughts about Boudicca and bosoms then straightened his spine and continued to school her in the proper way to address him.

"You are in England now, and we have a custom here that requires you to address members of the aristocracy with the reverence due them according to their rank. I am an earl ... therefore, you should address me as 'my lord' and you will address my grandfather as 'your grace'. A knight is addressed as 'sir'; not an earl and certainly not a duke," he said with finality, then promptly turned on his heel and left the room.

He had to get away from her and fast. He had never been so angry, offended, entertained and sexually aroused as he was now. The chit was alluring, maddening even, and if he wasn't careful, she was going to drive him insane with angry lust. *My God, so far she has cast up her accounts on my boots and tried to thrash me within an inch of my life, and it's just barely afternoon; what's next with this vixen?* He stormed to his library slamming the door behind him and went to the sideboard, grabbing a bottle of Scotch. He pulled the cork out with his teeth, spit it across the room and started guzzling the precious liquid straight from the bottle. He carried the bottle over to the sofa and plopped down on it, taking another satisfying drag. He held out his hand and saw that it was trembling as this was the first drink he'd had since last night. He needed this drink before he committed some unspeakable deed; the woman was a menace.

*****

The duke was a happy man; he had made the right decision with respect to the girl. She was exactly what his grandson needed, and by God, if she hadn't actually kicked his arse. He had it coming of course, insulting her, the way he that he did.

"Bravo!" he said, clapping his hands after his grandson stormed out of the room.

"Excuse me?" she said in confusion.

"That was excellent my dear. Keep up the good work, and for the record, I'm not so stuffy that I need to be called 'your grace' all the time. Perhaps you could just do it when we are in mixed company so as not to cause people to accuse you of being ill-mannered. In private you may call me sir or even

Mr. Crenshaw if you prefer; I really don't mind," he said with a wink.

"Thank you sir, I appreciate that. We Americans are not burdened with the same customs as you, and I fear that it will take me some time to adjust," she told him.

"You are doing fine my love, and might I say that you are quite a little pugilist," he said grinning.

The girl blushed beautifully and averted her very unique eyes.

"I have never been so insulted in all my life. I acted without thinking, I'm afraid," she said with eyes cast down.

"I would say that you certainly got his attention. He is no doubt in his library right now pouring Scotch down his gullet, thinking about what an arse he is."

She looked up at him then, and she was smiling.

"Do you really think so?" she asked with hope in her eyes.

"I know my grandson, and I know how he thinks. I guarantee that you are first and foremost on his mind at this very moment."

Chapter Four

Claire hadn't seen Dylan the rest of the day after the horrible scene at luncheon. It was just as well because she was embarrassed by her unladylike display of violence and wasn't sure she would be able to look at him again. She just needed to bide her time, avoid him as much as possible so she could get her money and her freedom. Never in her life had she demonstrated such behavior, but the man had provoked her beyond all reason when he implied that she was an immoral woman. And just what was wrong with her gown? She had many gowns with much lower decolletages than that one, and no one had ever insulted her when she wore them. Why, the one she had been wearing barely showed any cleavage at all, and in her minds-eye, was quite modest.

Perhaps things were different here, and women kept their assets more modestly covered. She didn't think so as she had kept up with all the current fashions, and many of her gowns were designs from France, which were popular in England too. Perhaps he was just very prudish and thought a woman should be wrapped up to her chin. True enough, she should have been dressed a little more warmly. The weather was cold and dank here, so she could probably benefit from going to a modiste and having some more gowns made that would be more suitable for England's climate.

When she had left Virginia, the spring weather had been quite pleasant, and the gowns that she had worn today were perfectly suited for that. Sure, it got rather cold in Virginia too, but the wet chill here seemed to penetrate much deeper, into one's bones. She had been a little chilled in the carriage and could have used a warmer wrap, she would have to admit, but she hardly felt that she had been indecent then or at luncheon either. She simply couldn't account for the man's irrational cruelty toward her except to say that he was simply a cruel man.

The duke said that he was usually quite pleasant, but she just couldn't see how that was possible given the way he treated her from the moment he first laid eyes on her. He was surly and brutish, and he had formed opinions about her morality that were completely unfounded. She had always regarded herself as a decent woman with a good set of moral principles. Sure, she bucked against social convention from time to time, but overall she would never allow herself to cast morality aside and compromise herself as he had implied.

Why, she had never even been kissed, even when she had been engaged to Barnaby. She knew all about what went on between a man and a woman with regard to sexual relations. The slaves on Melville Plantation had been quite open with their carnal impulses, and she had witnessed several shocking things as a result, but she was a lady and would never stoop to such behavior outside of marriage; it just simply wasn't done. One had to be forever mindful of their reputation lest they be labeled a woman of loose morals. Well, there was really no point in dwelling on the matter further; she had done all that she should and more to correct his crude assumptions. She would just have to avoid him as much as possible to ensure that such an occurrence never happened again.

It was late, and she was unable to shut her mind off long enough to fall asleep, and she wished that she had something new to read. She had already read the books that she had brought with her, and she wasn't in the mood to write on her manuscript. Perhaps she could slip down to the library now that the household was asleep and get something from there. Yes, that's what she would do; surely the brute wouldn't begrudge her a little reading material. She sat up swinging her legs off the side of the bed, put on her slippers and grabbed her wrap and the bedside lamp. It was unlikely that she would encounter anyone, so she wasn't too concerned about her state of undress. She was well-covered in any event.

She made her way down the stairs, stopping near the bottom to listen for sounds indicating movement or activity. When she heard nothing but silence, she proceeded into the foyer and set about searching for the library. She was sure there had to be one as the duke had indicated as much. She tiptoed quietly down the hall that she thought looked promising and tried a few door knobs along the way. After four tries, she located the room and peered inside the darkness to confirm that no one was there and entered. She quietly closed the door behind her and moved over to the desk in the center of the room. She looked around and noticed a sofa that looked rather worn and smashed as though someone spent a lot of time sleeping on it. It was very unsightly actually; then again this was a man's home, and he probably didn't care about such things.

She cast the thought aside as she spotted the bookshelves behind the sofa. There weren't a lot of books there, but perhaps she could find something of interest. She quietly moved forward, but when she rounded the sofa, her foot bumped up against something solid and heavy. A bit startled, she looked down, shining the lamp on the thing and gasped when she saw that it was Dylan; he appeared to be sleeping flat on his back upon the floor. There was an empty bottle of some kind of spirits overturned beside his head, and he was naked from the waist up.

She looked him over more thoroughly and realized that his trousers were unbuttoned, and he wasn't wearing any shoes or stockings. She held up the lamp so she could expand the radius of light and saw his clothing heaped in a corner behind his head, and his boots had been tossed all the way across the room. She couldn't leave him here like this, could she? At the very least, she should cover him with a blanket. She looked around and couldn't find anything to serve, so she walked over to the heap of clothes and picked up his coat; it would have to do. At least he wouldn't take a chill.

The poor man must have been in here all this time and had drunk himself into oblivion. What could cause such misery for such a young man to make him do this to himself? She set the lamp down on a small table beside the sofa and moved closer to him so she could spread his coat across him. Kneeling down, she very carefully placed it upon him so as not to disturb him. With the task done, she sat back on her heels and looked at him for a moment; he seemed so peaceful in his sleep. His hard, angry features had softened making him appear almost angelic and very handsome.

She knew better of course and wasn't fooled, but she couldn't help but feel a bit of pity for him with regret for the loss of the man he used to be. She continued her perusal for another moment then decided she would just leave him there to sleep it off. No doubt, this was a regular occurrence, and he would probably wake during the night and go on to his room; at least she hoped he would. It couldn't be very good for his back sleeping on the hard, cold floor.

She put her hand on the floor to lift herself up when suddenly her wrist was gripped hard, and she was pulled forward onto his chest. They were nose to nose, and his piercing blue eyes were trained on hers, causing a jolt of fear to course up her spine. She quickly began to struggle to free herself, but he grabbed her more securely about the waist, and she was quite helpless to move.

"Ah, so you are wanton after all," he rasped out.

"How dare you sir!" she growled as she renewed her struggle to get free.

He reached up, grabbing her face in between both of his hands and pulled her head forward, placing his lips on hers in a forceful kiss that was foul with spirits. She was stunned momentarily and froze, which allowed him to thrust his tongue into her mouth. The action made her jerk her head back, enabling her to free herself, but when she tried to get up, he grabbed her once again and brought her back down upon him.

"Unhand me you … you brute!" she shouted as she squirmed.

"What's your hurry?" he slurred. "Didn't you come here for a little sport with the earl?" he chided.

She managed to free her arm, and she slapped him hard across the face. He released her then, allowing her to jump up and start running toward the door. Just as she reached it, she was slammed hard up against it and found herself pressed between him and the door.

"Always trying to hurt me; I'm starting to think that maybe you like to play a little rough," he purred in her ear from behind.

She couldn't move as she was scared that he was about to force himself on her. She didn't think it would be wise to try to fight him further as it seemed to excite him all the more. She decided that she would simply become unresponsive in the hope that he would grow bored and release her. It seemed like the only thing that could possibly save her now. His hands started moving over her sides, feeling her every curve, but when he reached her rear-end, he rested his hand there and began to gather up the hem of her nightgown with his other hand. She whimpered in fear when his hands touched her bare bottom.

"So soft and smooth," he whispered in her ear as he caressed her.

When she didn't respond, he quickly stepped back, turning her around so that she was facing him now, but she was still pinned and couldn't get away. He pressed his pelvic into her stomach, and she could tell that he was aroused, but she still prayed that he would soon lose interest as she gave him no indicators that she would be responsive to his assault. He still hadn't seemed to notice, however, and began to untie her nightgown. She turned her head to the side and refused to look at him as he began to fondle her breasts, which he had exposed to his view. He groaned and placed his lips on her neck, kissing her ever so gently upon her jugular. He stayed with his mouth on her pulse a moment and his breath heated up her neck making her shiver. Then, after what seemed like forever, he very abruptly shoved away from her and spun around, walking away.

"Get out!" he shouted over his shoulder.

She didn't have to be told twice; she quickly opened the door, running as fast as she could until she reached the stairs where she practically flew all the way to the top. She ran down the hall quickly finding her room and dashed inside, slamming the door behind her. Once she was safely in her room, she leaned her back against the door trying to compose herself. Her chest was heaving up and down as she gasped for breath, so she closed her eyes in the darkness to shut out the vision of what had just occurred, to no avail.

He had spared her just like she had prayed he might; but why? He could have taken her right there against the door, but he showed mercy and allowed her to escape unharmed. He was drunk and should have been beyond reason, but he had somehow found a scrap of humanity within himself and allowed her to escape. Perhaps he had just wanted to scare her, but to what end? Whatever the reason, she was relieved, but more convinced than ever that she should give him a wide berth. If she had any sense at all, she would leave this place as fast as she could but then what? She would lose everything; she simply couldn't do that.

Maybe she should tell the duke of this, then he would see that it wasn't safe for her to stay here to help him with his grandson. The man was beyond all hope and had clearly chosen this path of self-destruction, so there was certainly nothing she could do to stop it. But would the duke refuse to help her then? She wasn't sure, but she suspected that he would. No, she would simply have to dig in and see this thing through. It was only a month, and one day was already gone; surely she could manage it. She would just stay busy with her writing to help pass away the time, and before she knew, it would be over, then she could leave this place and that cursed man behind with her freedom and her money. She was not so easily defeated as to throw in the towel after only one day. She was an American, made of sterner stuff.

*****

Dylan had known the moment she entered the room.

He had just lain down with the purpose of taking himself in hand, so he could get the relief that would allow him to sleep. He had been thinking about the insufferable woman all day and hadn't been able to stifle the painful erection that he had off and on throughout the day and night. No matter how much Scotch he consumed, he couldn't put thoughts of her out of his mind. One moment he felt guilty for what he had said at luncheon, and the next he was completely aroused by the ferocity that she had shown in defense of her own honor. He didn't want to have these thoughts about her because he was a dirty rotten scoundrel, and she was a lady of refined character; certainly more deserving than of a lecherous lout like him. He had to get her out of his system somehow, and he thought that if he gratified himself with thoughts of her, he could purge her from his mind for good.

That's when he heard her enter and he recognized her scent. His senses had been so tuned to her that he recognized the faint scent of jasmine and citrus, then when she closed the door, her essence wafted in the air, and he knew that she had come. He decided to pretend to be asleep so she would go away, but she had taken pity on his miserable carcass and thought to provide him with comfort and warmth. He was overcome by the kindness behind the action but didn't feel that he was deserving of it. That's when he knew what he had to do; he had to offend her again to show her that he was despicable and not worth her kindness. He had only meant to scare her, but when she struggled against him he became incredibly aroused and lost all sense of reasoning. He would have taken her against the door like an animal had she not turned her head away in disgust. He was relieved by that action as it prevented him from truly becoming the monster that he knew he was.

He should just go and get a whore so he was no longer so sexually repressed. He hadn't been with a woman since he had been with Wishy, and if he didn't get relief soon, he feared that he would do something stupid and irreversible to the girl. He didn't want a whore though; he wasn't even deserving of that. No woman deserved to have to endure him rutting about between their legs. He went and sat at his desk and unlocked the drawer where he stored his pistols. It was an almost nightly routine now that he would take them out and wrestle with thoughts of suicide. He lovingly caressed one and then the other before deciding that it would be Hank this night; Lester had the honor last night. He had named his two dueling pistols Lester and Hank and hadn't yet decided which one he would actually use to take his life, so he went through this ritual of selecting each night.

He sat back in the chair and held Hank in his hands and contemplated his life as he always did, but tonight he had the added agony of the girl to consider. She was the first woman he had really been around since that night a year ago and he had fully believed that he no longer had carnal desires; that he had somehow become immune to the fairer sex. Then she came into his life and threw him into lustful savagery and now he feared that he would harm her as he had Wishy. He never again wanted to allow himself to lose control as he had with her. He should be able to master his own wants and urges, but clearly he could not. He put the pistol to his head and closed his eyes; it would be so easy just to end it all here and now. He cocked the pistol and relaxed his shoulders; he could do this.

He thought about his brother then and fondly remembered all the times they had shared together. He missed his brother and his mother too. She had died when he was a young lad of only six, but he remembered her well. His mother had adored him and doted on him endlessly. David had been his father's favorite, but he never once doubted the love his mother had for him. He could see her plain as day smiling at him now, and he wanted to go to her. His grandfather's face came into view then, and he was looking sternly at him with disapproval in his eyes, but there was something else there too. Love was there in those silver eyes, and it was a love for him. He didn't deserve that love, but it was there nonetheless, and it wouldn't be denied. What would the old man do when he learned that he had taken his own life?

The thought gave Dylan pause as it always did. He couldn't do it to the old man; he just couldn't. He took the gun away from his head and carefully uncocked it. He laid it inside the drawer on top of the suicide note he had written long ago where it would be found to tell the world what a foul human being he really was. He put Lester in beside him and closed and locked the drawer then began to weep at his cowardice.

Resurrecting Dylan

Chapter Five

Claire and Adeline sat in the drawing room as had
become their custom over the last few days. Claire
would sit at the desk and work on her new
manuscript, and Adeline would sleep the day away
in her chair. Adeline was a nice lady, but she still
couldn't understand a word she said although they
had somehow managed to befriend one another and
quite enjoyed one another's company. Claire
wished that the lady didn't imbibe quite so heavily,
but she wasn't about to chastise a woman of her
advanced years about the sins of drinking spirits.

Three days had passed since that awful night in
the library, and Claire hadn't even seen a trace of
Dylan. She was relieved, she supposed, but his
absence was a little unsettling. How was she
supposed to help him when she didn't even know
for certain that he was in the house? She had
thought about what had occurred since that night,
and despite it all, her heart reached out to him and
she knew that he was a man crying out for help. He
had wanted to scare her away from him, she could
see that clearly now, but she was not so easily
cowed. She had made a deal with the duke, and she
fully intended to see her part of the bargain through.
It was her Christian duty to help this man if she
could, and she would not shun the task. True, she
hadn't been to church in several years, since her
mother passed away, but she still held firm to the
teachings she had received.

They had clearly gotten off to a rocky start, and
she thought that if they were to spend some time

together, she could smooth that over and perhaps they could start a friendship as the duke had suggested. Everyone needs a friend, particularly someone as lonely as Dylan seemed to be. She had been here for four days, and there hadn't been a single caller beyond his grandfather, and as far as she knew, he hadn't gone anywhere; clearly the man was lonely. Her thoughts were interrupted by Mr. Simmons entering the drawing room announcing the duke's arrival. She had not expected a visit from him, so she was rather surprised.

"Hello, Mr. Crenshaw how are you today sir?" she asked when he entered the room.

Mr. Simmons rolled his eyes and made a sound of disgust and promptly left the room. Presumably, he didn't approve of the way she greeted the duke and was letting her know in his familiar sarcastic way that she was lacking in decorum. She quickly stood and curtsied, realizing that was proper and most assuredly the cause of Mr. Simmons's stress.

"Hello my dear," he said, bending over her hand and placing a kiss on her knuckles.

"Forgive me sir, I am quite surprised by your arrival, and I have simply lost all sense of decorum," she said by way of explaining her bad manners.

"Worry not my dear; you are doing fine," he assured her with a soft pat on her hand.

"Please have a seat, and I will ring for some fresh tea," she told him.

"Don't trouble yourself; I came to see that grandson of mine. Adeline tells me he has been rather scarce, so I came to light a fire under his lazy arse," he said with a chuckle.

"I have not seen him since my first night here," she admitted. "Quite frankly sir, I don't even know if he's still in the house," she added.

Just then Adeline stirred with a snort and a sputter. The duke and Claire looked over expectantly at her, but she shifted herself into a more comfortable position and resumed her slumber.

The duke laughed and said, "I see she has been lively company for you my dear."

"Oh, we get along fine sir," she said with a smile.

"Poor dear never married and turned to spirits for comfort many years ago. I shouldn't have allowed it but … well suffice it to say, she is quite content as she is," he told her.

"Why did she never marry?"

"Oh, it wasn't for lack of suitors. She was quite a beauty, but there was a scandal, you see, and two of her beau fought a duel over her honor and she was quite overcome with the loss of the young man she had hoped to marry. She never forgave herself for his death and decided that she would honor his memory by remaining unwed," he solemnly told her.

"How tragic," Claire said as she cast a look at the old woman trying to envision her as a young woman. She could see that she probably had been lovely in her youth and felt a pang of pity for her and the young man.

"Yes indeed," he agreed simply.

After a moment of awkward silence, she

noticed that the duke was studying her closely. She felt a bit nervous and cast her eyes toward the floor.

"Why do you suppose you have not seen my grandson since the first night of your arrival," he prodded.

"It is most embarrassing to relay sir; I would prefer not to."

"Come child, you can tell me," he commanded gently.

After a moment more, she took a deep breath and relayed the story of the night in the library. She hadn't planned on telling him of it, but she saw no harm in it now.

"I suspected something similar must have occurred. Do you want to leave this place?" he asked.

"No, sir, we have a deal, and I intend to stick to it," she told him a little flabbergasted by the question.

"Even if I agree to honor my part?" he coaxed.

"Are you suggesting that I could leave here with my freedom and my money, now sir?" she asked incredulously.

"If that is your wish," he told her with kind, gentle eyes.

She thought about it for a moment. It would be easy to turn tail and run, but she wasn't a coward and that would be the coward's way. No, he needed her to help him, and she could not turn her back on him now.

"A deal is a deal, Mr. Crenshaw; I shall remain for the four weeks we agreed upon," she told him.

"Ah, that American spirit that I've heard so

much about," he said with a genuine smile.

"Yes well, we are not so easily defeated," she said with a big grin.

"Quite right!" he agreed.

Just then the door to the drawing room was flung open with a bang as it slammed into the doorstop with violent force, and in the doorway stood a disheveled and quite angry looking Dylan. He looked as though he hadn't slept or bathed since her arrival, and as she watched him stagger into the room, she realized that he was quite inebriated, as well. He looked about the room, and his eyes settled on her for a brief moment, where she could have sworn, she saw a touch of shame. He quickly looked away from her as if he knew that she could read his feelings and fixed his frosty glare on his grandfather.

"What do I owe the honor of this visit to Your Grace," he said with sarcasm dripping from his lips.

He swaggered before the duke and gave a clumsy sweeping bow that nearly toppled him over. The duke looked at his grandson with hurt in his eyes. Clearly, it was very upsetting for him to see his grandson in such a way, but he quickly recovered with a stiffening of his spine.

"Perhaps we should remove ourselves to the library, where we can discuss it privately," he said with firm authority.

"There is no need to remove ourselves; I'm sure whatever has to be said, can be said in front of Miss Melville, after all, she is soon to become my wife," he slurred.

Claire gasped at his words and was quite

unable to contain herself.

"I have no intention of becoming your wife!" she stated with righteous indignation.

"Oh, don't you?" he barked. "Isn't that why you threw yourself at me the other night in my library?" he asked snidely.

"I did no such thing, sir!" she said with a huff.

Dylan looked at his grandfather and smiled sardonically.

"Was it not your plan to have me compromise the chit and be forced to marry her?" he asked bitterly.

The duke looked at his grandson with tears welling in his silver eyes but said nothing.

"Well, your plan worked flawlessly; I have quite compromised her, you see. Did she not tell you?" he asked with venom in his voice.

"I have not been compromised, and had I been, I certainly would not agree to marry a drunken lout such as you," Claire said as she quickly placed herself before him, effectively shoving the duke out of her way.

She was angry and insulted, and she wasn't going to stand for this another minute. She stood before him with her shoulders back and her chest heaving with anger, glaring at him with the full intention of chastising him further until she noticed that his eyes were fixed firmly on her bosom. She became so incensed that he would treat her thusly that before she knew what she was about, she shoved him with all her might, sending him stumbling backward, where his fall was broken by the sofa.

"How dare you!" she shouted at him.

The insufferable man laughed at her then; he actually laughed! Well, she wasn't about to be mocked by him further, so she grabbed him by his collar, jerking him forward, and with a waggling finger in his face she proceeded to tell him just what she thought of him.

"You sir, are a despicable swine, and I would not marry you if you were the last man on earth. You stink to high heaven, you look like a vagabond, and you have the manners of a rabid dog," she said, then thrust him back against the sofa.

Dylan snickered and stretched his neck so he could see around her and looked at his grandfather.

"A match made in heaven, wouldn't you say?" he asked with a hiccup.

That was the last straw; she stomped on his foot with the heel of her shoe and turned and grabbed the teapot from the nearby table and dumped the contents on his head. He gasped and blinked his eyes rapidly from the shock of it; quite frankly it had shocked her as well. She supposed she was grateful that the tea had cooled so he wouldn't be scalded, but by God, he deserved it and worse. She cast him a glacial stare and then turned to the duke.

"I believe I shall remove myself from the room Mr. Crenshaw, because if I stay here another minute with this ... this animal, I will be tempted to do violence," she told the duke.

The duke was smiling ... *what was wrong with the men in this family*? She gave him a formal curtsey and turned to leave when she was tugged backward by her skirt and landed in Dylan's lap, where she was quickly imprisoned by his strong arms about her waist. She struggled to get away, but he held on that much tighter, and his hand was perilously close to her breast. Deciding the wise course of action was to be still, she froze and hoped that he would relax his hold so she could escape.

"Forced to do violence she says; I just love it when she talks like that in her crude American accent; it gets me all excited. Go and fetch the parson grandfather; I cannot wait another minute to claim my bride," he said just before he ran his tongue across her ear and then down the side of her neck.

The sensation sent a shock wave through her body that was not altogether unpleasant, but she was far to humiliated to allow it to go on, so she leaned her head forward and bit his arm. Needless to say, he released her then, and she quickly jumped up and ran from the room. Once out in the hall, she stopped and collected her wits. That's when she realized that she had given him exactly what he wanted. She spun around quickly and marched back into the room. She was not going to flee from adversity at the drop of a hat; she would simply beat him at his own game. She re-entered the drawing room and both men looked up with surprise. She walked back over to the desk where she had been sitting before the duke arrived, and before sitting down in the chair, she addressed the duke.

"He is quite right you know; we are an excellent match, and I agree that we should be married," she said with a boldness that shocked her.

As she expected, Dylan jumped up from the

sofa and seemed quite sober, then he stared at her as if she had gone completely mad. Maybe she had; she didn't know, but one thing she did know was that he was not going to send her cowering in fear. Of course, she had no intention of marrying the man, but if this was what it took to knock some sense into him, so be it. She could always cry off later, but in the meantime, she would become the overbearing fiancé and whip him into shape. Yes, that's what she would do, whip him into shape.

"Now wait just a minute!" he barked

"No, you wait just a minute. As you said before, you have quite compromised me, and I demand that my honor be restored, and the only way to do that is for you to marry me, sir," she told him while boldly glaring at him.

Dylan looked back at her with fire shooting from eyes as dark as sapphire and started advancing toward her. Upon reaching her, he towered over her in a very intimidating fashion, and if she were more imaginative, she could have envisioned that a fire-breathing dragon was about to consume her with his flames.

"Oh no, you don't; you'll not trick me into marriage!" he ground out with clenched teeth.

"Trick?" she asked coyly, despite her nervous agitation. "Why, I have done no such thing," she said with a sniff and a tipping up of her chin.

"Excellent!" the duke finally spoke.

Dylan and Claire both snapped their heads in his direction, and she was stunned to see that Adeline had gotten up and was now standing beside him. They were both smiling broadly as they looked at her and Dylan, and she suddenly realized she had fallen right in with the duke's plans. Oh, what a calamity! Well, there was nothing for it now but to forge ahead. She would simply explain to him later what her plan had been. He would see her reasoning and not hold her to the ridiculous idea that she would actually marry the man.

"This is perfect timing; I came over here to tell you about the dinner I have arranged for Claire to be introduced among certain members of the ton tonight, and now we shall be able to make it an engagement party," he said beaming.

Dylan made a choking sound, and Claire thought perhaps he was about to faint as he had lost all his coloring and was now a strange shade of gray. She reached out to take him by the elbow to steady him, but he snatched his arm out of her reach, spun away and stomped over to the window with his back to the room, where he grew very still and quiet. It had become a very awkward moment, and the tension in the room could have been cut with a knife. She looked at the duke, and he winked at her, which quite relieved her as it seemed that he understood why she had said what she did; at least they were on the same page. She winked back at him to indicate that they were a team in this and that the plan was a good one.

"I think that sounds lovely sir," she said.

"I have made all the arrangements for the dinner to be held here tonight at eight o clock and have invited all of Dylan's friends and a few other members of the ton. I had originally planned on introducing you to some eligible bachelors so the guest list is mostly comprised of men, but that shouldn't be too big of a problem. Once we announce the engagement, the gentlemen will realize that they are ... how shall I put this ..."

"Off the hook," Dylan rudely cut in over his shoulder.

The duke looked at his grandson's back and then back at her with an apologetic smile.

"Yes, for want of another phrase ... off the hook," he agreed with another wink.

"Good it's all settled then; I shall go upstairs now and see what I have to wear for the event," she said with a curtsy then quickly quit the drawing room.

She would have to pull the duke aside later tonight and confirm with him that this was only a ploy to help Dylan, and that she in no way planned to marry him. She was sure that he understood, but she wanted to clarify it with him nonetheless for the sake of prudence.

Chapter Six

When Dylan heard the drawing room door close, he turned to face his grandfather. The old man looked quite pleased with himself, and that made Dylan fume even more.

"This is a fine mess you have gotten me into Grandfather," he grumbled.

"I hazard to say that you have gotten yourself into this mess, young man," the duke retorted.

"It wasn't I, who insisted on bringing that ghastly woman here," Dylan growled.

"It wasn't I, who tried to force my attentions on the poor dear either," the duke said standing his ground.

Dylan sighed deeply, ran a hand through his already disheveled hair and shook his head in disgust. His grandfather was right; he had behaved badly, and now he would have to do the honorable thing and marry the chit. But damn and blast, he didn't want to marry her or anyone else. There had to be a way out of this madness before it was too late; but how? How was he to get away with dishonoring her further by refusing to marry her after the scene that had just passed, with witnesses no less?

"I will find her a husband," he finally said.

"You already have my boy; you already have," the duke said smugly.

"The hell I have! I will not marry that insufferable woman and no one, not even you, can force me to it," he shouted.

"Then what do you propose to do? Shame her

all over again?" the duke asked with anger in his eyes.

"Nothing has been formalized; I can still find her a husband and no one ever need know of any of this."

"I dare say the whole household knows of it and by tomorrow it will be all over the ton that you have taken advantage of the poor girl. No, you will have to do the honorable thing in this and marry the girl," the duke insisted.

Dylan let loose a foul string of oaths and turned back toward the window. His grandfather was right; the servants knew everything and by tomorrow, if not sooner, everyone would know of it, but that shouldn't stop him from trying to find her a husband. He could insist on a long engagement to keep the gossip down and covertly hunt for an unsuspecting victim to take his place at the altar. It would have to suffice for now to appease the old man as well as his own conscience. Were he a better man, he would be glad to marry her, but he was exactly what she said he was; a scurvy dog and he was undeserving of her. He wished he didn't suffer from this horrible attraction to her; the woman had gotten under his skin and had become a menace to his sanity.

He didn't know what came over him when he entered the drawing room, but he had taken one look at her and was quite unable to stop himself from becoming an arse. The way she had looked at him with her big, strange green eyes as though she could see into his soul had shaken him, causing him to lash out. He had purposefully stayed hidden in his room for the last three days to avoid her because he was ashamed by his behavior that night and he couldn't bear for her to look upon him. He realized his grandfather and his aunt Adeline were looking at him with interest, and he stiffened his shoulders.

"I will not marry her, and that is final," he said feebly.

"She will make a fine wife, and her dowry is rather impressive," his grandfather prodded.

"Then I shall make sure I find a proper husband for her; one deserving of her impressive dowry," he said snidely.

He and his grandfather glared at one another for a suspended moment. He could see the disappointment in his eyes too, and it sickened him.

"What makes you think that you are not deserving?" the duke asked.

"Can you not see what I am? Must I spell it out?" he barked.

"You are my grandson," was his simple reply.

"More's the pity for you," Dylan said then abruptly spun to leave the room.

"Just a minute," his grandfather said just before he could make good his escape.

He stopped with his hand on the doorknob but didn't turn around.

"Heed me well in this Dylan; you will marry the girl and soon, or I will disown you," his grandfather said.

Dylan didn't respond to that; he simply opened the door and left the room.

*****

The duke watched his grandson storm out of the room, and he smiled. Things were progressing quite nicely so far, and if he played his cards right, he would have Dylan and Claire wed before the month was out. The sexual tension between his grandson and the girl was explosive, even a blind person could see that they were meant for one another. He couldn't have picked a better candidate for Dylan if he had tried; it was as though the girl were tailor made for him. The girl had such fire in her spirit, and when her eyes sparked on Dylan and his on her, you could clearly see a merging of energies as though their souls were colliding in an epic battle for survival. It was quite a sight to see as they went at one another in such a way and reminded him of days gone by when he had first laid eyes on his wife, Joanna, God rest her soul.

They hated each other on sight as these two had, and after their hearts had been truly conquered by one another they had a love so great that it was the stuff of legends. Most people never had the privilege to know such passion as he had with Joanna, and he knew that what he was witnessing with these two young people would rival it easily. Dylan was so much like himself at that age, right down to the drinking, debauchery and subsequent depression, and there were times when he considered killing himself until he had found Joanna. That's why he so desperately wanted them to find love in each other; otherwise Dylan could be lost forever.

He didn't like issuing ultimatums to Dylan like he had, but he knew that Dylan revered him and that he would be giving him food for thought before he outright rejected the girl. He was banking on the fact that Dylan wouldn't want to disappoint him, but he may be so far gone now that it didn't matter. He hoped it wasn't too late to change the course of his life and before the letter had come from the girl's solicitor he had been trying to find a candidate for Dylan to wed. The girl practically fell from the sky and into his lap as the answer to the problem as though God had delivered her especially for him. He wasn't an overly-religious man, but he couldn't help but wonder if her arrival had not been a gift from heaven sent to save Dylan.

"You sly rascal," Adeline said with a chuckle.

"I can assure you that I have had to do very little to push them along. I was just thinking that it could be the hand of God," he said with a smile.

"They remind me of you and Joanna," she mused aloud.

"Aye!" he said softly.

"Do you think they will truly wed?" she asked.

"Oh, I have no doubt about it my dear sister; no doubt at all," he said as he leaned over to kiss her on the cheek.

"Is there anything I should do?" she asked.

"Just continue to observe and keep me informed as you have done thus far. I think the rest will work itself out quite nicely. As for me; I am off to retrieve the Crenshaw betrothal ring from my safe and will return in time for the party."

"Wonderful!" Adeline said clapping her hands.

*****

It was two hours before the party, and Claire was busy reviewing, in detail, all that had occurred between her and Dylan since her arrival. The more she thought about it, the more she was beginning to wonder if perhaps … no it was best not of think it. *He would make a terrible husband, but what if … no, I simply mustn't think it.* She looked through her clothes, trying to decide what to wear tonight and was having trouble deciding between the white muslin and the mint green silk gown. Both were equally nice and would be perfect for such an evening. She took them both out, draped them across the bed and stood back to study them. The white one would look lovely with her pearls, and she did have a new peach colored sash she had bought specifically for it; perhaps she should wear it.

That decided, she put the green one away and then set about deciding what slippers to wear. She should have something with an elevated heel as Dylan was quite tall and … there she went again. Why should it matter how tall Dylan is? She sat down on the chair beside the bed and looked at the gown. Why I am trying to impress him? Do I harbor a secret desire to marry the wretch? Surely not! She sat back in the chair and closed her eyes, trying to envision him as he might have been a year ago before he was taken over by the depression. She could see him smiling and laughing, and the image nearly took her breath away.

She would love to have him smile at her in such a way or to laugh at something she said rather than snarl and chide her for it.

What did this mean? She wasn't sure, but she was starting to feel a little uneasy about her actions earlier. She didn't want to be married or at least she hadn't wanted to be married to Barnaby, but she had been a girl of just sixteen. She had rebelled against her father's demands, turning Barnaby away from her by bragging about her writing, knowing full well that he didn't approve and that it would provoke a quarrel. She was a woman grown now, and the idea of marrying wasn't quite as scary as it had been then, but would she really want to saddle herself with a man such as Dylan. She was physically attracted to him yes, but the man was insufferably rude and clearly had a drinking problem. Perhaps with the love of a good woman, he could mend his ways, but she wasn't so sure that he really wanted to. He seemed quite content to wallow in his misery and lashed out at everyone around him so they wouldn't get too close and interfere with his self-destruction.

Did he want to die? Could that be the reason that he acted the way he did? If he continued on thusly, he certainly would die, sooner rather than later and the thought made her sick at heart. Perhaps tonight, when she met his friends, she would get a sense of who he really was and what he was like before and that would help her determine whether he was worth salvaging. But then what? Would she really marry him? Could she? Oh, it was too much to contemplate and it made her angry that she could think of nothing else. He had gotten under her skin so quickly that she hadn't even noticed it happening. How had she gone from hating him to

… loving him? No, surely it wasn't love … was it? She groaned and sat up in her chair. This was madness; she shouldn't even be thinking in such terms about such a man.

She would stick to the plan, and the plan was to stay here and offer friendship for four weeks, and at the end of that time she would be free and wealthy. It was what she wanted, and she wasn't going to allow herself to be sidetracked like this. The idea that she could possibly love the man was ludicrous and not to be borne. She should have taken the duke up on his offer to allow her to leave now, but no, she had to be noble and stick to their bargain. This would teach her not to be so goose-brained again. The man didn't want her friendship; all he wanted was his Scotch. Well, let him have it and good luck to him if that be his true desire.

Desire? What would a man like that desire? Did he long for happiness with the love of a good woman? Could a man like that ever be happy? She sighed deeply and walked over to the bell pull and tugged. It was time to bathe and get ready for the party. There was no sense in wondering such silly things anyway. She would just stick to her plan … it was what she really wanted.

*****

"You can't be serious!" Dylan snarled at his grandfather.

The duke had come to his room a half an hour before the dinner party was to begin and given him the Crenshaw betrothal ring, demanding that he give it to the chit for their engagement, and it was all he could do not to throw him out on his ear.

"Of course, I'm serious. You are engaged to the girl, and I would not have her embarrassed to explain the absence of her engagement ring," the duke said with complete sincerity.

He was right of course; once the announcement was made, the women would gather around and insist upon seeing the ring, and if she didn't have one, speculation would run rife. He sighed deeply and held out his hand for the ring. He would give it to the chit, but he would be damned before he went on bended knee to do it.

"How many bachelors did you invite tonight?" he barked at his grandfather.

"Besides Jasper and Luther, there will be three others," he said with what Dylan was sure was a smirk.

"Who might those three be?" he inquired calmly.

"Lord Kenwick, Lord Jefferies and Sir Matthew Hyde," he said.

Dylan didn't like the idea of Kenwick; the man was a rake and would probably try to get beneath her skirt at the first opportunity. Why should he care?

"Why would you invite Kenwick?" he found himself asking.

"He has deep pockets and is in search of a bride," was his simple answer.

That was news to Dylan; he hadn't heard that he was actively seeking a bride, so perhaps there was no real cause for alarm. The other two were decent sorts from what he knew of them. He particularly liked Matthew, though he was surprised that he would be seeking a wife so soon after his first wife's death in child bed. He didn't have any doubts about Jefferies, however. The man had been searching for a bride for the last five years and was so selective that he hadn't even come close to making an offer for anyone. Well, it was none of his business who she married; he just wanted to be rid of her with all possible haste. He would go through this charade tonight and then he would actively start petitioning his friends and acquaintances to take her off his hands. He had given a lot of thought to his grandfather's threat to disown him, and when the words were said, they had cut him to the core. But he had come to the realization that he would be dead soon, and his grandfather's opinion of him wouldn't matter anymore, so it really didn't matter if he disowned him.

"You look very nice Dylan, and if I didn't know better, I would even think you sobered up for the occasion," his grandfather said casually.

Dylan had sobered up, but he wasn't sure why. Somehow, he just didn't want to drink this afternoon and decided he would wait until the party.

"The night is young," he promised.

Chapter Seven

"Miss Melville," a soft voice from behind called to her.

Claire had just reached the landing at the top of the stairs so she could descend for the party when she heard the voice. She snapped her head around in surprise, and her knees nearly buckled when she saw that it was Dylan standing there. He was impeccably dressed in formal black evening attire, his hair was pulled back neatly, and he was cleanly shaved. He smelled of bay rum soap and some other spice she didn't recognize, and she could tell just by looking at him that he was sober. Had it really been his voice speaking her name so softly? It must have been because there was no one else nearby. She straightened her spine and looked at him expectantly.

"Yes?" she said as casually as she could manage.

"Please accompany me to the library before we go to the party. I have something that I must give you and would like to do so in private," he said.

She was instantly suspicious of his behavior and wasn't sure it was such a good idea to be cloistered away with him in the library; the very place where such an unpleasant scene had passed between them just days before.

"We are quite alone here," she suggested.

He looked her over from head to toe, and the slowness that his eyes caressed her body made her shiver inwardly. No, it would not be a good idea to be alone with him; nothing good could come of it.

"I'm afraid that I must insist," he said after he was through perusing her figure.

"I do not think that it is wise to be ..."

"You will come to no harm by my hand," he said, cutting off her words.

She drew in a deep breath and her heart thudded in her chest when he came up beside her and extended his arm for her to take. She hesitantly accepted, and they started their silent progression down the stairs. The whole way down the stairs, her nerves were quaking, and she couldn't imagine what he would want to give her or the transformation that seemed to have taken over. He was actually behaving as a gentleman should, and she found it quite alluring. She would not be fooled by this, however; he had shown her time and again what a brute he really was; therefore, she would continue to regard him with suspicion. He led her down the hall, and when they reached the library, he halted just outside the door as if he suddenly realized that it might not have been wise to bring her here. She looked up at him, and he was looking back at her; for a moment, she thought she saw something there, but he quickly averted his eyes and opened the door.

The room was dark, but he remedied that with expedience by lighting a lamp on the table beside the door. He turned back to her, urged her to step further into the room and closed the door behind them. Her heart skipped a beat as she remembered what had occurred right here in this very spot, and he seemed to be aware of it too as he leaned in toward her as though he were going to say something, then he caught himself and took a few steps back before turning to go over to the desk. He stopped there at the corner of the desk and turned back toward her to find that she remained exactly where he'd left her. She didn't want to go any nearer, and she felt comforted knowing that the door was right behind her in case she needed to flee quickly.

"Come," he said.

"I prefer to stay right here," she said with an uncertain voice.

He stood there a moment as if trying to decide what to do or say, so she took mercy on him.

"What is this about?" she prodded.

He cleared his throat and looked away from her as he dug into his pocket. He pulled out a small box and looked down at it, then began turning it over and over in his hand nervously. She could see that it was a black box, the kind that ... oh no; not that. Her body reacted instantly, and she quickly turned toward the door. She had to get away from him because this was far too embarrassing. She opened the door, but he had come up behind her and extended his hand above her shoulder to prevent her from opening it further. She froze, and after a moment he quietly closed the door. She stood there facing the door, and she could feel his breath on her neck. Her heart was about to break free of her chest as she remembered the last time they had stood just like this. She didn't dare turn around to look into his eyes because if she did she would surely swoon. He reached for her left hand, and she felt him slide the ring on her finger. Her knees buckled, and she would have fallen had he not pressed himself against her from behind to prevent it.

He placed his hands on her shoulders, and she could feel that he was trembling, or maybe it was her, and he was simply suffering the vibrations. She leaned forward and placed her forehead on the door in resignation of what would possibly occur. Would she fight him this time? Did she want to fight him? They stood this way for what seemed an eternity and all the while her senses were tuned more acutely than they had ever been before. Then he placed his lips on the back of her neck, and the feeling was like a sizzling bolt of lightning throughout her entire being. Warmth radiated down her spine and from there it coursed slowly through her body, and it was the most delicious feeling she had ever had. He slid his lips around to the side of her neck, and when he reached her ear he rested. After a moment he spoke, and everything she had felt up until then suddenly evaporated.

"You think you have won but you haven't," he breathed into her ear.

She immediately stiffened, but he still had her trapped as he pressed his whole body against hers from behind.

"I have no idea what you mean," she said with rising anger.

"Don't you?" he breathed as he licked her earlobe.

She tried to buck him off of her, but she quickly learned the error of it when he laughed softly and pressed himself harder against her.

"I have a problem Claire. You see, I want you desperately but not enough to marry you and having you about is somewhat ... maddening. I can hardly resist the urge that I'm having, to take you here and now. But I must you see as I am not so stupid as to allow you a complete victory over me," he said with a thrust of his hips against her behind.

"Move away from me ... you ... beast," she struggled to demand.

"No, I think I am quite comfortable as we are; at least this way you cannot kick and thrash me as you seem to love doing," he purred in her ear.

"I will thrash you, just you wait," she promised.

"Maybe so but for now, I'm in control," he said then licked the side of her neck.

She was angry now; humiliated beyond belief, and against her will the tears began to flow out of her eyes and down her face. He turned her face so that he could see her then; he must have known that she was crying and wanted to bask in the glory of his achievement. He reached up and ran his thumb down the path her tears had taken then put his thumb to his lips and licked the tear away. She shivered as she watched him do this, and when she looked into his eyes, she saw something there that saddened her. He hated himself for what he was doing even now, but for whatever reason, he was quite unable to stop himself.

"Tears; is that what my mighty American warrior has been reduced to?" he asked with a silky voice.

"You said I would come to no harm by your hand," she reminded him.

"I have not harmed you," he said with another thrust of his hips against her backside.

"Unhand me now or I will scream," she threatened.

"No one would care that a betrothed couple has engaged in a little love-play," he said softly.

"Why are you doing this?" she asked calmly.

He grabbed her by the shoulders then and flipped her around so they were face to face. They stared at one another, and for a moment she felt as though she could see deep into his soul. Suddenly, everything came to her clearly with total understanding, and she knew without a doubt what she had to do. She reached up and laid her palm against his cheek and smiled with warmth radiating.

"Let me help you Dylan," she said softly.

He reacted as though her words were acid in his face. He shoved away from her, and then with a violence that surprised her, he stood glaring at her as if she were the very Devil, and had she been smarter, she would have taken the opportunity to flee, but she couldn't bring herself to do it. Instead, she advanced toward him until she reached him, then she once again placed her palm upon his cheek.

"I can help you if you would let me," she insisted.

He shoved her hand away from his cheek, "What makes you think that I need help?" he barked at her.

"You are killing yourself a little bit more each day, and when I look at you, I can feel the bleak agonizing sadness in your heart and soul. It reaches out to me, begging me to bring you close and wrap you safely in my arms. I cannot explain it, nor do I even like that I have these feelings about you because you are the most infuriating man I have ever met in my life, but Dylan there is something there between us, and I know if you would give it a chance we could be … friends at the very least."

Dylan stood there looking at her with an unfathomable expression in his eyes. For a moment, she thought that perhaps she had reached him, but then his expression of anger returned, and he stiffened his back, glaring at her.

"I don't know what you think you see when you look at me, but I don't want or need your … friendship. I wish I had never met you and that you would simply go away, but I am stuck with you now out of a sense of honor and duty to the duke, but heed me; I will not marry you, so you can put all such foolish notions aside.

"We will go through this farce for the sake of your reputation, and when the dust settles, you will quietly cry off and marry another. Tonight, you will look over the candidates that my grandfather has invited, and if you don't find someone suitable there, we will go to every party and ball that London has to offer until you find someone. Is that understood?" he demanded.

"No! I will marry you Dylan and that is the end of it," she found herself saying.

The words that flew out of her mouth were pure madness, but she knew this was her course, the course given to her by God or fate, she didn't know, but she would stay on it. She knew without a shadow of a doubt that he would kill himself if she did not stop him. She realized then that she loved him, and why she did she would never understand, but she knew it unequivocally.

With lightning fast movements, he grabbed her and brought her to him and crushed his lips against hers in a punishing kiss. Her first reaction was to fight, but she refused to do it. He needed her, and she would give herself to him so that he would see that he was worthy of life and of the love of a good woman. He prodded against her lips with his tongue, and she opened up to receive him and with a groan he deepened the kiss and began to explore her curves with his seeking hands. He reached around her bottom, drawing her closer into his embrace, and with a savage hunger he continued to consume her. She threw her arms around him in an effort to hang on as the force of the man was so powerful that she felt as though she would be swept away in the current of his passions. That had been a mistake as he suddenly stiffened beneath her embrace, broke the kiss and pushed himself away.

"Damnation woman; this cannot be!" he shouted.

"Why?" she shouted back.

He looked at her as if she had gone mad, and she was starting to suspect that maybe she had. This whole situation had spiraled beyond her control and she didn't even recognize herself anymore. He growled at her then, and rushed at her; sweeping her up off of her feet, he took her over to the sofa and laid her down, then came down upon her. He never broke eye contact with her even when he began to lift her skirt. She trembled as she imagined what he was about to do. He slid his body down the length of hers, stopping to run his tongue along her leg before he moved toward her thigh. He was a savage and she helpless as the look in his eyes was mesmerizing. When he reached the top of her thigh, just where it joined with her private center, he stopped and stared at her with hot desire in his eyes.

"Fight me Claire," he breathed raggedly.

"No," she said breathlessly.

"Stop me, or I will take you here and now," he demanded.

"Take me then because I will not fight you," she vowed.

He made an agonizing sound in his throat as he pushed himself off of her. He turned and kicked over the table that was at the end of the sofa, startling her into a sitting position from the shock of the action.

"I will not do this; I will not!" he shouted.

"Why do you fight against yourself so?" she asked.

"You don't know what I am or you would fight me as I have begged you to do," he told her with pain etched in his face.

"What are you Dylan?" she prodded.

He rushed back to her, dropped to his knees and took her hand in his. He looked at her with tears welling in his eyes.

"I am a monster," he said.

"I don't believe it. Why would you say such a thing?"

He lowered his head, coming to rest on her

knees where he began to weep as though his soul were tortured. She ran her fingers across his brow and allowed him to cry. She knew that she was close to finding out what she so desperately wanted to know.

"I killed her," he finally rasped out.

Her heart lurched in her chest, and her stomach clenched. She had not expected those words and yet they explained so much.

"Who did you kill Dylan," she asked softly.

"Wishy … I killed Wishy," he said with a groan.

Was it true? Was she embracing a murderer? She didn't believe it, but something had happened; of that she was sure. She simply couldn't imagine him a murderer.

"How did you kill her Dylan?" she asked cautiously.

"It doesn't matter; she is dead, and I am responsible," he said.

"I don't believe that," she told him calmly.

He lifted up his head, and his eyes pierced her like a blade through the heart.

"Believe it!" he said harshly.

"Is that why you feel that you don't deserve to have love in your life?" she prompted.

"Listen to me Claire; I don't want or need your understanding, and I don't want or need you to love me. I only need you to leave me alone and find someone else to marry. I am no good for you, and if you continue to persist, I will destroy you, just as I did her. Do I make myself clear?"

She didn't have an answer to this as she still

had so many questions of her own. She knew in her heart that he wasn't a murderer, yet he was holding himself responsible for the death of this girl.

"We shall discuss this later Dylan; it is time for the party, and I'm sure the guests are waiting," she improvised.

He looked at her with pain in his eyes for a suspended moment as if he were trying to see into her thoughts. She kept her gaze locked on his until he finally nodded his head that he agreed, and together, they silently left the library and on to the drawing room where by now all the guests had gathered, awaiting their arrival.

Chapter Eight

Dylan needed a drink. He hadn't had a drink since late last night, well early this morning rather and had made it all the way through dinner without so much as a sip of wine. He didn't know why it was important to him to refrain, but he had, and it was starting to show. He was ready for this farce to be over so he could go to his room and drink his Scotch, but he had to stand around and act like he was the happy fiancé to the lovely American with deplorable manners. Well, they weren't really so deplorable except to say that she refused to call anyone 'my lord' or 'my lady' and she kept referring to his grandfather as 'Mr. Crenshaw'. God, he needed a drink.

His nerves were wound tight, and his heart was filled with sorrow along with a dull aching thud in his head that was making him queasy. He hadn't meant to reveal so much to Claire, but somehow the words had poured forth beyond his control. It scared him to think that she had that kind of power over him, and he didn't know how to protect himself from her. He hadn't meant what he said to her about not wanting or needing her; on the contrary, he did with a fierce passion that burned like hot coals in the center of his being. When he saw her in the hallway about to descend the stairs earlier, the sight had taken his breath away. She was so beautiful dressed in her white muslin gown that for a moment, he thought he was seeing a living goddess. At that moment, he had been filled with such intense desire for her that he wanted to take her into his arms and make love to her as he had never wanted to before. He wanted to feel her body wrapped around his while he filled her with his entire being. The feeling had nearly been his undoing, and it was all he could do not to whisk her away into his chambers and ravish her.

Why was she so intent on having him for a husband; couldn't she see what he was? God knows, he had shown her his true nature over and over again, but she seemed to desire him all the more for it. What would he have to do to make her see that he was beneath her, unworthy of her affection? She would have allowed him to take her there on the sofa or against the door even, and he couldn't imagine why. She wasn't just after his title or his fortune as he had first thought; she wanted him, the man, but who did she think he was? He sensed in her a goodness that he had never encountered in another woman before. Most females of his acquaintance were cold and conniving, but she was different. She had depth of character and an inner beauty that was blinding to the beholder. He was starting to suspect that he was in love with her, but he couldn't allow those feelings to grow. They had to be snuffed out before they destroyed such a magnificent creature. He had to find her a husband and put her out of his life, out of his world entirely.

He watched her now mingling with the guests, and when she spoke to Kenwick, it was all he could do to suppress the feelings of possession and not go over there to snatch her away from the rogue. He didn't like the way he looked at her as though she were the main course of a sensual dinner.

"I think you should marry her," Jasper Townley, the Earl of Pembrook's voice intruded on his brooding.

Dylan snapped his gaze to his friend whom he had not really associated with in over a year. He was tall and thin with golden brown hair with streaks of blond, and his keen hazel eyes that missed nothing were probing his own, and he realized then how much he had missed his friends.

"If the duke has his way, I very well might," Dylan grumbled.

"I'll take her if you don't want her, mate," Luther Rollins, the Marquess of Huntley said with a huge grin.

Luther was another of his long-time friends and to know him was to love him while wanting to kill him at the same time. He was a huge, overgrown boy in a man's body with wild, unruly reddish blond curls and green eyes. He had the face of a cherub, complete with dimples and the soul of a loyal lion who would die for those he loved.

"You can only have her if you are willing to marry her," he said with a pang of jealousy at the notion.

Luther grinned, but said nothing further. Luther was the last person he could envision settling down in domestic bliss; he loved the ladies too much to settle down with one in particular. He looked again at Claire as she was still talking with Kenwick. Couldn't she see the danger she was in being so close to the man? He felt a surge of anger course through his body, and his fists clenched with the urge to do violence. He tore his gaze away; it was not his business who she married. If she wanted a rake like Kenwick, so be it.

"She's beautiful," Jasper mused aloud.

"She is the bane of my existence," he said with heat he had not meant to show.

"I could be persuaded to settle down for a woman like her," Jasper prodded.

Dylan snapped his gaze to his friend. He was serious; he could see it in the way he was devouring Claire with his eyes; he wanted to kill him for daring to want her. He had to get away from here before he turned into a homicidal lunatic.

"Why don't you want her?" Jasper asked, never taking his eyes off Claire.

"Stay away from her Jasper," he found himself saying.

Jasper turned his attention to him then, and the two men glared at one another. Jasper had a way of looking beyond a situation and envisioning the eventuality. Dylan knew that he could see the struggle within him and the knowledge of it made him angry. He couldn't hide anything from Jasper or Gabriel, either one, which was why he had refused to see them for over a year. He didn't want them to see that he was suicidal and try to interfere with his plans.

"You said you wanted to find someone to pawn her off on; why shouldn't that someone be me?" he finally asked.

"Because I want her out of my life, not married to one of my best friends," he growled.

"Ah!" was his simple reply.

"What is that supposed to mean?" Dylan barked at him.

"You love her," Jasper stated.

Just then Gabriel Hawkins, the Duke of Windhaven walked up to the group. He had a broad smile on his face, and he was looking at Dylan as though he were bursting with pride. Pride in what? Dylan was getting more irritated by the moment, and if he didn't get a drink soon, he would explode.

"Ah Hawk, Dylan was just telling us how he wants to be rid of his fiancé, but she is off limits to me; can you imagine such a thing?" Jasper told him.

Dylan had to suppress the urge to strangle his good friend. He knew he was trying to provoke him, and he was in no mood to be part of his mischief. Gabriel's expression changed from one of pride to one of absolute revulsion. Oh well, there was nothing he could do about it; he was an arse, he knew it, and it was high time everyone else did too.

"How could you not want her Dylan?" Gabriel asked incredulously.

"Oh, he wants her; he is besotted with her," Jasper goaded.

"He said I could have her if I were willing to marry her," Luther put in cheerfully.

Dylan could feel the tension mounting, and if he didn't get out of here soon, he was going to make a huge spectacle of himself. He tried to ignore his friends and turned his attention back to Claire and was relieved to see that Alyssa was with her now.

"Dylan?" Gabriel persisted.

"I don't want to discuss it," he growled.

Dylan was torn between wanting to escape the

room and wanting desperately to keep an eye on Kenwick as he was still looking at Claire as though he wanted to secret her away and toss up her skirts. The only thing preventing him from acting on his urges was Alyssa, and he didn't know how much longer her protection would last. He needed a drink … but he needed to wait; he didn't know why, but he instinctively knew this. He held out his hand and saw that it was trembling and knew that time was running out. This didn't go unnoticed by his friends, and the next thing he knew, he was being whisked away out of the drawing room and led to his library. Gabriel had a death grip on his arm, and Jasper and Luther had closed ranks around him so he couldn't escape.

Gabriel dragged him into the library, shoved him down on the sofa and walked over to the sideboard; he poured some Scotch into a glass and brought it to him, then thrust it at him. Dylan looked at it as though it were an evil thing before turning his head away in revulsion.

"What's going on with you Dylan?" Gabriel demanded.

"Nothing is going on with me," he gritted out between clenched teeth.

"Why are you trembling?" he persisted.

Dylan refused to answer, but Gabriel wouldn't let the matter go.

"How much have you been drinking?" he demanded.

Dylan didn't answer.

"Take the drink before you go into shock," Gabriel demanded.

Dylan looked at the drink again and unconsciously licked his lips. There was sweat on his upper lip, and he reached up to feel his head. It was clammy and moist.

"I can smell the liquor oozing out of your skin. You are suffering, and if you don't take this drink you could go into shock," Gabriel persisted.

Dylan didn't want the cursed drink; he needed it, but he didn't want it. He couldn't understand why he felt that way, but he just couldn't bring himself to take the drink.

"I don't want the drink, damn you," he shouted.

"Take the drink Dylan or we will hold you down and force it down your gullet," Gabriel persisted.

He ignored the threat and refused to take the drink.

"If you are trying to quit, I find that admirable, but you can't just stop and not suffer the consequences of withdrawal. You must take it slow; take this one drink, and you will stop trembling and your sweats will go away," he implored him.

Dylan grabbed it from him and quickly tossed it back. His stomach wanted to rebel against it, but his body's response was immediate. He could feel a calm settling over him, and the irritation that he felt was starting to slide away.

"You have a problem Dylan, and you need to address it before it kills you," Gabriel said calmly.

"The only problem I have is meddlesome friends and an unwanted fiancé," Dylan grumbled.

"Talk to me," Gabriel softly commanded.

"There is nothing to say; why can't you leave

me alone," he pleaded.

"Because you're my brother, and I love you," Gabriel said with tears in his eyes.

"We are all brothers," Luther put in solemnly.

Dylan didn't want to hear this. He loved them too with all his heart, and he couldn't stand for them to see him this way. He leaned forward with his elbows on his knees and buried his face in his hands. He felt intense shame and disgust with himself and wanted to crawl into a hole and die. He knew they wouldn't leave him alone until he gave them what they were after.

"I killed her," he said quietly.

"No you didn't!" Gabriel's response was swift and sure.

Dylan looked up at his friend who believed in him so much that he refused to see the truth.

"She wouldn't have died had it not been for me, and you know this," he stated.

"It was a tragic situation to be sure, but you cannot hold yourself responsible for the actions of others. One of those men killed her Dylan, not you. You were viciously wounded and could have died yourself, but you were spared. You avenged her death, and now you need to forgive yourself and begin to live again."

Dylan put his face back in his hands and made an agonizing sound deep in his throat. He didn't want absolution; he wanted to suffer. He didn't deserve life when she had been denied it.

"Tell us about Claire," Jasper commanded softly.

Dylan jerked his head up and looked at him; the

impulse to jump up and strangle him surged through his body again.

"You will stay away from her Jasper, and so will you Luther," Dylan snapped.

"Tell us about her," Gabriel prodded.

"She is my father's ward, and the duke has taken it into his head that I should marry her. I do not want to marry her or anyone else," he snarled.

"But you want her," Jasper prodded.

"Yes, damn you, I want her, but I cannot have her," he shouted.

"Why?" all three asked in unison.

Dylan put his face back in his hands; why were they doing this to him?

"We are not going away Dylan," Jasper said.

Dylan began to weep.

"I am unworthy," he said on a sob.

"That is ridiculous," Gabriel said.

"Why did you agree to marry her if you don't want her?" Luther asked.

Dylan looked up at his friends, and he felt raw and exposed. They were the few people in the world that could see him for what he really was if they would only look.

"I compromised her," he said with bitterness dripping from his lips.

"Then there is no question that you should marry her," Gabriel said.

"I didn't … it's not like it sounds," he said.

"What is it like then?" Jasper asked.

"Damnation! Why must I explain myself?" he growled.

"Because you need to conquer this demon

within you Dylan, and in order to do that you must confront it," Gabriel explained.

"The demon has already won," Dylan said sardonically.

"I refuse to believe that rubbish. You will marry this girl Dylan, and you had better do it soon. Kenwick is lusting after her and will no doubt snatch her away if you do not," Gabriel told him.

"Let him have her; damnation, let him have her," Dylan shouted.

He quickly stood, shoving past Gabriel and walked over to the sideboard and grabbed the bottle of Scotch, uncorking it with his teeth. He paused and looked at his friends ... *let them see what I have become*. He spit the cork out and turned the bottle up to his lips, threw back his head and let the precious liquid flow. He quickly drained the contents of the bottle then hurled it across the room where it smashed into thousands of pieces. He wiped the excess liquid from his mouth on his coat sleeve and roared like an animal.

"Now can you see that she is better off with Kenwick?" he snarled.

The response from his friends was immediate. Before he knew what had happened, he was picked up; Gabriel and Jasper had an arm and Luther had his heels. They were toting him through the room and through the French doors of the library. He knew where they were headed and started to twist and turn to get out of their grasp. It was futile; he was held firm and before he knew it, he was airborne and then the rude shock of cold water washed over him as he was submerged in the garden pond. He briefly considered just sinking like a stone and drowning himself, but he knew his friends wouldn't allow that. But he would stay here a while nonetheless; the cold darkness was a comfort.

"Should we go in after him?" Luther asked.

"No," Gabriel commanded.

"We will have to keep a closer eye on our friend from now on," Jasper mused aloud.

"Yes, we must have a meeting to discuss our next plan of attack. We shall meet at Whites after the party; I don't believe we have time to waste," Gabriel said.

Chapter Nine

Claire lay in bed thinking about the evening and all
that had transpired. She couldn't stop thinking about
what had happened between her and Dylan before
the party and was quite sad that he had chosen to
virtually ignore her for the remainder of the night.
Oh, sure he had done his duty and stood by her
when the duke had announced their engagement,
but his demeanor had been rather frosty, and he
made no attempts to act as though he were actually
pleased by it. Instead, he had chosen to brood
silently in the corner until his friends had sought
him out. She thought it was strange that the four
men had all disappeared, and when they returned an
hour later Dylan was not among them. There was no
explanation given for his absence, and she was sure
that something must have occurred between the
men that had caused Dylan to retreat to his
chambers. The party hadn't lasted long after their
return, and for that she was rather grateful. She had
learned something very significant about Dylan
through the Duchess of Windhaven, and she needed
time alone to consider it all.

The duchess had been quite forthcoming with
information as she regaled her with the tale of how
she and her husband came to be married, and in the
telling of the story she had learned about the terrible
death of the girl named Wishy. As she had known,
Dylan had not killed the girl, but the details of why
he blamed himself were rather sketchy. When
Claire had asked the duchess to clarify certain
points of the story, it was clear that she didn't have

all the details herself. From what she managed to gather, Dylan must have had a tryst with the girl, and she was subsequently killed by some ruffians. Dylan must have felt that he should have protected her from harm, but he had been assaulted and was unconscious when she was killed, so he could not have done anything different.

He must have loved the girl to have been affected so profoundly that he would spend a year wasting his life away in such a self-destructive manner. Somehow, that didn't sound right though as he had only known her for a day. How could feelings become so deeply engaged in such a short time? Was there really such a thing as love at first sight? Could he ever love another after having suffered such a loss? She knew that a man didn't have to feel love for a woman in order to want to have carnal relations with her, so perhaps he was just ridden with guilt for not being able to protect her. She hoped that was the case because if he were still pining away for the girl, he would never be able to love her. How can one compete with a ghost? Perhaps he did really love the girl after so short a time. It had only been a few days, and she loved him. The thought was not a comforting one, and she felt the beginnings of despair creeping over her.

What if what he said to her was true? He said he didn't want or need her and that he wanted to be rid of her with all possible haste, even to the extent that he would take her to every single ball until she found a proper suitor. She knew that he desired her; she had felt the evidence pressed against her bottom in the library. She knew that he fought against that desire and loathed himself for having it. He had wanted her to fight him, but why? Did he like it when she abused him as she had before? She couldn't imagine why anyone would, though he had seemed rather excited by it when it was happening. She sighed deeply and rolled onto her side and looked at the glow of the moon as it shown through her window. Perhaps she should be cruel to him more often to see how he responded. Perhaps that would get a response from him quicker than anything else. She didn't think it would be hard as he would no doubt provide plenty of provocation to incite her to violence, but she wasn't sure she could bring herself to do it now that she had seen his bleeding wounds.

Her instincts told her to wrap him in love and compassion but would that be the best way to break down his defenses? Tonight, he had revealed quite a bit, and she hadn't used violence at all. She had threatened to, but she hadn't actually done it. He had been angry at the turn of events and wanted to push her away with his crude behavior. Had she not had the moment of understanding that she had, she would have lashed out at him with all of her might. What would have happened if she had? Would he have forced himself on her then? The thought made her shiver but not with fear. She wanted to know what it would be like to have him inside her; did that make her a bad person?

She had never had this feeling before and thinking about it now made her burn low in her belly, and she could feel the flesh between her legs grow taut with a dull, aching throb. Was this desire?

Is that how he feels when I am near him? She pressed her hands on her woman's mound and clamped her thighs down hard to keep the throbbing at bay. She felt uncomfortable now as though she had a void that needed to be filled. Her breast felt full, and her nipples were tightened into hard nubs, and they ached too. *What is this?* She kicked off her covers because she suddenly felt hot and stifled. It felt like she had a fever, but her body was covered with goose pimples as if she were cold.

What was that? She grew still and listened closely. She had heard a tinkling sound at the window; there it was again. She quickly sat up and looked at the window thinking perhaps a bat or a night-bird of some sort were out there pecking at the window, but she could see nothing. There it was again; someone must be down below throwing pebbles at the window. She stood up and put on her wrap and cautiously approached the window. She stood at the side of the window and stretched her neck so she could take a look below. There was a man down there, but she couldn't quite make out who it was ... oh, it was Mr. Kenwick from the party ... a marquess or some such, she wasn't sure.

Why, he just threw another pebble at the window; what on earth is he doing that for? She stood in full view in the window now, and he saw her then and gave her a courtly bow and started motioning for her to open the window. She thought about it for a moment and then decided the best way to be rid of him was to open the blasted thing and tell him to go away. She hastily opened the window and leaned out so she could better project her voice.

"Have you gone mad, Mr. Kenwick?" she called out as quietly as she could.

"Yes, I have gone mad with passion for you my lovely American rosebud," the devil in disguise said.

"Sir, you had better remove yourself at once before you wake the entire household," she warned him.

"Allow me to properly re-introduce myself. I am Robert Ensley, the Marquess of Kenwick; your most humble and devoted servant," he said with another courtly bow.

Claire realized he was politely correcting her mistake and thought it was done in a rather grand fashion, and it made her giggle.

"Yes, well, Mr. Ensley, you had better leave before someone calls the watch," she said with a smile.

"I would go to prison with a smile on my face were you to bestow your sweet kiss upon my lips," he said with a seductive grin.

The man was handsome; she had to give him that, and he certainly knew how to flirt. He was tall and dashing with dark brown hair, styled in the Brutus fashion that was so popular, and if she remembered correctly he had green eyes. He seemed rather full of himself, however, and that simply didn't interest her.

"I feel that I must inform you that you shall go to prison a very disappointed man," she told him with a bit of a giggle.

"How you wound me, your loveliness. How might I persuade you to have mercy on a poor wretch in love?" he said with another wicked grin.

"In love?" she asked. "Surely you jest, sir."

"Love is no laughing matter, my lady. I find that I am quite besotted and will die a thousand deaths until you free me from this malady that has so suddenly stricken my heart by agreeing to become my wife."

"Mr. Ensley, I am sorry that you are suffering sir, but I must remind you that I am engaged to Mr. Crenshaw," she told him with a bit of a flush.

Was she really engaged to Dylan? She wasn't so sure that he believed it, but it seemed right to her. At any rate, it was the perfect excuse to rid herself of this nuisance.

"That is why I must act swiftly. I mustn't let him make away with such a fair prize. He is undeserving of such a fine exquisite beauty as you," he told her.

Now she was angry. How dare he say such a thing about Dylan?

"Sir, I will have you know that he is ten times the man you could ever hope to be, and I love him with all my ..." Oh my God, there he is.

Her heart fluttered in her chest as she saw Dylan walking up behind Mr. Ensley. Had he heard everything that had been said? She hoped not, but she suspected that he must have because he looked like a beast fit to kill.

"Please my lady, don't stop talking; your voice is like silk caressing my soul," he told her, totally oblivious to the predator behind him.

Dylan was stalking him like a panther stalks its prey before the kill. She felt tendrils of fear spike in her blood, and she was truly afraid for Mr. Kenwick or whatever his name was. Before she could warn him, Dylan tapped the man on the shoulder, and he spun around and was met with Dylan's fist. Dylan laid a savage blow somewhere on the man's handsome face, but she wasn't sure where it landed. He stumbled backwards and landed on his backside, and Dylan advanced upon him again and grabbed him up by his lapels and slammed his face with another savage blow.

"The next time you think to sniff around the skirt of my fiancé, you had better be prepared to name your seconds, Kenwick!"

She heard the threat that he issued, and her heart soared. He had called her his fiancé, and it sounded as though he truly meant it. She shook off the sappy thought and continued to observe the scene below, fearing that it would escalate. Mr. Ensley scrambled to his feet and quickly fled. Dylan stood staring after him until he had completely disappeared in the darkness. He glanced up at the window and the look in his eyes sent chills down her spine.

"Go to bed Miss Melville," he calmly said.

Claire was paralyzed by the sight of the man as she realized that his coat was unbuttoned and beneath, his chest was bare. He wasn't wearing a shirt beneath, and his hair was down about his shoulders, and he looked quite savage standing there; almost like an Indian, native to her country. She shivered and drew her wrap tighter around her bosom but didn't leave the window. They stood staring at one another for several moments as if locked in a spell. It felt as if time stood still, and they were the only two people in the entire universe, she wanted desperately to go to him. What would happen if she did? Would they make love? The spell finally broke, and Dylan turned and walked toward a tree that partially shaded her window. He sat down beneath it, facing her and tilted his head up to look up at her. What was he doing?

"What are you doing?" she had to know.

"If you are going to refuse to go to bed then I must take up a sentinel position until you come to your senses," he said.

"You are going to be my protector then?" she asked with a smile.

"Don't read too much into it, Miss Melville," he said snidely.

Well what did she expect? Of course, she was talking to Dylan, and he was an arse, so naturally he would act like one to correct her of any false delusions she would suffer from with regard to him.

"Of course, I realize that you would never do anything so chivalrous for me simply because you desired to do it. Don't waste your time, just go back to your scotch and wallow in it," she snapped.

He said nothing to this, only continued to stare at her with unfathomable eyes. What was going on in that brain of his?

"Go Dylan, just go," she said.

"Go to bed and I will," he said softly.

"Leave and I shall go to bed," she retorted.

"Must you be so difficult about everything, Miss Melville?" he asked with a sharp tone.

Oh the nerve of the insufferable man; he calls

me difficult when all he has done is snap and bark at me since my arrival.

"You sir, are the one that is difficult. I cannot even have a conversation with you without wanting to thrash you. Why do you suppose that is?" she asked.

"Because you are a violent American that thrives on war and dissent," he offered sarcastically.

"How dare you say such things to me, sir," she huffed.

"See what I mean? You always posture and stomp your feet like a bull ready to charge whenever someone says something that you don't like," he told her with a crooked grin.

The sight of that smile took her breath away; he was smiling, and he was smiling at her. She found herself unable to speak, and she realized that she was smiling back at him. It didn't last, however, because he must have realized that he let his mask of anger slip. He quickly wiped his smile away then resumed his hostile stare. She was making progress with her combative stance just as she suspected she might. It encouraged her.

"What about you, sir? No one can even speak to you without being insulted or slandered for their efforts," she said with a hostile glare of her own that she did not feel. What she really felt was joy. They were having a conversation and so far it seemed to be going rather well.

"Speak proper English with the proper homage due to your betters, and I might not need to be so insulting," he retorted.

"My betters?" she barked.

"Yes, your betters. I am a lord yet you refuse to acknowledge it or anyone else of rank. Take poor Kenwick for example; you were calling him Mr. Kenwick. It is Lord Kenwick, you silly goose," he said with another crack in his armor.

So he had heard the entire exchange. He must have even heard her say that she loved him; had he? The thought made her shiver.

"I have told you sir, that I will call no man lord. There is no man alive that is my better, and I refuse to allow you to force me to behave so submissively."

"Somehow, I could never picture you behaving submissively," he said with silk pouring off his tongue.

Was he trying to seduce her? She shivered again.

"I would fight to the death before I allowed myself to be subjugated," she told him.

"It must be an American thing to want to fight so much; perhaps there is something in the water there that affects the brain," he suggested with his armor fully lowered.

She gasped at the sight of the most magnificent smile she had ever beheld, and it brought tears to her eyes.

"Speechless now, my mighty warrior?" he asked with a touch of concern in his eyes.

Claire shook her head and fought to hold back the tears that threatened to rush forth. If she needed confirmation that she loved this man, she had it now.

"What is it Claire?" he asked as he stood and

advanced toward the window so he could see her better.

She shook her head again but managed to speak.

"I find your insults about my fine country to be quite feeble," she choked out.

He smiled again, and her knees nearly buckled.

"Go to bed, my mighty warrior," he said softly with a wink, and then he was gone.

Chapter Ten

"Luther Rollins, the Marquess of Huntley to see you, Miss Melville," Simmons said.

Claire was startled by the interruption as she had been deeply absorbed in her manuscript and hadn't expected any callers. She wasn't sure, but she thought perhaps this was one of Dylan's friends. Why would he be calling on her?

"Show him in, Mr. Simmons," she said.

A moment later, a very large man with unruly hair came through the drawing room door, and she remembered that he was indeed one of Dylan's close friends. He was clutching a nosegay of flowers in his giant hand, and he had a very large grin on his baby-like face. What a charming man, she mused.

"Hello Mr. Rollins; how are you today, sir?" she asked.

"Hello Miss Melville; I am doing quite well. Thank you for seeing me," he said.

Claire really had to crane her neck to look at this man as he advanced toward her; he must have been six and a half feet tall. She realized that she was gaping and quickly pulled her wits together.

"Won't you please sit down, Mr. Rollins?" she said, indicating that he should sit on the sofa.

He moved with more grace than Claire would have thought him capable of and took his seat on the sofa. He realized he was still holding the flowers and unceremoniously held them out for her.

"Oh what lovely flowers, Mr. Rollins; thank you very much," she said taking them from him.

She brought them to her nose and closed her eyes at their delightful scent. She loved fresh cut flowers, especially daisies.

"You are quite welcome, my lady," he said with a huge grin.

"Oh please, do not call me 'my lady'; I am just Miss Melville or Claire if you prefer," she said, a little embarrassed by the way he had formally addressed her.

"I believe I shall call you Claire, and you should call me Luther," he told her.

"That is a lovely name, Luther, and it suits you perfectly."

"I called today to see if perhaps you might like to take a ride about the park. It's a lovely day, and I have my curricle available. It would be a great way for you to meet more of society as everyone who is anyone goes to the park," he said with deep dimples in his cheeks.

The man positively gleamed when he smiled. Such a sweet innocent face he had too.

"That sounds grand Luther. I have been cooped up in this house for nearly a week working on my manuscript and would really appreciate the diversion," she told him.

"Wonderful … uh … er … is Dylan about?" he asked.

"I have not seen Dylan since last night," she said with a touch of disappointment in her voice that she tried to conceal.

It was three in the afternoon, and she hadn't seen hide or hair of the man in question, and she was really quite depressed by it; she had such high hopes for today after all that had occurred last night.

"Perhaps he is at his club," Luther suggested.

"Oh no, sir, he never leaves the house. He is either holed up in his library or in his chambers, but he is definitely here," she said.

Luther had a strange look on his face at the information she had imparted, and she wondered if perhaps she had said something wrong.

"You say he never leaves the house?" he asked.

"Never, and yesterday was the first time I had seen him in three days. He just stays hidden away from everything and everyone round the clock," she said, wondering now if it was wise to tell him of his habits.

"Hmmm … Perhaps I should go and take a look and see if he is alright," he suggested.

"You are certainly welcome to, but I have found that when he is disturbed by visitors he becomes quite surly," she said.

"Well, perhaps we should not disturb him then. Are you ready to go to the park?" he asked.

"Oh yes, I just need to get my wrap, and I will be ready," she told him.

"Take your time Claire … we have all the time in the world," he assured her.

Claire dashed out of the drawing room and up the stairs to retrieve her wrap and nearly ran into Dylan on her way. He was standing on the landing at the top of the stairs, and he looked somewhat angry but … sober.

"Hello, Mr. Crenshaw, how are you today?" she said with sunshine in her voice.

"Who is that in the drawing room?" he asked

gruffly.

"Why, it is Mr. Rollins and he has come to take me for a ride about the park," she said.

Uh oh … she didn't like the look in his eyes or the tightening of his jaw.

"Is that the way of it, Miss Melville?" he asked.

"The way of what, sir?" she asked confused by the question.

"Have you found your future husband?" he asked sardonically.

"He is your friend, Mr. Crenshaw, and he has come out of courtesy to take me to the park," she said, getting angry now.

"And did his courtesy call bring those flowers that you have clutched in your hand?" he asked.

Claire had forgotten that she still had the nosegay in her hand and looked at it bewildered.

"As a matter of fact yes, Luther brought the flowers," she told him.

"Luther is it?" he said with a dangerous glint in his eye.

Claire realized she had made a mistake just then and wasn't sure how to recover from it. He very clearly didn't like the idea of his friends courting her or that she would be on a first name basis with them.

"Really, Mr. Crenshaw; I hardly see what your complaint is. Didn't you tell me that you wanted to be rid of me as soon as possible?" she sniped.

With moves so fast she hadn't had time to react he had advanced on her and grabbed her wrist, yanking the flowers out of her hand. He threw them behind him, lunged forward and placed a punishing kiss upon her lips. She quickly threw her free arm around his neck, bringing herself closer into his embrace and deepened the kiss. Her knees were so weak with desire that if he were to let go of her she would slide into a heap on the floor at his feet. He smelled clean, and there wasn't a trace of whisky on his breath, and it was after three o'clock. With the same suddenness that he had kissed her, he had broken the kiss and pushed her away from him.

"If he kisses you, I will know, and I will kill him," he said menacingly.

Claire's knees had nearly buckled, and she was shocked by his statement and gasped. She quickly recovered with stiffening shoulders, and then with a tilt of her chin she laid into him.

"How dare you say such a thing? How am I to find a husband if you continue to threaten to kill every man that dares to approach me?" she goaded.

"See that he doesn't kiss you, Miss Melville," he said.

He stood there and dared her to say anything further for a moment, and then he spun on his heel, went back into his room and slammed the door loudly in his wake.

Claire smiled.

*****

The ride through the park had been wonderful and Luther had been right that everyone was there. She couldn't help but notice all the curious looks that they had received, and Luther had stopped several times to introduce her to this person or that, most of whom she would never remember. She had never heard so many titles in her life; *how do these people keep track of such things*? Her mind was truly scrambled with the effort of trying to figure it all out.

"Would you care for a quick tour about Mayfair before I return you home, Claire?" Luther asked.

"That would be lovely Luther, but are you sure we should?" she asked.

"I don't see why not; it's still early," he replied.

She wasn't sure it was such a good idea, but he seemed to be a nice fellow, and she didn't think he would do anything untoward with his friend's fiancé. He had been very polite thus far, so she didn't see any real harm in it.

"A quick tour would be fine," she conceded.

"Very good," he said smiling.

He deftly maneuvered the curricle through the traffic, and before she knew it, they were whizzing through the streets of Mayfair. He seemed to enjoy pointing out houses of people they had just met as well as friends of his.

"Would you mind if I asked you a personal question Claire?" he asked out of the blue.

Claire had a moment of irrational panic that he might be about to make a proposal or something equally ridiculous and tried to relax so he wouldn't see her alarm.

"That would depend upon the question, Luther," she hedged.

"Do you love Dylan?" he asked.

She snapped her gaze at him from the shock of

the question.

"Very much," she replied without thinking.

"Good, you'll do nicely then," he said.

"Nicely for what?" she demanded.

"My dear lady, we are going to bring Dylan back to life, and you are going to help us," he said.

"Who is we?" she asked.

"You, me, Jasper and Gabriel," he told her.

"How can I help?"

"You and I are going to become lovers," he told her.

Claire sputtered and coughed.

"I beg your pardon?" she demanded.

"Oh not in the real sense, forgive me for frightening you. We are only going to make him think we are," he explained.

Claire understood what he was saying. They planned on making their friend mad with jealousy so he would become possessive over her, and in so doing … what?

"What is this supposed to accomplish?" she asked.

"It's to sober him up, Claire," he explained.

"You may not believe this, but I think your plan is already working," she told him.

The big man laughed jovially.

"I knew it would work … what do you mean, it's already working?" he asked suddenly perplexed.

"I saw him when I went to retrieve my wrap, and he was perfectly sober and very irritated by your arrival to take me to the park."

Luther smiled and slapped his leg.

"Perfect. Now tomorrow, Jasper will come to

court you and you will allow it. The two of us plan to become somewhat of a nuisance so be prepared for things to get a little rocky," he explained.

"Am I supposed to be Jasper's lover too?" she couldn't help but ask.

Luther laughed and nodded his head.

"I think this plan has a big gaping hole in it," she said.

"What might that be?" he asked.

"Dylan will not want to marry the town trollop," she told him frankly.

"Well, we don't have to be lovers, I suppose, but you will have to let us court you," he said.

"Courting is fine," she agreed.

After a moment of companionable silence, Claire began to wonder about things.

"Luther? Why is Dylan so angry at himself?"

Luther drew in a deep breath and held it for a moment then very slowly let it out.

"Promise you won't tell him that I told you?" he asked.

"Of course."

Luther told her everything. More than she had bargained for, actually. She didn't like the part about virgins, debauchery and brothels, but she supposed that this kind of behavior was fairly common in bachelors, so she decided not to judge too harshly. The part about Wishy was much as she had suspected, and she had a complete understanding of his self-loathing now. She tried to block out the image of him cradling the poor dead girl in his arms and wailing like his soul had been ripped apart. She didn't want to think of that because it made her soul feel torn too, and she hadn't even experienced it, though she had certainly seen the aftermath.

"The poor dear man," she said when he finished the sordid tale.

"They don't come any better than Dylan, Claire and if you will bear with him, he will be a devoted husband. You will never have to worry about him straying because he is as loyal as they come," he assured her.

"He smiled at me last night, did I tell you?" she said, and then began to sob.

That smile had probably cost him dearly now that she knew it was probably the first in nearly a year.

"Please don't cry Claire, I didn't mean to upset you, and if I take you home with your eyes swollen with tears, Dylan will kill me," he pleaded.

He was right, Dylan would. He had already threatened to do it if he thought that Luther would try to kiss her; he would become unhinged if he thought that Luther had hurt her somehow. She dried her eyes and sniffed in an attempt to hold them at bay.

"I'm alright now," she told him.

"That's good because we are about to go down Dylan's street. It's getting late, and I don't want to face Lester and Hank when I bring you back.

"Who is Lester and Hank?" she asked.

"His dueling pistols," he told her with a smile.

"He named his pistols?" she asked incredulously.

"Men are funny like that, Claire … sometimes

we even name our ... never mind," he blushed again.

Claire didn't need to have it spelled out; she knew what he had been about to say. Men; she would never understand them, but she certainly had a better understanding of Dylan now, and she was grateful that Luther was such a rattletrap that she had been able to learn so much.

Luther stopped his curricle in front of Dylan's home, and Claire nearly fell out of the seat at the abruptness of it. She collected herself and was about to jump down when he stayed her hand by placing his large one over hers. He jumped down and ran around to assist her down and walked her to the door. He took her hand in his, placed a very tender kiss that he lingered over a little too long for her comfort, and then made a sweeping bow and promised to call again on the morrow. With a wink and a grin, he turned about on his heel and bounded to his curricle while whistling a cheerful tune, and then he was gone.

She stood there for a moment and watched him go, realizing that all the farewell drama had been for Dylan's benefit, so she assumed that he had probably been watching the whole time. She took a deep breath and turned to the door just as it was opened by Mr. Simmons who practically snarled at her as she entered. As she expected, Dylan was waiting on the landing at the top of the stairs. He took one look at her then turned and walked away.

Well, it wasn't going to be easy, but the wheels were in motion and they seemed to be headed in the right direction. He had been steaming mad when she returned and most likely had brooded the whole time she had been gone. *I wonder if he is sober now*?

Chapter Eleven

Claire was beginning to despair that they had
miscalculated Dylan's feelings for her because it
had been six days since the day Luther took her to
the park, and she had not seen him since. Once
again, she wasn't even sure he was in residence.
She was sitting in the drawing room trying to
concentrate on her manuscript but was having a
difficult time of it. She didn't feel all that well and
kept having an uncomfortable feeling in her right
side. Adeline seemed a little agitated too as she had
been wide awake every day for the last four days
and mumbled incessantly. Her chief complaint
seemed to involve the lack of Scotch within the
household, but that didn't make any sense unless
Dylan had consumed it all. Was it possible that he
went on a really bad binge and may very well be
lying there dying in a drunken stupor?

The wondering and the waiting were driving
her mad, and if it hadn't been for the daily visits by
Jasper and Luther, she would have already been fit
for the funny farm. Jasper assured her that the plan
was working and not to worry, but how did he
know? No one had seen him and for all she knew he
was totally oblivious to their ruse. Jasper assured
her that Dylan knew every move they made and that
she was not to worry. It was all so frustrating. Even
the duke was getting frustrated as he had come by
yesterday and told Mr. Simmons to summon Dylan,
but he ignored it completely, and the duke left
angry. Something was wrong; Claire could feel it in
her bones. The house seemed to be vibrating with

tension; even the servants were a nervous wreck.

Mr. Simmons was the only one allowed in Dylan's chambers, and it was absolutely impossible to get information out of him. The man seemed to take a perverse pleasure in keeping her in the dark about Dylan's well-being, and if she had the power, she would fire him immediately and storm the fortress. That awful Mr. Ensley sent her flowers again and between him, Jasper and Luther the house was taking on the impression of a funeral parlor. She should throw them all out. Of course, there was no point in the exhibition if Dylan didn't even see it.

Tonight, Jasper was escorting her to a ball and it was her hope that she would have been able to tell Dylan of it in the hopes that he might want to go too. He had promised to take her to balls, but so far there had been nothing; just cold silence behind a closed door. Claire sighed deeply and put away her quill and ink. Trying to write with her mind so entangled was impossible. Her head hurt, and her neck was stiff, she felt like she could use a rest.

"Adeline, I believe I will go and take a nap to rest up for the ball this evening," she said.

Adeline smiled and nodded her head and said something that sounded like, 'peasant shreams muddier'. Hard to figure with her, but if she had to guess, she would think that she had just wished her to have pleasant dreams. She had become more coherent over the last few days, and it was getting easier to understand her.

"Thank you dear, I will certainly try," she told her.

Claire left the drawing room feeling a bit defeated and fatigued and with a numbed mind she made her way up the stairs. She had her head down when she was walking down the hall and didn't realize that Dylan was standing there until she bumped into him. She jerked her head up and was about to say something when he put his finger to her lips and shook his head, no. He took her by the wrist and led her to his room and gently prodded her to enter. Once inside, she whirled on him to demand some answers, but he was advancing toward her, forcing her to walk backward further into the room. She bumped into the bed and her knees gave way, and she promptly sat on the edge.

"What do you think you are doing?" she demanded.

"I wanted to speak to you," he said.

"You could have spoken to me anytime you wanted for the last six days Dylan; why the urgency now?"

"I wanted you to be the first to know what I have done," he told her with a crooked smile.

"What have you done?" she asked cautiously.

"You'll never guess, but try," he said with mischief in his eyes.

"Did you steal the crown jewels?" she asked with a raised eyebrow.

He tossed back his head and laughed. She was stunned; the man was laughing.

"No you silly goose, I didn't steal the crown jewels though now that I'm sober I probably could," he said with a wink.

"Sober?" she asked.

"Yes, I have been sober for one week. Today is the seventh day … well, actually the sixth; the first day doesn't really count because I did drink that night before I purged myself of it after an impromptu swim in the garden pond, but that's another story," he said.

Claire couldn't believe what she was hearing. He had stopped drinking a week ago, and he wanted her to be the first to know. What did that mean?

"Dylan this is wonderful news. How come you have been hidden all this time; I was so worried about you," she told him.

"It wasn't a very easy thing to do. It made me very sick for the first few days, and I didn't want anyone to know what I was up to in case I failed," he explained

"You have been sick?" she asked perplexed by this information.

"Yes, I had to get the poison out of my system, and it didn't want to release its hold on me. I can't really explain it, but I was quite addicted and had to go through a process," he explained.

"It sounds positively awful, but I'm so glad you pulled through. You look … radiant," she said, then dipped her head in embarrassment.

He did look radiant … he was beautiful in fact. He looked so healthy and clean, and his eyes were clear and bright. His smile was so heartwarming that she could feel its warmth all the way to her toes.

"I did it for you, Claire," he told her softly.

She looked up at him with disbelief written all over her face.

"For me?" she asked.

"So I could be the man you deserve," he said with a devastating smile.

She burst into tears then. She couldn't believe what was happening. It was as though she were in a dream, and any moment she would wake up and find that it had all been an illusion. He dropped to his knees and wrapped his arms around her waist and gently laid his cheek against her bosom. She reached up and ran her fingers through his soft, silky hair and cried harder.

"Shhh ... Claire don't cry," he crooned.

"I can't believe that this is happening," she said on a sob.

"Believe it Claire; it is true. I would not have you saddled with a drunkard for a husband," he told her.

She pulled away from him, and when she did, he looked up at her with his chin resting on her knee.

"Husband?" she asked.

"We are engaged, are we not?" he asked lifting his head.

"I don't know; are we?"

She felt him stiffen, and he pulled away from her. He stood up and walked away and started pacing. What had she said wrong? What was happening?

"Do you not want me, Claire?" he asked.

"The last time I spoke to you about our

engagement was with hostility, and you didn't give me much to hope for, if you will recall," she said bristling.

"Have you been having such a grand time with Luther and Jasper that I mean nothing to you anymore?" he barked.

"That is absurd," she said, her temper rising.

"Is it really? All those flowers in the drawing room indicate a grand time being had by someone, and oh yes, Kenwick has been sending them, as well. I suppose you are seeing him too," he said snidely.

"I have not been seeing him; why do you make such ugly accusations?" she demanded.

"What else am I to think? You have gone out every day with one man or another, gallivanting all over London, without a chaperone, I might add," he shouted.

"I am a woman grown; I can see to myself. I hardly need to be tended to like a child while I go gallivanting all over London," she mocked.

"Surely, America is not so backward that it allows unmarried women to go out with unmarried men without benefit of a chaperone," he chided.

"How dare you sir?" she said standing up now, fully prepared to do battle.

She advanced toward him like the bull he said she was as she saw nothing but red.

"Oh, I dare my warrior princess … I dare," he said as he advanced toward her.

They met in the middle of the room, and they were nearly chest to … well … stomach, and the tension was so thick you could choke on it.

"You have no cause to talk to me like this sir, no cause at all, and I demand an apology now or so help me God I will thrash you," she threatened with her fists curling into tight little balls.

"Don't hold your breath, sister," he chided.

Claire reared back on her heels and drew her arm back, and just before she would have tipped over backward she flew forward and let her fist fly. Dylan ducked the punch easily and grabbed her wrists, pinning them at her sides.

"Careful … I'm sober now, and my reflexes are fast," he warned.

"Unhand me ... you … savage brute!" she shouted.

She twisted and turned trying to free herself from his hold, but he reached around her like a bear hugging a tree and lifted her from the ground. He walked with her kicking and thrashing about in his arms and dumped her unceremoniously onto his bed and fell down upon her. He grabbed her by the wrists and forced them up over her head and bound them in the grip of one of his very powerful hands, and with his free hand he brushed the hair out of her eyes.

"I was wondering when I would see my mighty warrior again," he said just before he lunged forward and took her lips in a ruthless kiss.

She resisted at first, but he grabbed her by the chin and forced his tongue into her mouth and started massaging hers with his own. It was so intoxicating that it stunned her into submission and she found herself being very cooperative.

"Does Jasper kiss you like this?" he breathed

into her mouth.

Claire whimpered and shook her head as best she could; he thrust his tongue back in, and she began to arch and twist trying to get closer to his body.

"Does Luther kiss you like this?" he said with a punishing reminder of who was kissing her now.

Her lips felt bruised, but she didn't care; all she cared was that he was devouring her, body and soul.

He pulled away from the kiss, and she tried to chase after him, but she was still immobilized by his grip and the weight of his body. He stared into her eyes as though he were trying to see inside her mind.

"Answer me," he demanded.

What did he ask me? She couldn't remember; all she knew was that her body was hot and in terrible need of his kiss.

"So it's Luther then, is it?" he asked shoving away from her.

He stood up beside the bed, and she quickly sat up in response.

"What are you talking about," she asked in bewilderment.

"Don't play innocent now, Miss Melville," he said with absolute disgust written all over his face.

"Perhaps you had better start drinking again, so you can speak more clearly because you aren't making any sense at all," she shouted.

"Oh, you would like that wouldn't you? Totally oblivious to the fact that you are shagging my friends because I am too drunk to notice," he growled.

Claire jumped up so fast she surprised even herself, and the next thing she knew she was airborne and had wrapped herself around him and was pulling his hair.

"You are an animal … I hate you … I hate you … you filthy dog!" she shouted.

Dylan wrestled her off of him and thrust her to the floor, but she jumped up like a cat and rushed at him again with her fists flying so fast he had no time to react. He stood there while she banged on his chest as though he were a drum until finally she was exhausted and slid back to the floor in a heap at his feet.

"Collect yourself and get out!" he said with a coldness that made her shiver.

Claire couldn't understand what had gone wrong. How could things have come to this when moments ago they were lost in each other's embrace?

"Dylan, I don't understand what happened here," she told him.

"You tried to make a fool of me, Miss Melville; that's what happened here," he gritted out through clenched teeth.

"I would never do such a thing Dylan, I swear."

"Just leave," he said stiffly.

Claire stood to leave and her knees buckled, and she nearly fell. Her whole body felt as though she had been wrung out and left to dangle in a harsh breeze. She reached the door, and she stopped to look back at him. He had turned away and all she could see was the cold stiff spine he had presented her. She gasped and silently sobbed, then quietly opened the door and left. Once in the hall, she ran as fast as she could to her room and flew inside, then threw herself upon her bed. Her guts felt twisted and on fire, and she thought she would die from the pain of loss that she felt. She had lost him somehow, but she didn't understand how; what had gone wrong? What was she to do now? She closed her eyes and continued to sob.

****

"Miss Claire, don't ye want to get a bath afore the ball?" Lucy asked.

"The ball?" she asked confused.

"Aye, it's seven o'clock and if ye don't get ready now, ye'll miss the 'ole thing," she said with a soft smile.

The ball? How could she have forgotten the ball? Had the whole incident with Dylan been a dream? Did it really happen at all? How long had she been sleeping?

"Are ye alright Miss Claire?" Lucy asked.

"I don't know Lucy … something is wrong," she said, still feeling strange and confused.

Lucy reached out and placed a hand to her forehead.

"Miss Claire, you have a raging fever," Lucy exclaimed.

"A fever?" she slurred as the room started to spin and everything went black.

Lucy ran from the room screaming for help.

"Lord Sumersleigh, come quick," she screamed.

Dylan opened his bedroom door, and she

grabbed him by the hand and started leading him down the hall. She kicked open the door to Claire's room and dragged him over to the bed. He was shocked at the sight before him. Claire was as red as flames, and she was unconscious … what had he done?

Chapter Twelve

Dylan took one look at Claire and nearly fell to pieces. Why had he treated her so poorly? Now look what had happened; she was sick and he was to blame. He must have upset her tremendously to bring on such a condition.

"Go tell Mr. Simmons to fetch a surgeon immediately … the duke's surgeon," he told Lucy.

Lucy ran out of the room, and he crawled in the bed beside Claire, pulling her into his arms and starting to stroke her hair. What if she dies? He made an agonized groan and pulled her hot and limp body closer to his.

"Claire wake up!" he commanded her.

She moaned and whimpered, and her eyes fluttered. His heart leaped in his chest, and he thought she might come around, but she went silent again. She was burning alive; he had to do something. He carefully laid her down and began stripping her clothes off. Once he had her disrobed down to her shift, he grabbed the pitcher of water from the sideboard and a cloth to set about wiping her down with the cool water. He heard a shuffling noise behind him and turned to look up, and Jasper was standing there in the doorway.

"Get out!" he shouted.

"What's wrong with her Dylan?" he said, ignoring the command.

"I have no idea, but I have called for a surgeon, now please go because she isn't dressed," he said trying to shield her from Jasper's view with his own body.

"Perhaps I can help," Jasper persisted.

Dylan thought about it for a moment. Was Jasper in love with Claire too? Perhaps he was.

"Are you in love with her Jasper?" he found himself asking.

"No," he answered simply.

That was a relief to Dylan, and he felt like a selfish bastard for even caring about it now when Claire was so ill. He sighed deeply and motioned Jasper forward. Jasper moved to the side of the bed and lifted Claire's arm to take her pulse. He closed his eyes while he did this, and after a moment he lowered her arm then laid his ear to her chest so he could listen to her heart. After a moment of listening to her heart, he looked up at Dylan.

"Could she be with child?" he asked.

"I don't think so, at least not by me," he said.

"I need to see her stomach," Jasper said.

"Why?" Dylan asked defensively.

"I want to check for distention in the abdomen," he said softly.

"Perhaps we should wait for the surgeon," Dylan suggested.

"She is your woman Dylan ... rest your mind," he prodded.

"What about Luther, is he in love with her; is she with him?" Dylan asked.

"No," he answered simply.

Dylan felt like an arse for even asking, but he had to know. He had treated Claire so badly when he accused her of it, and he was desperately seeking a balm for his conscience.

"We quarreled, and I accused her of sleeping with my friends while I was too drunk to notice," he said with shame in his voice.

"She is a good woman Dylan … rest your mind," Jasper told him softly.

"I haven't had the chance to tell her that …" he cut his words off.

"That you love her?" Jasper suggested.

Dylan nodded his head. He did love this woman; he knew that now without a doubt.

"Move aside Dylan and allow me to examine her," Jasper insisted.

"Why are you here?" he found himself asking as he moved aside.

"I was going to take her to a ball to make you jealous," he explained.

"Why would you want to do that?" he asked as he watched Jasper pressing about on her beautiful stomach.

"To bring you back to life," Jasper told him.

Tears that he didn't even know were there rolled down from his eyes. His friends had been courting Claire because they loved him, and the notion was overwhelming.

Jasper finished his examination and lowered her shift and turned to him.

"Her appendix is about to burst and may have already," he said.

"What does that mean?" he asked in alarm.

"It means that if we don't remove it very soon she will die from the poisoning," he explained.

"The surgeon is on his way," Dylan told him.

"Let us pray that he is not too late," Jasper said softly.

Dylan's heart jumped in his chest; he couldn't let her die. He would be lost without her, and he had just been found; he needed her like he needed air to breathe. He knew now that she was essential to his own survival, and he would do whatever it took to save her.

*****

Doctor Hilliard came in a timely fashion and concurred with Jasper's assessment but added that there must be some kind of secondary infection to account for the high fever; perhaps a kidney infection, he suggested. After a heated argument with Dylan, the surgeon agreed to remove the appendix with the assistance of Jasper, who was well versed in medicine, though self-taught. He wanted it understood that he only did so under duress and with the understanding that she would probably die from the infections and that he could not be held accountable in that event.

Dylan was beside himself with grief at the prognosis and had become unmanageable. He argued with Jasper and the doctor to no avail as he wanted to stand by in case she died so he could be there with her to see her through it. Luther and Gabriel had arrived, and it took both men to physically remove him from her bedside so that Jasper and Doctor Hilliard could get started. They dragged him away and took him to his library where they now sat in relative silence. He needed a drink, but Gabriel and Luther were watching him so closely that there was no way he could slip away, and even if he could there was no liquor in the house. He had it all thrown out when he set about cleaning out his system so he wouldn't be tempted.

"She is going to die and my last words to her were an awful accusation," he said to no one in particular.

"She is not going to die; she will live to fight with you for many years to come," Gabriel told him.

Dylan wished that he could have Gabriel's positive outlook, but his luck hasn't been too good over the last few years and he simply couldn't believe that God would have enough compassion for his sorry arse to spare him the grief.

"She told me she hated me," he said.

"That woman loves you Dylan," Luther put in.

"How do you know?" he asked.

"She told me," he said with a smile.

"I don't know why she would love me; I have done nothing but ridicule, mock and treat her as if she were scum on my shoes since her arrival," he said with a bit of a crooked grin forming on his lips.

His mighty warrior was a hellcat and gave him as good as she got and then some, and the thought comforted him because it proved that she had a strong will and might possibly fight to survive. There was a knock on the library door, and the three men looked up anxiously.

"Enter," Dylan called.

The door opened, and the duke walked into the room.

"I'm sorry it took me so long to get here, but your father has taken a turn for the worse, and I had to make sure all was taken care of. How is the patient?" he asked.

"They are performing the surgery now, but the surgeon doesn't think she will live. What of my father?" he asked.

"I don't think he will live much longer Dylan; you had best prepare yourself," the duke said solemnly.

Dylan looked heavenward and sighed deeply; what else could go wrong? He had a moment of regret for never having been close with his father. They had been virtual strangers since he was a young boy, but he didn't want him to die.

"How much longer?" he asked.

"A day, maybe two but unlikely," the duke said.

"I'm sorry, Grandfather; I know this must be hard for you to accept. What can I do to help?" he asked.

Dylan loved his grandfather and would do anything for him; all he had to do was ask. Dylan had not always been cooperative of late, but he had never failed him, even when he was at his worst. His grandfather placed a hand on his shoulder and smiled.

"Keep doing what you are my boy. I am very proud of you, and I love you very much," he told him.

Dylan stood up and embraced him, and the two men stood in this way for a long comforting moment.

"Thank you," he said pulling away from the embrace.

"She will make it Dylan; have faith. God has sent her to us, and I firmly believe that. He will not be so cruel as to take her away now," he told him with a warm assuring smile.

Had God really sent Claire to him? He had never been a spiritual man, but he had to wonder if there was truth in what his grandfather said. She had been here for less than two weeks and touched his life so profoundly and had inspired him to want to be a better man. Maybe she was an angel, and God was bringing her home now that her work was done; he didn't want to believe that. He was selfish, and he wanted to keep her here with him forever. He sat down in his chair, and his grandfather took a seat on the sofa; the four men sat in silence while they waited for word on her condition. All Dylan could do now was have faith in the will of his mighty warrior and the kindness of the God he had virtually ignored his whole life.

*****

An hour later, Jasper and Doctor Hilliard came down and both of their faces were grim. Dylan's heart fell in his stomach, and his body tensed in preparation of hearing the worst.

"The surgery went well, and if she makes it through the next twenty four hours, she may live," Hilliard said.

Dylan let out the breath he had been holding.

"Do not get your hopes up my lord; she has a long way to go yet. As I said before, there was a secondary infection of some kind. I believe that she has a kidney condition with this as well. Could be just an infection, but it could be something else; I have no way of knowing for sure. She should have nothing but water for the next two days and only in small increments. On the third day she may have broth and other fluids, and you should maintain that diet for about a week."

Dylan was thankful that she was still alive, and he wanted to go to her now. He would see to it that the doctor's orders were followed to the letter, but he needed to go to her now to see for himself that she would live.

"Excuse me," he said, then promptly left the room and ran up the stairs.

He burst into her room expecting to see her awake, but she was still unconscious. He realized there was no way she could have been awake and felt stupid for thinking it in the first place. He quietly walked over to the bed and slid in beside her so he could watch her sleep. He hadn't realized that Lucy was there in the room until she spoke.

"My lord, she still 'as the fever so we need to keep applying cool compresses to 'er body throughout the night," she told him.

She must have been trying to politely tell him to go away, but he was having none of it.

"I'll do it Lucy; go and get some sleep. You will need to be rested up so you can take over tomorrow," he told her.

Lucy reluctantly left the room and went to her

small room which was situated off of Claire's room. He was glad she would be nearby just in case, but he fully intended to care for Claire himself. It was the least he could do after what he had done, and he needed to have something to do to occupy his mind. He sat up and slid out of the bed, careful not to shift her around too much and started to work with the cool compresses. She was so beautiful laying there with her hair spread out and her cheeks burning with fever. Would she forgive him? The thought pressed hard into his mind and took hold, making his hands shake with fear. He would do whatever it took to get back in her good graces if only …

No, he wouldn't think it; she would live.

*****

During the early morning hours the fever finally broke, and Claire seemed to be resting well. She had opened her eyes once and looked at him with a sweet crooked smile before her eyelids fluttered and closed again. That smile gave Dylan some much needed reassurance that she still loved him and charged his body with a renewed energy, and he felt more alive than he had in a long time. That one sweet smile stroked his soul like a loving caress and he felt a profound sense of contentment. When she recovered, they would marry right away, he decided. He couldn't imagine his life without her now, and he wanted to let the world know it. She would make the most beautiful bride the world had ever seen, and he would be honored to stand beside her.

One day she would be a duchess, and the thought tickled him as she had such an aversion to titles. How would she respond when someone called her 'your grace'? He chuckled softly and kissed her forehead.

"I love you Claire. Thank you for coming into my life when I needed you so desperately," he said softly.

She didn't respond of course, but that was alright; he would tell her again when she was awake. He stood up and put away the wet cloths he had been using throughout the night and walked over to the window. The moon was still out, but the sun was about to rise. He could see a lavender haze over to the east. She had made it through the night, and she would live; he was sure of it. He looked up at the sky and closed his eyes in communion with God and thanked him for the blessing. Lucy would wake soon, and he would have to go and see his father one last time. His father would have liked Claire; who wouldn't like her?

He was about to turn from the window when a flash of movement caught his eye below. He froze and looked closely. Someone had been there beneath the tree; he was sure of it. Who would have been out there at such an hour? He continued to look out the window and started scanning the lawn. That's when he saw the silhouette of a man walking quickly away. Kenwick! He would know him anywhere. Why was he out there? Could he and Claire … no he refused to think it. The scoundrel was probably lurking about because … something wasn't right here.

He looked over at Claire as she lay there sleeping, unaware of all that had occurred, and couldn't help but wonder if perhaps it hadn't been Luther or Jasper at all, but Kenwick she wanted.

But Luther had said she loved him, and he had heard her tell Kenwick that himself. No, she didn't want Kenwick, but one thing was clear … Kenwick wanted her.

Over my dead body, he silently vowed.

Chapter Thirteen

By the time Dylan had arrived at his father's house just after dawn, he had already passed on. The duke told him that it had been a quiet passing, and that he hadn't suffered. Dylan was relieved and felt a pang of loss for the man that he hardly knew. He was the Marquess of Wentworth now, whether he wanted to be or not, but he didn't feel any different for it. He hadn't even gotten used to the idea of being Sumersleigh, so Wentworth wouldn't be too much effort to assume. The duke said that he would handle all of the funeral arrangements and that Dylan should keep his focus on Claire until she was out of the woods. He was relieved to hear those words because that was where his focus was, and now he didn't have to bear any guilt over it.

First, he had something he needed to take care of. and it couldn't wait. He left his father's house and headed to Whites to see if he could link up with Kenwick and find out the man's intentions toward his fiancé. It was just after nine o'clock, and Whites was virtually empty. Dylan went in anyway and decided he would break his fast there; he was hungry and realized he hadn't eaten in two days. While he waited for his breakfast, he read the Times for the first time in over a year and was surprised that with the exception of America declaring war on England, nothing had really changed while he had been buried alive in his home. The same people were causing the same scandals as they were when he had fallen out of society.

The waiter brought his food, and he ate it with gusto and topped it off with a large glass of milk. It had been delicious, and if truth were told, he could have eaten more. He decided against it, however, as he didn't want to tax his body too heavily after all he had been through over the last week. It was best to ease along gradually, or he could have a huge stomach upset. That wouldn't do at all because he had too much going on to become indisposed. There was Claire to consider and his father's funeral, so he had better do what he could to stay fit. He looked across the room and noticed two men drinking ale, and for a brief moment he would have liked to have one, but he knew if he did, he wouldn't stop there, he would want something more substantial. It was time to leave and put the temptation behind him. Kenwick was most likely at home now, anyway

He got up to leave and speak of the Devil; there he was, coming in the door. Kenwick spotted him right away and turned to exit quickly. Dylan laid his coin on the table and ran after him, catching up with him just as he was about to round the corner.

"Hold there, Kenwick; I would have a word with you," he told him.

Kenwick stopped but didn't turn around. Dylan advanced from behind and spun him around by his shoulder, and the two men glared one another.

"What is your interest in my fiancé?" he asked him.

"Come now Sumersleigh, you don't really want the chit. Everyone knows you are a drunken sod and have no real interest in being leg-shackled," he said snidely.

"Your impressions of me are a bit out of date; allow me to bring you up to speed. First, I should inform you that I am Wentworth now and secondly; I am no longer a drunken sod and third; you had better stay away from my fiancé. If I catch you lurking about outside her window again, I will kill you," he told him with a cold ruthlessness that would have frightened the average person, but Kenwick didn't seem too concerned by the intimidation.

"I saw how you treated her at the dinner party Wentworth, and I am of the opinion that the girl deserves better. I am better, and I will have her. I know what you really are, you see, and it is my duty to save the girl from marrying a monster like you," Kenwick said calmly.

Dylan lost all sense of reason and before he knew what he was about, he punched Kenwick in the gut, sending him to his knees.

"You will have her over my dead body, Kenwick," he growled.

"Perhaps that could be arranged," he grunted.

"It will take a better man than you to kill me, but you're welcomed to try," he told him.

Kenwick wasn't a stupid man; he knew that Dylan was a superb marksman with a pistol and refused to issue a challenge for the insult Dylan had just given him. This made Dylan angry, but there wasn't much he could do about it.

"What? You don't want your honor avenged Kenwick?" he prodded.

Kenwick rose to his feet and dusted off his

trousers then stood straight and tall before Dylan.

"If I were to meet you on the field of honor I would be a dead man. There are other ways for vengeance to be appeased," he threatened.

"I am all ears," Dylan snarled.

"I wouldn't turn my back if I were you because as soon as you do, I will be there with a knife that will fit quite nicely right in the center," Kenwick said with cold sincerity.

"I'll be waiting," Dylan told him.

Kenwick made a mocking bow, spun on his heel and quickly extricated himself from Dylan's menacing presence. Dylan wanted to do murder and his hands curled into tight fists as he watched Kenwick disappear down the street. God, what he wouldn't do for a drink! Dylan sighed and tried to release the tension in his body. He didn't want to go back to Claire with murder and rage in his heart; she deserved better than that.

*****

Dylan was disappointed to see that Claire's fever had spiked again. He was also unhappy that he had missed an opportunity to speak with her as she had been awake before he returned home. She was in quite a bit of pain, so Lucy had given her some laudanum, and she was sleeping once again. Lucy said that she had been in good spirits and had asked about him. She told him that he had stayed with her all through the night and that he had to go to his father's house. Lucy didn't know that his father had passed and was quite sad to hear it when he relayed the news to her. He needed some sleep, but he wanted to be there when she woke up again, so he called for a cot to be set up in the room at the foot of her bed. He gave Lucy instructions to wake him should Claire wake again or if her condition worsened in any way.

Lucy was in stern disagreement with his sleeping there, but after much clucking and huffing she gave in and took up her place in the chair in the corner of the room to do some mending and to keep a close eye on him, no doubt. He knew it wasn't proper for him to sleep in here, but he didn't want to miss anything. He wanted to be there when she woke so he could tell her that he was sorry and that he loved her. He promised Lucy that after she woke and he said his piece, he would go to his own room and that seemed to mollify her somewhat. He had a sneaking suspicion that Lucy wasn't as upset as she pretended to be as she had known him since he was a boy and had always liked him.

He was glad that Lucy was here to keep such a close watch on Claire, and he made a mental note to talk with his grandfather about keeping her on here once they were wed, with an increase in pay, of course. He could tell that Lucy adored Claire and would serve her well, so she was the perfect candidate for the position. He settled himself down on the cot, but sleep didn't come easy as he had so much on his mind. Kenwick was a thorn to his peace of mind; he didn't think he would be rid of him easily. The man was bold in his pursuit of Claire, and he wondered why.

Did the man love her? Men did foolish things when they were in love, and he could certainly understand how he could have fallen in love with her so quickly, but part of him wondered if he just viewed her as a conquest of some sort. He had heard negative things about Kenwick over the years with regard to young women. It was rumored that he had stolen the virtue of many a young maid, and that he had several bastards lying about. Well, one thing was certain ... he wouldn't get his hands on Claire. Dylan closed his eyes and tried to shut out all the noise inside his head and before long he had fallen into a restless sleep.

*****

A few hours later, Dylan sat straight up in the cot when he heard a terrible moaning. He was confused at first about his surroundings and then he remembered where he was, and he looked over at Claire; she was awake but in terrible pain. Lucy was standing beside her with her head cradled in her arms, and she was trying to give Claire some water. The movement must have hurt her, but she was drinking the water now. He quickly got up and went to the other side of her bed noticing that her eyes followed his movements. Lucy gently laid her back down when she was through drinking and fussed a bit with the covers.

"Do ye want some more laudanum Miss?" Lucy asked.

Claire shook her head, no, and closed her eyes for a moment and tried to conceal a pained expression, but it was obvious she was hurting.

"Perhaps you should take it Claire," he suggested softly.

She opened her eyes and looked at him and shook her head, no, again.

"I don't want to become addicted," she rasped out.

"We won't let you become addicted, but you are in pain and you were operated on just last night. Please take the laudanum," he said.

"In a little while," she finally conceded.

Dylan decided to let the matter rest. He sat on the edge of the bed and moved a stray strand of hair out of her eyes.

"You had me very worried Claire," he said softly.

Lucy took that as her clue to leave the room, and he was grateful to her. He had things he wanted to say to Claire, and he wanted to say them in private.

"I'm sorry that I have caused so much trouble," she told him.

"Don't be silly; you were very sick," he admonished.

"I am not silly sir," she bristled.

"I love you Claire," he told her when he realized they were about to quarrel.

She snapped her gaze to him and gasped at his words.

"Yes, I love you, and I don't want to quarrel with you anymore. I want us to be married as soon as you recover because I have discovered that I am quite lost without you," he told her.

She began to weep, but she said nothing. Dylan had a moment of panic that she had not forgiven him or that perhaps she didn't love him anymore. He took her hand in his and brought it to his lips.

"Please say that you still want me Claire," he said, just before he laid a soft kiss on her palm.

"Oh, I do Dylan; I want you desperately. I love you so much, and I was sure that I had lost you after our last quarrel. Luther is not my lover, I swear," she told him.

He chuckled and kissed her palm again.

"I know; I am a fool for ever thinking that either of you would betray me in such a way. Forgive me," he said.

"Jasper and Luther hatched a silly plot to make you jealous. They thought it would spark you to life and that it would make you want to fight for me," she told him.

"I know love, and I thank them for it. I have come back to life, and it's because of you. I had already decided that I had to change my ways and become the man you deserved, so all their efforts were for naught," he said kissing her palm again.

She winced and closed her eyes again, trying to stifle a moan.

"You will take the laudanum now, Claire; I insist," he told her.

He gently slid off the bed and went to the door to call for Lucy. She was in the room so fast he barely had time to say her name. She knew what the problem was without him even having to direct her.

"Lucy, would you like to stay on with Claire when we are wed," he asked, thinking now was the perfect time to ask her.

Lucy jerked her head around and gasped.

"Is it true? Ye really are to be wed?" she asked.

"Indeed, just as soon as she recovers," he said with a smile.

"Oh, that's wonderful; praise be to the saints," she exclaimed with a large toothy grin.

"So you will stay with us then?" he prompted.

"Ye don't even 'ave to ask my lord," she said while putting a couple of drops of the laudanum in a glass of water for Claire.

"Good; I'm glad that's all settled," he said.

He watched as Lucy gently lifted Claire's head to give her the medicine and gently lay her back down.

"I suppose I should go now; I promised Lucy that I would go back to my room once I had an opportunity to speak with you, Claire. I want you to rest well so you can recover quickly; I am eager to claim my bride," he said with a seductive grin.

She blushed prettily and nodded her head. He leaned over and kissed her on the forehead and reluctantly took his leave. He was a happy man, and it was great to be alive.

Chapter Fourteen

The next two weeks passed agonizingly slow for Claire. She was feeling much better now, but the doctor insisted that she have at least one more week of bed rest before she tried to resume a very limited routine for another three weeks after that. His main concern was that the stitches on her belly could burst, which could cause infection and a very ugly scar. The surgeon assured her that once she was healed completely the scar would be barely noticeable, and she hoped he was right because as it was now, it was quite unsightly. They never did figure out what the secondary infection had been, but whatever it was seemed to be gone now as the fever had not returned in nearly a week. She was quite relieved that she appeared to be on the mend as she was eager to recover so she and Dylan could wed.

The betrothal announcement had already been placed in the Times, and next week Dylan was going to start having the banns read, putting the wedding just under a month from now. Dylan had arranged the date for the wedding to give her a full six weeks of recovery, per the doctor's recommendations. She had the feeling that had the doctor suggested a full two months to recover, Dylan would have used Lester or Hank to change his mind. He had been such a dear man over the last two weeks, showering her with gifts and dancing attendance on her as if she were the most important thing in his life. The transformation in the man was marvelous, and she had no doubts that he would be a kind and loving husband. He spent most of his time in the room with her, reading to her or just simply talking the day away long into the night, where most nights he would fall asleep on the bed beside her. She knew it was scandalous, but she didn't care; he would soon be her husband.

Claire was very sad that Dylan's father had died and that she couldn't attend the funeral with him. It was a very modest affair, though many members of the ton and family turned out to bid farewell to Jonas Crenshaw, the Marquess of Wentworth. Dylan didn't seem to like that he was the new Marquess of Wentworth, but he told her that there was nothing he could do about it, and that he would simply remain Dylan Crenshaw in his heart. He told her of his aversions to titles as he had been born a second son and never expected to obtain one. She had known that he was a second son, but she hadn't known that he would prefer to be untitled; learning that quite impressed her as he considered himself a simple man with no more special qualities than the next man. She teased him and told him he would make a fine American, and he lifted his brow and said that he wouldn't go quite that far.

She told him of her writing, and he seemed impressed with her talents but really didn't offer a lot of encouragement to pursue the idea of becoming a published authoress. She sensed that he wouldn't stand in her way if she were to insist, so for now she wouldn't make an issue of it. He had actually read her current work and the two others she had brought with her from home and told her that they were very good, but that was the end of that. It was more than Barnaby had done, so she was hopeful.

The duke and Adeline were ecstatic over their upcoming nuptials, and between the two of them planning the wedding, it was bound to be a huge affair complete with a ball to be held the weekend before the ceremony. She never imagined that Adeline could have so much energy, but it seemed that since Dylan had quit drinking so had she. Claire could even understand what she said now, well most of the time at any rate, and the two of them had become the best of friends. She wished that her mother and father were still alive to share in her happiness, but she felt them close in her heart and knew that somehow they were happy for her.

The Duchess of Windhaven had come to visit her on a couple of occasions, and they, too, were becoming the best of friends. She said they were to be family now as the four men were like brothers, so that now made her, her sister. Claire liked the idea of having brothers and sisters as she had grown up an only child. All in all, she was quite happy here in England with her new friends and family and hardly missed Virginia at all. There was nothing there for her after all since her father had died and the plantation had been sold.

After the first day of her arrival in England, she would have never envisioned that she would have found such happiness here and marveled that she could have ever hated the place. Of course, she hadn't really seen much of it being cooped up in a sick bed, but the people in her life had more than made up for it.

*****

Dylan was sitting with Jasper and Luther at Whites, and the three men were discussing what should be done about Kenwick. The man continued to send flowers to Claire every day and had even been so bold as to call on her when Dylan had been out of the house yesterday. Dylan gave Simmons strict instructions to dispose of the flowers that had been sent and turn the man away when he called. He had hoped that when he put the notice in the Times that he would have given up, but still he continued to be a nuisance. He had caught a glimpse of him a time or two outside Claire's window, but by the time he had gotten down there he had disappeared, and he had so far been very careful to avoid another confrontation with Dylan. He supposed that short of calling him out, there was very little that could be done. Dylan hoped that once he and Claire were wed he would see that he had lost and move on, though he would prefer that he give up now.

"Why don't we have him trussed up and placed on a ship for America," Luther suggested after a long silence.

"Damnation Luther, I think you just had a stroke of genius," Jasper said smiling.

"We couldn't do that," Dylan said.

"Why not," both his friends asked in unison.

Dylan didn't have an answer for that, and now that he thought about it, the idea did have its merits. It would take months before he could return to England, and he and Claire would be well and truly wed by then, perhaps they would even have a child on the way.

"It would have to be a last resort," Dylan allowed.

"I think it's a grand idea Luther; I'm quite impressed," Jasper told his friend with a slap on the shoulder.

Luther beamed at the compliment. It was rare for him to be the one to come up with a good idea, and he was relishing in the moment.

"Thank you Jasper; that means a lot coming from you," Luther told him.

"Perhaps, Luther and I could scare him off for you," Jasper offered.

"No, he could be dangerous," Dylan warned.

He remembered the look in Kenwick's eyes when he made his threat about a knife in his back and thought that he might try to harm his friends too.

"Luther could snap him like a twig," Jasper said haughtily.

Luther beamed again, "Perhaps when you get that flying contraption built, we can load him up and send him to the moon," he said with a chuckle.

"I don't think it will fly quite that far, but ... no I would have to have some kind of rocket propulsion," Jasper said with a faraway look in his eyes.

Clearly, he was onto an idea for his latest invention, and it would be difficult to get him back on task.

"Please don't tell me you are considering strapping your arse to a rocket, Jasper," Dylan groaned.

"Not my arse; Kenwick's," he replied with a cheeky grin.

"We will not be strapping anyone's arse to a rocket and that's final," Dylan said.

"Luther might like to volunteer. Wouldn't you like to take a ride to the moon, Luther?" Jasper asked mischievously.

"You will not be using that overgrown child in any of your dastardly schemes," Dylan chided.

"I am not a child," Luther argued.

"Says you," both his friends said in unison.

Luther's moment in the sun was covered by a dark cloud now, and he sat glumly with his shoulders slumped forward.

"We're getting off point," Dylan said after a moment.

"Short of sending him for a boat ride to the colonies, all we can do is to keep a close eye on Claire to make sure he isn't given any opportunities to be alone with her. It shouldn't be that much of a problem considering she is bedridden for another week and housebound for another three after that," Jasper said.

True, Claire was safe and had no idea that Kenwick was still in pursuit of her. The man hadn't been bold enough to throw rocks at her window again since that first night, but he was sure he was still lurking about during the night. He had decided after seeing him there again that he would stay with Claire at night. Most nights, thereafter, once she had fallen asleep, he stood vigil in the window for several hours so he could be seen by Kenwick.

Perhaps that would be enough to keep him at bay. Claire wouldn't be leaving the house on her own any time soon, and they would be marrying in a few weeks, so perhaps Kenwick wouldn't have any real opportunities to get near her. He would like to have married by special license but the duke wouldn't hear of it, so he had agreed to allow the banns to be read so he and Aunt Adeline would have time to prepare for a proper wedding.

"I could move in with you until the wedding to help you keep guard," Luther offered.

Dylan's first reaction had been to say it wasn't necessary but seeing that his friend seemed to want to prove his worth, he decided to consent.

"I would appreciate that Luther; it's very kind of you," he told him with a warm smile.

Luther was beaming again.

"You are welcome too of course, Jasper," Dylan told him.

"I think I'll pass. I have some ideas that I need to put into play with my flying machine," he told him.

"Try not to blow yourself up, would you?" Dylan asked with seriousness.

"No worries, mate," Jasper said with his signature grin.

That was easy for Jasper to say, but they all worried about him when he was inventing. Jasper had a tendency to become totally absorbed in his work when he was in one of his modes and often would go without sleep, food or drink for days on end. To think about him tinkering around with rockets and gravity defying flying machines was positively horrific.

"Just see that you stay in orbit," Dylan cautioned.

*****

"You are going to make me fat Dylan," Claire admonished as Dylan presented her with another box of chocolate confections.

"I love a woman with a little meat on her bones," he said with a sexy smile.

Claire felt a shiver travel down her spine, and she knew that she was blushing; the man is a menace.

"Did you have a nice time at your club?" she asked, trying to regain her composure.

Being so near him every day and not being able to throw herself in his arms was taxing on her nervous system. He had been a perfect gentleman and kept his amorous attentions to a safe peck on the forehead or a kiss on the palm here and there, but she wanted more.

"I had a fine time. I brought home a house guest, however," he told her.

"A house guest?" she asked with surprise.

"Luther will be staying with us until the wedding," he told her.

Claire thought that was strange. Luther had a townhouse in Grosvenor Square, which was only a few minutes away. Why would he need to stay with Dylan?

"Does he have an infestation of rats at his townhouse?" she asked with a teasing smile.

"No ... I felt a little sorry for him after Jasper

and I poked a little fun at him. I wanted him to feel useful, so I told him he could come here and help me with the preparations for the wedding," he fibbed.

She knew he was fibbing, but she couldn't imagine why. Perhaps she shouldn't concern herself with it. They had been friends since childhood and there were bound to be things between them that they wished to keep to themselves.

"That's very nice of you dear," she said with a smile and a raised eyebrow to let him know she didn't completely buy it.

He sighed and cleared his throat.

"The truth of the matter is that we have had someone lurking about the property at night, and Luther is going to stay with us for awhile to be sure that we all stay safe. I didn't want to alarm you, but I can see that I cannot lie to you either," he told her.

Claire was alarmed.

"Do you think it's a burglar?" she asked with concern.

"I don't believe so," he said averting his eyes.

"Tell me what is going on Dylan," she demanded.

"It's Kenwick; he's been lurking about outside your window for two weeks, and he sends flowers everyday and has even dared to call on you when I left the house," he rushed out in frustration.

Claire gasped at this information; she had no idea that this was going on.

"What does he want?" she asked alarmed.

"You," he said simply.

"That's absurd," she protested.

"I assure you that it's true. He told me so himself and said that you deserved a better man than a drunken sod like me," he told her with sadness in his voice.

"Well, you just tell him that I wouldn't have him if he were dipped in gold and trimmed with diamonds. The very nerve of the man," she huffed.

He leaned forward so quick that she didn't have time to react and kissed her on the lips ardently. She threw her arms around his neck and pulled him closer, urging him to deepen the kiss. He massaged her tongue with his own, and her whole body heated up in response. She whimpered and moaned her appreciation, and he quickly pulled away.

"I'm sorry Claire; did I hurt you?" he asked with panic on his face.

"No, quite the opposite; please don't stop," she begged.

"I think I had better before I do hurt you," he said sheepishly.

She wasn't sure how he could possibly hurt her by simply kissing her, and then she realized the implication behind his words.

"I wish I were well now Dylan, so you could hurt me," she purred seductively.

His answering smile was wicked. He reached up and stroked her cheek, then leaned forward, placing a soft kiss on her lips.

"Soon my love; only I promise to be gentle," he told her.

"I look forward to it with an aching in my heart," she told him with a husky voice.

"I should go and see about your dinner my

sweet," he said, sliding off of the bed.

She looked him over from head to toe, and she could plainly see that he was aroused, and the knowledge made her shiver. She would be his wife soon, and she would finally get a glimpse of what lay beneath the strained fabric of his trousers. She imagined that he was very well endowed, though she didn't really have a frame of reference to base it on. Perhaps in another week or two she could encourage a little heavy petting, and she could get a peek. The thought made her giggle.

"What are you laughing at," he asked with a crooked smile.

He could see where her eyes were focused, and he stood there with his hands fisted at his hips to allow her to look her fill.

"I was just wondering when I might get a peek at what lies beyond the strained fabric of your trousers," she admitted with a blush.

"On our wedding night and not a moment sooner, young lady," he said with a wink.

"You are a cruel man, Dylan Crenshaw; a very cruel man indeed," she pouted.

He threw his head back and laughed, then made a sweeping bow and took his leave.

Chapter Fifteen

Things went very well over the next two weeks and Claire had healed up quite nicely. The doctor removed her stitches, and she was no longer restricted to her bed. It felt good to be up and about, though she wasn't allowed too much activity beyond sitting in the drawing room and the occasional short walk in the garden. Dylan still hadn't let her go up or down the stairs, insisting on carrying her to and fro. It was a sweet gesture on his part, but she felt sure that she could do it herself. When she protested this morning, he told her that next week he would allow her to try and do it on her own. She didn't argue about it as she loved seeing him so chivalrous with regard to her care.

He had become quite handsome over the last week or so, and Claire thought it was probably because he was gaining weight now that he no longer wasted his life away with drink. His muscles had bulked up, and some of the hard angular features in his face had softened, giving him a more youthful appearance. He had resumed his daily fencing exercises with Luther and had even gone to a boxing club with Gabriel a few times. She was glad to see him doing so well, and he seemed so much happier than he had been when she first met him. Before he was a foul tempered, foul smelling ogre, but now he was full of mischief and humor, and he smelled absolutely divine.

He still had not allowed her to have a peek inside his trousers, always maintaining a very gentlemanly demeanor when he was in her presence. He quit sleeping in her room when she was no longer confined to her bed, and she missed his presence there immensely. When she pouted at him about it, he assured her that he would make it up to her once they were wed and never leave her side again. That would have to do, she supposed, because apparently he was determined to guard her virtue. She would no doubt have already lost her virtue had he not moved out of her room because she had become quite amorous toward him, and he was finding it harder and harder to resist her attempts to seduce him. She didn't know what had come over her behaving in such a way, but she couldn't seem to control herself. Even now she was quite warm and moist in her woman's flesh just thinking about him.

At one point, Dylan had asked her if she were still a virgin, and she became insulted and they quarreled. It had been their first quarrel since the night she became sick, but it didn't last very long. He apologized for asking and told her that she was behaving like a woman with some experience and that he had been confused by it. She didn't know about that; all she knew was that her body burned for him, and she felt like she would die if he didn't make love to her very soon. That was the night he moved out of her room telling her that if she was a virgin, she wouldn't be so long if he remained, and since then he had kept their visits to a more courtly routine. That had been a week ago, and she missed him terribly.

She would have to wait two more weeks to know the wonders of the marriage bed, and with each passing day she grew more eager. She had started dreaming of making love with him, and many nights she would suddenly wake up and her body would be aching with a terrible need, like it was this very minute. She was lonely right now as Dylan had gone to his club and Adeline was taking a nap; she had no idea where Luther was, but she didn't think he left with Dylan. There was nothing to do but write on her manuscript and she wasn't really in the mood for that, so she decided that a walk about the garden was in order. She could use the exercise since their betrothal ball was a week away, and she would need to be strong for dancing. The weather was perfect for it; not too cool, and there wasn't a cloud in the sky. She knew that Dylan didn't want her walking alone, just in case, but she couldn't see any harm in it; she didn't plan on being out there long.

*****

Claire loved the garden, though it was in serious need of attention. She supposed that a bachelor wouldn't care whether his garden was well tended, but once she was mistress here, she would see that some improvements were made. She would bring in more roses and some lilies, perhaps a few more azalea bushes. Some irises and jonquils wouldn't be a bad idea either; the place could use a splash of color. She would like to see some more statuary brought in too; perhaps some of those Greek mythological characters would go nicely. There was a nice little pond, but it lacked a fountain. She would see about that as well; she really loved fountains. Why, she could have the whole thing completely reworked and make it a romantic spot for when they entertained guests or just each other.

She stopped short when she saw a flash of movement below the hedgerow and thought perhaps a cat had come to visit. He was probably after a bird no doubt, and she wanted to discourage that. She walked over to the hedge and squatted down so she could see below, but whatever was there was gone now. She stood back up and walked a little further along the hedge, thinking perhaps she had scared the little scamp because she saw no further sign. With a deep sigh she decided she had gone too far away from the house and was no longer in view of the drawing room windows. She didn't want anyone to become alarmed when they couldn't see her; if anyone were there to look, that was. She turned around to go back and collided with a wall of flesh, and her heart nearly leaped out of her chest when she saw who it belonged to.

"Mr. Ensley, what are you doing here sir?" she demanded.

He grabbed her by the arms and pulled her into his embrace so fast that he caught her quite off guard and moved in for a kiss. She turned her face just in time to avoid his lips on hers and began to struggle against his hold in earnest.

"Unhand me sir, or I shall scream," she shouted.

"My lovely Claire, please do not scream. I have been trying to see you for weeks, and I am quite distressed over the long absence of the woman I love from my life," he pleaded.

"You do not love me sir; unhand me I say."

He did as she demanded, and she quickly took steps back to put some distance between them. Her heart was beating so hard that she could hardly catch her breath, and she was more than a little frightened. His eyes roved over her body and settled on her heaving bosom, and she began to feel as though he were undressing her with his eyes.

"What do you want from me, Mr. Ensley?" she demanded in an attempt to redirect his eyes.

He looked into her eyes for a suspended moment.

"Run away with me, Claire. We can go to Gretna Green and be married right away. You do not want to marry him; marry me instead," he told her.

Claire gasped at his words as her mind reeled from the very idea of it. The man must be insane to think that she would do such a thing.

"You had better leave this minute, Mr. Ensley. I am to be married in two weeks, and I am quite in love with my fiancé," she told him indignantly.

He advanced on her, then pulled her into another embrace, and this time she was so shocked by the swiftness of it that he was able to land his kiss upon her lips. She struggled to pull away, but he had her imprisoned in his arms, and he tried to deepen the kiss. She turned her face away from the intrusion of his tongue into her mouth and tried to scream, but he quickly put his hand over her mouth and pulled her down to the ground, crushing her between him and the earth. She panicked then as he began to grope and tug at her bodice with his other hand until he managed to get inside. He squeezed her breasts hard and started kissing her about the neck and chest. She tried to scream but was unable to, so she tried to bite his hand to get him to release her. That seemed to excite him as he pulled his hand out of her bodice and began trying to lift up her skirt. She cringed and tried to buck him off when she felt his hand upon her naked thigh, but she was quite unable to remove him from atop her. He tore her drawers and began to probe her woman's flesh, and the feeling of it made her blood turn cold as she feared she was about to be taken by this madman, and she could do nothing to stop him.

"So hot and moist; I knew that you would want me as much as I want you," he breathed in her ear.

He started fumbling with the buttons on his trousers, and she tried again in vain to buck him off of her. He managed to get his trousers unbuttoned and threw her skirts up to expose her stomach so he could commit his crime against her. He rose up so he could view her body and froze with the focus of his gaze settling on her scar. He swallowed hard and shook his head as if confused before looking into her eyes. He took his hand away from her mouth and stroked her cheek fondly.

"It's true then; you have been ill?" he asked with kindness she had not expected to see in his expression.

Afraid to speak, she simply nodded her head, and what he did next surprised her as he gently removed himself from atop her and began to right her clothing. He stood up then, and she was stunned as she lay there on the ground watching him button up his trousers, and when he was finished he offered his hand to her so he could gently pull her to her feet as if she were fragile.

"Forgive me Claire, I quite lost myself. Can you forgive me?" he asked.

The man must be insane; how could she forgive such a thing?

"I do not forgive you sir, and I would beg that you leave this instant," she growled at him.

"It was never my intention to harm you. I only wanted to show you how wonderful it could be between us so that you would come away with me," he told her.

Claire felt violated from what he had done to her; there was no way anything between her and this man could be wonderful.

"I want nothing to do with you Mr. Ensley. Please leave," she told him defiantly.

What he did next repulsed her to her very core. He slowly ran his fingers under his nose and breathed her scent in deeply, and then he placed them in his mouth and closed his lips around them. He closed his eyes as though he were savoring the taste of manna from heaven and made a groaning sound deep in his throat. She shivered and gasped at the action, and he opened his eyes and slowly removed his fingers from his mouth, piercing her with his gaze.

"I have tasted your passion, Claire, and I know that you want me; the evidence is on my tongue," he said with a wicked grin.

Claire felt as though a lightning bolt coursed

down her spine at the horror of his words, and she bolted and ran as quickly as she could. She didn't look back as she made her way out of the garden, but she could hear his words as she fled.

"You belong to me now Claire, and I will have you," he called after her.

She cried out, not only from his words and what he had done, but from a terrible throbbing in her stomach as she reached the French doors that led to the drawing room. Once she was safely inside, everything went black, and she slid to the floor in a heap.

It was Luther that found her moments later, and he brought her around with gentle patting upon her cheeks. Her eyes fluttered open, and when she saw his face she was startled and quickly moved up into a sitting position.

"Please Claire, be careful; you have swooned," he told her with a gentle, caring voice.

Her head was spinning, and she felt confused, and she started looking about her surroundings. Had it been a dream? Had she swooned and while unconscious, imagined the whole thing with Mr. Ensley?

She wasn't sure as her mind was so foggy at the moment.

"I would like to go to my room, Luther; could you assist me please?" she asked.

Luther scooped her up into his big strong arms and swiftly carried her up the stairs and to the door of her room. He gently lowered her to her feet and held on to her arm to make sure she was steady before he released her.

"Will you be alright, or do you need help getting to your bed," he asked with a blush.

"I think I will be fine now Luther, thank you," she told him.

She opened the door, and once inside, she turned back and bid him goodbye then closed the door. She walked over to her privacy screen and lifted up her skirts and her knees nearly buckled when she saw that her drawers were torn.

It had really happened!

* * * * *

When Dylan returned from Whites, Luther met him at the door and told him about Claire. He ran up the stairs and was going into her room, but the door was locked and he couldn't get in. He knocked on the door, and Lucy opened it and blocked him from entering.

"How is she?" he asked.

"She is resting my lord, though she 'as been very upset and she won't say what the trouble is," she told him.

"Has the doctor been sent for?" he asked.

"She wouldn't allow me to call for 'im, my lord," she told him.

"We shall see about that, please allow me in Lucy," he demanded.

She quickly stepped to the side, and he walked over to the bed. Claire appeared to be sleeping, and he debated whether he should wake her. He turned to Lucy.

"Have Mr. Simmons call for the doctor, Lucy,"

he said.

Claire's eyes popped open, and she quickly sat up.

"No you mustn't; I am fine," she said.

"You are not fine Claire; you swooned. Tell me what happened," he demanded.

She didn't say anything, and Lucy hadn't moved to follow his order.

"Now Lucy!" he barked.

She quickly scurried out of the room, and he looked back at Claire.

"I will have an answer, Claire," he told her firmly.

"I went for a walk in the garden, and I guess I overdid it because I swooned; that is all," she said defensively.

He put a hand to her brow, but she didn't appear to have fever.

"Are you in pain?" he asked.

She averted her eyes and shook her head to indicate that she wasn't.

"Were you alone in the garden, Claire?" he probed.

She snapped her eyes up at him and nodded her head that she was.

"I told you that you were not to go out unaccompanied; now you see why," he said with stern, barely contained anger.

She nodded her head but said nothing; something didn't seem quite right. She seemed awfully nervous about something.

"Is there something you aren't telling me," he prodded.

"No!" she answered quickly.

He looked at her and tried to discern whether or not she was being truthful. Perhaps she didn't want him to think she was too sick to marry in two weeks and feared he might want to postpone until she had a chance to recuperate more completely. It was a thought worth considering. He didn't want to rush her and have a problem down the road as a result.

"Shall we postpone the wedding for a couple of more weeks?" he asked.

"Oh no please Dylan … no, please don't do that. I am fine, really I am," she begged.

He breathed a sigh of relief knowing that was the cause of her nervousness and not something else.

"I love you, Claire, and I want you to be fully recovered before we wed. It wouldn't do at all for you to rush yourself and suffer consequences later on," he explained.

"I wanted to exercise to build up my strength for the ball, and I simply overdid it. I will stay in bed for a few days and rest up, and I will be good as new. Please don't postpone, I beg you," she pleaded.

Dylan thought about it. He supposed they could wed and postpone the wedding night. He just wanted her well and would do whatever it took to protect her.

"Alright my mighty warrior; we shall not postpone," he told her then kissed her on the brow.

She exhaled a long breath and nodded her head then lay back down on her pillows.

"I shall sleep now Dylan," she told him.

"That's my girl. The doctor will be here soon to have a look at you, but you can rest until he arrives," he told her.

She nodded her head and closed her eyes.

Chapter Sixteen

Claire breathed a sigh of relief when Dylan left the room. She was relieved that he wasn't going to postpone the wedding as she had feared. She was terrified that something would go wrong because of what Mr. Ensley did, and she wanted to be sure that she was safely wed in any event. She had decided that she would never tell Dylan what happened out there in the garden because if she did, he would kill Mr. Ensley, and she didn't want him to be hanged. Surely, Mr. Ensley would give up once she was wed, and it was too late for him to convince her to wed him instead. She thought about what he had done to her with a cringe at the memory. He was a handsome man, but his touch had repulsed her because he wasn't Dylan. Claire just couldn't imagine herself with anyone but him.

The man must suffer from some kind of mental malady to behave as he did. Stalking around here for a month then accosting her that way just didn't seem normal at all. Why had he become so obsessed with her? She had done nothing to encourage his attentions, and she had barely been interested in talking to the man at the dinner party and was quite relieved when the duchess had come to rescue her. The man had a way of looking at her that made her feel uncomfortable, and now she knew what it was. She was grateful that he had showed mercy to her when he became aware of her illness, so he couldn't be a complete lunatic. A real madman would not have taken pity and spared her from rape.

It was all very perplexing, and she hoped that nothing happened between now and her wedding to cause Dylan to learn of it. She hoped she never saw the man again, but she suspected that she hadn't seen the last of him. She would just stay indoors avoiding the garden until after she was wed so as not to have any more unplanned encounters with him. Perhaps she could talk Dylan into a long honeymoon; say six months or so. Maybe by then she would be with child and the crazy man would lose interest in her. Would he stop obsessing over her even after she was wed? The notion was too terrifying to contemplate. What if she were never free of him?

*****

Dylan met with the doctor after he examined Claire, and the tension left his body when the doctor pronounced that she would be alright. He said that it wasn't unusual for a person to swoon after trying to exert themselves after a prolonged illness such as hers. He said that she should continue to exercise, but in smaller increments, and to always have someone present in the event that she became overtaxed. He said that she was well on the mend, and that there should be no problem at all with them going forward with their marriage plans including the marriage night. With a wink and an elbow to Dylan's ribs, he suggested that they keep their activities to one or two times a day with nothing too rigorous for at least another two weeks after the wedding. He was comforted by that because the idea that he could hurt his bride was more than he could stomach, and knowing that they could still have their wedding night lifted his spirits considerably.

"Thank you very much Doctor; you have given me much comfort," he told him as he was seeing him out.

"Anytime my lord; all you have to do is call," he assured him.

Dylan watched him go and turned back to his library. He had some things he needed to get caught up on with regard to his estates as he had sorely neglected them for the last year. Now that his father was gone he had inherited two other estates, and if he didn't get on top of things and stay there he could have some real problems on his hands later on. He would have already been in the poorhouse had it not been for his able stewards, and he made a mental note to increase their salaries for all their hard work. His most recent acquisition of properties was very nice, and he thought that perhaps Claire would enjoy living at the one in Kent. Wentworth Manor was a spacious country home with plenty of room for a growing family, and he had always liked the place.

Of course, she might not like the place, but before they left for their honeymoon trip he planned to take her there to see what she would think about living there. Of course, they would still have their two properties in Mayfair and would reside part of the year here. He would probably rent his father's home out as he had no desire to keep that particular property for himself. He preferred his home to that one, though the other was significantly larger. He supposed he should talk that over with Claire as well, but he didn't think she would be opposed to keeping this one as their London home.

He thought about Claire being his marchioness with a smile. She hadn't expressed any feelings about becoming a titled lady, and he wondered if the full weight of it had settled in her mind. He wasn't very socially active with the ton, but once she became his wife, other titled ladies would start issuing invitations for tea and various parties. He couldn't imagine her in such a setting and wondered if she would have a hard time adjusting. She would probably rather skip all those silly engagements and continue with her writing. He hadn't told her yet, but if she were going to continue with the notion of becoming a published authoress, she would have to do so under a man's name as she would likely never be published otherwise.

There were a few women who had been published, but it was still largely a man's world in that arena. He had been quite impressed with her talents, and her stories were very creative. She had a real flare for the dramatic, and her villains were always despicable monsters. He wondered where she got her inspiration for such characters and hoped that she had never encountered such villainy in her life. He didn't think she had though she had been raised in a country that had seen war, and her father owned a slaved plantation so he could imagine that there were some pretty cruel sorts associated with that. Perhaps that was where she contrived such monsters, though he hoped not.

If she were to pursue her writing openly, she would no doubt be shunned by her peers, and he hated to be the one to have to tell her that. The peerage was a strange lot in that they thought earning one's own living a sin. He didn't subscribe to such stupidity and would stand by her no matter what she decided; she was to be his wife, therefore, he could do nothing else. He would do so with pride, and may God have mercy on anyone who ever slighted her in his presence.

*****

Robert Ensley, the Marquess of Kenwick, sat under the tree outside Claire's window in the early morning hours just before dawn. He was angry at himself for what had happened the day before as he would never have intentionally hurt her. He had heard that she had been ill and had some kind of surgery, but he had really believed it to be a lie put out by Wentworth to keep him at bay. Though he had suffered a moment of conscience when he had seen her scar, he didn't intend to be put off very much longer. He would have her, and he would have her very soon. He knew that she wanted him now as he had felt the evidence with his own hand and had tasted her sweet essence on his lips. She was playing coy, hard to get, but he knew better now.

He realized that he was going to have to figure out a way to abduct her, and he would have to do it sometime before her wedding day. Wentworth was obviously a tyrant that kept her under lock and key, guarding her very closely. He would get around him and rescue her from having to spend the rest of her life with a man like him. He was a murdering drunk with a penchant for violence and rape, he just couldn't stand by and allow him to have such a sweet girl as Claire.

The stories about Wentworth were quietly whispered in pubs, and each telling of them seemed more unbelievable than the last, but he knew the truth of what happened as Diana had told him when he went to visit her in Bedlam. He had raped and killed that poor maid and then killed those two men while they lay unconscious with cold calculating cruelty before trying to kill Diana. She was spared when Windhaven intercepted him, but his intent had been clear. Diana had been his lover back then, and he had tried to help set her free, but it had proved hopeless. Now that he had found Claire, he didn't want her anymore. Claire was all that mattered to him now, and he couldn't allow that madman to have her. But how was he going to get to her?

After today she would probably be too scared to go back into the garden … then again she might return with the intention of seeking him out. He doubted it because he knew that he had frightened her, which he never intended to do. He had just wanted to show her how it could be between them, and he had to keep her from screaming so as not to bring attention to their tryst. How ironic that he was trying to prevent her from marrying a murdering rapist, and now she probably thought that of him. He would make it up to her as soon as he got her away from here. He just had to figure out a way to do it. He didn't think he could get into the house undetected with that overgrown ape lurking about when Wentworth wasn't around.

When the modiste shops opened this morning, he planned to have some gowns made up for her and purchase all the other things she would need so that when he took her, she would have need of nothing. He didn't have her exact measurements, but he felt sure he could communicate his desires effectively to outfit her decently until such time as he could have more things made for her. That should take a few days to complete, so perhaps he could come up with a way to abduct her by then. If worse came to worst, he could steal her away from the ball they had planned. He wasn't invited, of course, but he felt sure he could slip in undetected. That seemed like his best option from what he could see, but he didn't want to wait that long. He wanted to grab her as soon as he could before that monster hurt her. He hoped that he hadn't already forced himself on the poor girl, but if he had, he would just have to accept it; he wanted her regardless.

He knew that the blaggard had been staying in her room nightly but that was probably to keep vigil while she had been ill. Surely, he wouldn't have forced himself upon a woman who had just undergone surgery, and he didn't think that he had done so prior to that. He had been keeping a close eye on things, and the one servant he had communicated with said that Wentworth and Claire fought like cat and dog every time they were in the same room. It was comforting to know that she had spurned him that way, as it gave him hope that once he rescued her she would be receptive to his attempts at seduction because he had saved her from a life of misery. She would see what a kind and loving man he could be and fall madly in love with him as he had with her. He just needed to have time to convince her of it.

He didn't think that she was in love with him now, but she certainly was attracted to him; that he knew for sure. He closed his eyes at the memory of her soft flesh in his hands. She was soft as silk, and her breasts were perfectly suited for his hands; he had always admired a large bosom, and hers was perfection.

Her legs were so shapely, firm and with the exception of that scar, her torso had been delectable. It would fade with time, of course, so he wasn't worried; she was perfect just as she was, scar and all. He adored her American accent and the way she dragged out her vowels was very sexy. She reminded him of a cat with those unusual eyes, and her hair looked like spun gold.

He clenched his fist at the thought of running his hand through her tresses as he drove his shaft deep into her warm sheath. Heaven couldn't offer anything sweeter, he was sure of it. He couldn't wait to undress her and kiss his way along her body, stopping to pay homage at the freckles on her bosom. His naughty miss must have lain nude in the sun at her American home as the sun had kissed her on the very spot that he ached to. A woman like that would probably enjoy making love outdoors, and he looked forward to taking her back to his home in

Lancashire and doing just that. His estate was secluded and offered a beach with ponds and even a stream where they could swim naked and bathe in the sun until their hearts' content. He was sure that she would be happy there, and perhaps he would even take her to America for their honeymoon, and she could show him her home. Maybe he could even purchase an estate there, and they could live there part of the year from time to time.

Whatever she wanted would be fine with him; as long as she was his wife, he could want for nothing else. A flash of movement caught his eye on the terrace. It was time to go before he was caught. He looked up at her window one last time, sending a silent message of love to Claire, and with that he slunk into the darkness and made his way to town. He wanted to be at the modiste as soon as she opened because he didn't have a moment to waste in preparation.

Chapter Seventeen

Claire was excited about the ball as Lucy prepared her hair. The modiste had arrived with her gown late this afternoon, and it was absolutely breathtaking. She had never before owned a gown, quite so exquisite. It was made of pastel rose muslin with a mint green sash that fit just under her bosom. The skirt draped down her hips just so, putting emphasis on her shapely figure. The décolletage was rather low, but she didn't think Dylan would mind too much, or at least she hoped he wouldn't. Her slippers were the same color as her sash with little rosebud accents, and Lucy was busy decorating her hair with matching roses. Her hair was intricately braided and fashioned into a lovely top knot with ringlets flowing about her neck and face.

Dylan had presented her with a lovely ruby set of jewels from the Crenshaw collection, and she had been quite pleased to see how nicely they went with her ensemble. The necklace was fashioned like a choker with a cascade of rubies that rested just above her cleavage. The earbobs matched perfectly, and the bracelet was magnificent; she felt like a queen with such finery.

"There ye are miss; ye'll be the most beautiful woman at the ball," Lucy said stepping back to admire her work.

Claire gazed at herself in the mirror and couldn't believe how beautiful she really was. She had never regarded herself as a beautiful woman, but tonight she knew that she was absolutely gorgeous. She stood up and went over to the cheval glass to take in the whole picture, and she beamed at Lucy in the reflection.

"You did a wonderful job, Lucy. How would I ever get by without you," she told her.

"Thank you miss; of course, I 'ad wonderful material to work with," she said smiling.

"Oh Lucy I hardly recognize myself; I never knew I could be so … pretty," she said with a blush.

"Pretty 'ardly describes you miss; yer a true vision, ye are," Lucy assured her.

Claire could hardly believe that she would be married in six days, and she was looking forward to it with barely contained eagerness. It all seemed so surreal that she was sure it must be a dream.

"Well, I suppose I should get downstairs now; I don't want to be late to my own ball," she said smiling.

"Aye, 'is lordship is no doubt wearing a path in the foyer as we speak," she agreed.

"Thank you again Lucy. Don't wait up for me; I shall tell you all about it in the morning," she told her as she turned to gather her wrap and her reticule.

"Thank you, miss," Lucy said.

"I wish you would call me Claire, Lucy; I would feel so much better about it as I feel that you and I have become such good friends," she told her.

"Aye mi … Claire, that we are," she said with a quick curtsey.

Claire smiled and touched her friend on the cheek.

"Sleep well, Lucy," she told her.

With that she left the room and made her way downstairs where Dylan awaited her.

*****

Dylan stopped in his tracks at the sight of Claire descending the stairs and sucked in a breath at the vision before him. She was absolutely magnificent; he had never seen a lovelier woman in his life, and she was his. He couldn't believe his good fortune.

"You look ... ravishing, Claire," he said as his eyes perused her from head to toe.

He took her hand as she descended the final step and placed a sultry kiss upon her gloved knuckles. She blushed deeply and smiled the most devastating smile, making his heart skip a beat in response. She would be his wife in less than a week, and he looked forward to it with an aching in his loins and pure joy in his heart. He never felt a stronger sense of pride than he felt at this moment as he looked at the woman he loved, and he decided he must be the luckiest man in the world.

"Come, let us go to the ball and celebrate our good fortune," he said as he extended his arm.

She placed her hand on his forearm, and he led her to the door and out into the night where the carriage awaited them. He assisted her inside, and once she was comfortably ensconced he followed; sitting across from her, he tapped on the roof with his cane, and they were off. They gazed at one another as the carriage made its way through Mayfair, and Dylan was glad the ride would be a short one as he had the uncontrollable urge to draw her into his lap and ravage her.

"I want to kiss you," he said.

She blushed prettily.

"There is nothing to stop you," she said with a husky voice.

He leaned forward, taking hold of her wrists and gently tugged her forward then kissed her ever so sweetly. She whimpered and pulled her hands away to drape them about his neck and deepened the kiss. His shaft flinched in response, and he knew then that if he allowed this to continue, they would never make it to the ball as he wanted to take her here and now. With great reluctance, he reached up and took her wrists in his hands and put them at her sides then broke the kiss.

"Careful my sweet or we shall miss the ball entirely," he threatened.

"That would be divine," she purred.

"Behave!" he admonished with a wicked grin.

"Why must I behave when I want you so desperately?" she pleaded with pouting lips.

"One of us has to," he responded.

She huffed and sat back to continue her pout, she never looked more adorable than at that moment. He was sorely tempted to let her have her way, but he knew that his grandfather would have him by the cods if he did.

"Don't pout love; we shall be married in less than a week, and I will never deny you again," he promised.

Her answering smile was dazzling, and he was quite mesmerized by her radiance. He was glad that the doctor had told him that she needed a full six weeks to recover because the knowledge that he could cause her harm was the only thing protecting her virtue. Thankfully, the ride was mercifully short, and they quickly arrived at the duke's residence. The carriage came to a stop, and with a sigh he assisted her out and offered his arm to escort her inside. He had a brief moment of guilt as the butler announced them, knowing that they were breaking with tradition by not observing the usual period of mourning, but he wasn't about to wait a year to claim his bride, and his grandfather supported the decision. He hoped that people would be gracious and not make too much of it because he wanted this to be a special night for Claire. It was her first real outing since she had been in London, and he wanted everything to be perfect for her. There were at least two hundred guests, most of which were very good friends of the family, so he didn't expect too much fall out for their indiscretion.

When they descended the steps into the ballroom, a hush went over the crowd as everyone looked at them. The women gasped and the men made grunts of approval at the sight of Claire, but everyone was smiling. He relaxed his shoulders then, and they made their procession into the crowd.

"All of London approves," he murmured in her ear as they made their way towards his grandfather.

"Are you sure?" she asked nervously.

"How could they not?" he retorted.

Claire smiled and blushed but said nothing more on the matter. The crowd murmured their well wishes as they made their way along until he reached his grandfather's side, and once there his grandfather embraced Claire and kissed her on the cheek then shook Dylan's hand. He turned to the crowd then and made the wedding announcement. After the announcement, cheers and applauds rang through the room, and when the crowd settled down the first strings of the opening waltz were struck and Dylan held out his arm to escort Claire to the dance-floor.

"This is my dance, I believe," he said with a big smile.

"You won't step on my toes will you?" she teased.

"Not too hard," he teased back as he whisked her into the dance.

She threw her head back and giggled as they twirled their way around the room, and as they made their way other couples trickled in and soon the floor was full, along with his heart.

*****

She was beautiful he observed from his position behind a statue on the terrace. He could see inside the ballroom, and he watched with deep anticipation as Wentworth twirled her about the dance-floor. He was going to make his move tonight and get her away from that animal if it was the last thing he ever did. He would wait until she was alone and then he would convince her to go with him. He couldn't believe that the hour was upon him and that he would soon have the woman he loved by his side. He had dreamed of this moment for over a month now, and he wasn't about to let anything stop him from his objective. He had everything prepared, and his carriage awaited them out front. The trip to Gretna Green would take about three days, and then they would be married. He had imagined what it would be like the first time he made love to her and even now, as he gazed upon her in that lovely gown, he felt an aching deep in his loins. They would share a grand passion; he could feel it deep in his soul.

*****

Claire was getting tired as the night wore on and about a half an hour ago, she thought she had caught a glimpse of Mr. Ensley; now she couldn't shake off the feeling that she was being watched. She looked around the room fearing that he might be here to ruin her chance at happiness, but she couldn't see him. Surely, the man wouldn't be so bold as to show up here with Dylan and two hundred witnesses, but somehow she sensed that he was near. Dylan had gone to fetch her some lemonade and left her in the care of his grandfather and Adeline. She wished they could go home now as they had been here for over two hours, her feet were tired, and her nerves were shot. She didn't know how to ask Dylan to take her home without causing hurt feelings with the duke and Adeline, but she really wanted to go back to the safety of Dylan's home.

She felt silly for thinking that she was being watched, but somehow she knew that she was. She didn't think that Mr. Ensley would waste an opportunity like this to try and make contact with her again, and with her wedding so close, she felt that he would do something rash out of desperation. She breathed a sigh of relief when Dylan returned with her refreshment as she knew she would be safe at his side.

"You look tired," he said as he handed her the lemonade.

"I am very tired; I wish we could go home," she admitted.

He looked closely at her for a moment, and then he turned to his grandfather.

"I am afraid we may have overtaxed Claire; I believe I should take her home now," he told him.

"I agree; we must consider her health as you will want a healthy bride next week," the duke said with a wink and a smile.

"Will you give our regards?" Dylan asked.

"Absolutely; you two go on home, and I will explain your absence," he told them.

Dylan nodded his head and offered his arm to Claire and led her away. Once outside, he called for the carriage to be sent around, and they stood in silence as they waited. Then she saw him, and Dylan saw him too. Her heart plunged to her stomach, and her body began to quake. Dylan stiffened and grabbed hold of her arm, pulling her closer to him.

"Kenwick, what brings you here?" he asked with venom dripping from his voice.

"I have come to claim my bride," he said calmly.

Dylan put her behind him and advanced on Mr. Ensley, grabbing him by the lapels.

"I told you to stay away from her," he growled at him.

Mr. Ensley leaned forward and said something in Dylan's ear. Claire strained her ears to hear what was being said because Mr. Ensley had dropped his voice very low. She had a deep sense of dread that her life was about to be irrevocably changed. Dylan stiffened in response to whatever was said, and after a moment he turned to glance at her with a look of betrayal on his face. Her knees buckled, and she dropped to the ground making a gut-wrenching sound of horror. She knew what was said; no one had to tell her. Dylan knew now what happened in the garden that day and from the look upon his face he blamed her.

"I didn't mean for it to happen," she cried.

"Oh but it did, Claire, and your lover has just told me all about it," he snarled.

"He is not my lover, I swear," she denied hotly.

He was towering over her with such hostility in his stance that she feared he would strike her. Her body began to shake uncontrollably, and she was desperately searching her mind for a solution to this terrible situation.

"That is not the way he tells it, and you just admitted it a moment before. It's too late to change your story now," he shouted.

"Please Dylan, let us go home and talk about this; I'm sure I can explain it better when we are alone," she implored him.

"It is no longer your home; I want nothing to do with a whore," he said with cold harshness.

Claire uttered a sound of terror, and she jumped to her feet. She threw her arms around his neck trying desperately to hold him.

"Please Dylan, listen to me. You mustn't believe what he told you; it is a lie, I swear," she pleaded.

He stood there for a moment with a pained expression in his eyes, and for a brief moment she thought that he might believe her, but suddenly without warning, he flung her away, and she fell to the ground.

"Take her," she heard him shout, and then he jumped in his carriage, and he was gone.

She stayed on the ground in a heap sobbing as though her heart had just been ripped out of her chest. In fact, that was exactly how it felt, and she wanted to die. She felt a hand on her arm and looked up to see Mr. Ensley standing beside her, and then he bent over to assist her to her feet. She stood there in stunned disbelief as he helped her with her wrap, then picked up her reticule from the ground as though all that had occurred just then was completely natural. The man had just ruined her life, and he had the nerve to be smiling.

"Get away from me," she growled at him.

"No, my dear, I shall never leave your side. We will be married in just a few days now that all the obstacles have been removed to our happiness," he told her with a twinkle in his eyes.

The man must be insane to think she would want anything to do with him. He took her by the arm and tried to lead her to his carriage, but she pulled away from him then tried to run. He caught her quickly, whisking her up, and then started walking with her in his arms.

"Put me down you … you … madman," she shouted as she twisted and writhed in his arms.

A moment later, he set her down in front of a carriage and opened the door. She realized that he expected her to go with him as he had positioned himself so that her path to escape was blocked. Her only option was to go inside the carriage and that, she refused to do. When she refused to do as he wanted, he grabbed her by the arm trying to force her inside, so, with blind panic, she lifted her knee and thrust out with her foot making contact with his groin. He yelled in agony as he dropped to his knees, and she didn't waste a moment before she ran. She ran as fast as she could in her slippers, but she had no idea where she was going; she just knew she had to get away and somehow find Dylan.

Chapter Eighteen

She hadn't been fast enough she soon realized as a carriage pulled up beside her, and she was accosted by two men and quickly tossed inside. Once she was inside the carriage it quickly took off, and she found herself sitting across from a very angry looking Mr. Ensley.

"You didn't have to kick me," he grumbled.

"I will do a lot more to you than that if you do not release me this instant," she threatened.

"I cannot do that Claire. Whether you believe it or not, I have just rescued you from a madman," he told her.

Claire laughed incredulously at his words.

"This coming from a madman," she said with irony.

"I didn't want it to come to this Claire. I had hoped that I could find time to be alone with you to make you see reason, but Wentworth kept you under lock and key, this was the only way I could get to you," he explained.

"Did it ever occur to you that I didn't want to be rescued?" she asked.

That made him pause, and he looked at her as if she had gone daft.

"Surely you know what kind of monster he is," he said.

"The only monster I know, is you sir," she retorted.

He shook his head in frustration and took a deep breath.

"Listen to me because I am about to enlighten

you Claire. Wentworth is a murdering rapist, and he would surely harm you if given a chance," he told her.

"A murdering rapist?" she asked with exasperation.

"Yes, he raped and murdered a poor maid before going on a killing rampage where he killed two helpless men. He nearly killed … he nearly killed another woman whom I admire, but she was spared when Windhaven intervened. The man is a lunatic, I assure you Claire," he told her.

Claire couldn't believe what she was hearing. His version of events and Luther's didn't quite match up. She regarded him with suspicion for a moment.

"How do you know of this?" she finally asked.

He sat quiet for a minute as if trying to decide what to say next.

"The other woman, Diana, she was my lover, and she told me what happened; she was there you see," he admitted.

Claire knew about Diana and that she was presently in Bedlam because she had tried to have Alyssa killed. She wasn't about to believe her accounting of anything.

"Luther told me what happened. He did not rape and murder that girl," she said with conviction.

"I assure you that it's true. Only Diana was witness to it all, and they tried to shut her up by putting her in Bedlam. But she told me what happened, and I tried in vain to get her out, but I was unsuccessful," he told her.

"What do you mean they put her in Bedlam to

shut her up?" she demanded.

"They all conspired to protect Wentworth; even her own father," he snarled.

"I don't believe any of this," she said hotly.

"Suit yourself, but it's true nonetheless, and I went to great effort to rescue you from him," he retorted.

"Stop this carriage and let me out at once," she demanded.

"No my dear, you must allow me to protect you," he told her with conviction.

Claire launched herself at him and started savagely pounding his head and shoulders. He tried to restrain her, but she was like a whirlwind that could not be contained. The next thing she knew she felt a blow to her chin, and then she fell into blackness.

*****

Dylan couldn't believe that Claire had betrayed him but she must have as she admitted it herself. When Kenwick whispered all that had taken place between them and proved it by telling him about her scar on her stomach and the mole on her inner thigh, he knew that he was telling the truth. She had allowed Kenwick to make love to her in his own garden as soon as his back was turned, which explained why she had been so nervous that day. She said she had overtaxed herself and now he knew how. He felt like a fool for ever trusting her as he knew her for a trollop the moment he laid eyes on her. She was a clever whore, he would grant her that, but she was a whore nonetheless. He had started to suspect that she was a woman of easy virtue the way she always pawed at him and tried to encourage him to bed her. She no doubt wanted to cover her arse in the event that she was pregnant with Kenwick's bastard and thought to fool him into raising the brat as his own. Well, good riddance to them both.

The carriage pulled up in front of his house and he quickly exited telling his groom to ready his horse. He was going to leave this place and the memories of the harlot behind and never look back. He ran up the stairs to change and packed a small bag, then went to his library and opened his safe to retrieve a large bag of coin and his bankbook. He would start a new life somewhere else where no one knew who he was; where he was just a man and not a cursed marquess with responsibilities.

There was a knock at the door, and Dylan knew that Simmons had come to find out what was going on. He didn't want to deal with him right now, so he ignored the knock. Simmons, being who he was, didn't let that stop him from coming in.

"My lord, what is amiss?" he asked with concern in his voice.

"I am leaving for a while Simmons, and I don't know when I shall return, if ever. I want you to see to things in my absence and tell my stewards to continue on as they always have," he said.

"What of the woman, my lord?" he ventured.

Dylan didn't care what happened to her.

"It's not likely that she will return, but if she does, allow her to get her things then send her on her way," he said.

"But you are her guardian, my lord," Simmons pointed out with shock in his voice.

"She will no doubt be the Marchioness of Kenwick when she returns, and if she isn't, tell her to take it up with the duke. I want nothing to do with her," he barked.

"What should I tell his grace?" Simmons asked.

"Tell him that he was wrong about the girl, and that I have escaped the mistake of my life," he told him.

With that he picked up his bag and made his way out of the library with Simmons following at his heels.

"My lord, I wish you would reconsider; no woman is worth leaving your home and your life behind," he told him.

"I cannot stay here Simmons and that is final," he said as he opened up the front door.

He turned back to look at his bewildered butler and valet, and for a brief moment he wondered if he was making a different kind of mistake. He shook off the unwanted thought and mounted his horse.

*****

Claire woke up alone sometime later in a strange bed in a strange room, and she wasn't sure but she thought she might be at an inn. It wasn't the cleanest of places, and she could hear loud celebratory voices below. She sat up gingerly as her head was aching, then she realized that her chin and jaw felt somewhat bruised. She remembered what had happened now and she darted her eyes around the room to confirm that she was indeed alone. She swung her legs over the side of the bed then stood up, causing her head to spin as though she could faint, but she shook it off and went to the door and turned the knob to find that she had been locked in. She turned and looked to see if the room had a window and was disappointed to see that it would be too small for her to get through. She walked over to it anyway and looked below to see that it was pitch black outside, and she couldn't tell how high up she actually was.

She turned and looked into the room again and noticed a trunk sitting at the foot of the bed. She walked over to it and opened it, seeing that it was full of very fine women's clothing. Very strange, and where was Mr. Ensley? She closed the trunk then went over to the sideboard to see that there was a pitcher of ale and some water in a bowl with some washcloths out beside it. She dipped the washcloth inside the bowl of water, wrung it out and started to wipe her face in an attempt to rouse herself.. She felt slow, sluggish and was beginning to wonder if perhaps Mr. Ensley had given her some kind of drug.

What was she to do now? She had no idea where she was, she had no means of escape, and even if she did she had no money to get home with. Home; she didn't even have a home now as Dylan never wanted to see her again. She felt tears stinging her eyes, and she felt as though her soul had been torn apart. How was she ever going to live without Dylan? She turned and walked back over to the bed, sitting down on the edge to contemplate her situation. There had to be a way to escape Mr. Ensley, but how? She jerked her head up as she heard someone turning the door knob. She quickly stood in preparation for the door to open; she wanted to greet her assailant on her feet instead of sitting there like a helpless dove.

"Ah, you're awake my love," Mr. Ensley said as he cautiously entered the room.

"I am not your love, and I insist that you let me go this instant," she told him with her shoulders squared for battle.

"I'm sorry that I struck you Claire, but you were quite unmanageable in the carriage, and I was afraid that you might hurt yourself," he told her.

Claire would make him sorry alright; the nerve of the man. She advanced toward the door with the intention of leaving, but he quickly placed himself in front of her, blocking her exit.

"If you do not let me go, I shall scream," she growled.

"Scream if you like; there is so much noise below, no one will hear you," he told her smugly.

She raised her hand to strike him across the face, but he caught it and twisted her arm behind her back, crushing her against him.

"There will be no more violence, Claire; enough is enough. Now be a good girl and get back in the bed. I am tired and wish to go to sleep," he told her.

He released her, and she turned as though she were going to do as he bid, but then she quickly spun around and launched herself at him. She jumped up, wrapping her legs around his waist, grabbed a handful of his hair with one hand and pounded him about the head and face with the other.

"My God,woman, you are mad!" he shouted as he tried to pry her off of him.

Claire was mad; at this moment, she was a woman with nothing to lose, and she would do whatever it took to escape. He tried to pull her hand out of his hair, but she lowered her head and bit his neck, drawing blood into her mouth. He spun them around, pressing her up against the door, pinning her and allowing him more control of the struggle. He used his lower body to hold her in place and grabbed her by the wrists, forcing them down between them and pressed hard with his hips to keep them pinned. She struggled like a wildcat and continued to try and bite him, but he was strong and kept her at bay.

"You like to play rough; we can play rough," he breathed in her ear just before he ripped the front of her gown, exposing her stays to his view.

The shock of it stunned her momentarily and that gave him an opportunity to grab her stays, ripping them, exposing her bare flesh. He groaned at the sight and lowered his head, then kissed her on her breasts; the feeling of it brought her back to her senses, and she began to struggle anew.

"Unhand me, or I shall thrash you," she shouted.

He lifted his head and looked at her with a crooked smile.

"You are quite helpless now my kitten," he purred.

Claire realized the futility of her situation and slumped forward, hanging her head low; he was going to have his way with her, and there was nothing she could do to stop him. He lifted her chin and ran his tongue along the side of her neck as he began to fondle her breast, kneading and pinching with an urgency that scared her.

"Please don't do this, I beg of you," she pleaded.

"Let me love you, Claire," he said softly in her ear.

"No please, I cannot bear your touch," she told him.

He pushed away from her then and looked at her as if her words had wounded him deeply. The man honestly thought she would welcome his advances after what he had done?

"You would prefer the touch of a murderer to mine?" he asked, stepping back from her.

"Yes, because I love him," she shouted.

"He will never have you now," he told her smugly.

Claire fumbled with her torn clothing and tried to cover herself from his view. He put his hands on hers and moved them away, allowing the cloth to fall away again.

"The dress is quite ruined now; take it off," he commanded.

"I shall do no such thing," she told him.

"Take it off, or I shall take it off for you," he threatened.

Claire realized that he had already seen her body and there was no point in trying to be modest now, but she didn't want to fully disrobe before him. She didn't want to do anything to encourage him further.

"I have nothing to wear," she told him.

"You have a trunk full of clothing that I had made special for you," he told her.

He held out his hand, but she refused to take it.

"I wish you no harm Claire; I only want to show you what's inside the trunk," he told her.

"I shall do it myself," she told him.

He stepped aside, and she cautiously walked past him then dropped to her knees in front of the trunk to open the lid. She dug around inside looking for something suitable to wear when she escaped, but all she could find were delicate gowns and lingerie that looked as though they were made for a trollop. He had brought nothing practical to wear at all. Why, there wasn't even a single night gown inside.

"There is nothing practical to wear," she grumbled.

"Practical is for servants; you are a lady and soon to be my marchioness. Those clothes will be perfect for you," he told her.

"There is nothing to sleep in, and you have torn my only shift," she argued.

"You shall have no need of anything to sleep in," he said with a sultry voice.

She slammed the lid closed on the trunk and stood up and faced him with her shoulders squared.

"I don't know what you think is going to happen here, but if you think I will willingly bed down with you, you are quite mistaken sir," she spat the words.

"Oh, you will sleep with me Claire, and you will do so this night. I have waited a long time for you, and I shall not be denied," he told her as he slowly advanced toward her.

Claire desperately searched her mind for a way out of this madness, and she was suddenly struck with a thought. He had showed mercy on her before when he saw her scar.

"I have not been released by the surgeon yet," she told him.

He halted and gave thought to her words.

"How long has it been since you had the surgery?" he asked.

"Just a few weeks," she fibbed.

"When are you to be released by your doctor?" he asked.

"He was to examine me again next week," she told him.

He ran his hand through his hair, closed his eyes and sighed impatiently.

"I shall have to be gentle then," he said.

Claire panicked; he fully intended that she would sleep with him.

"What if you do damage to me, and then I cannot have a child as a result?" she threw out in desperation.

"Damnation!" he growled and spun on his heels storming out of the room, slamming the door closed behind him.

Chapter Nineteen

Claire couldn't believe her luck; she had been spared again. How long would he wait before he insisted that she bed him? She didn't know, but she suspected that he would be back, and he would pester her anew. She hurried over to the trunk and rummaged around until she found a gown that would have to suffice, and she quickly put it on then grabbed her wrap and put it around her shoulders. She realized that she still had on the jewels that Dylan gave her and that they would be a magnet for cutthroats, so she took them off and searched for her reticule. She found it on the night stand, dropped the jewels inside, and then closed it up tightly tying the drawstring around her wrist; that would have to do.

She walked over to the door and tested the knob. Surprised to find that it was unlocked, she knew this was her chance to escape. Cautiously, she stuck her head out into the hall and saw no one about, then ventured along testing doors as she went. She found one unlocked and quietly opened it then breathed a sigh of relief to find that it was empty. She quickly closed and locked the door behind her before going over to the window. This window was bigger, and she thought that she could probably squeeze through it. She unlocked it then lifted it up, careful not to make too much noise before taking a look around outside. It would be daylight soon as she could see the beginning of sunrise to the east. She still couldn't really tell how high up she was, but she figured it couldn't be more than twenty feet, maybe less. She would probably sprain her ankle when she landed, but she would have to take the risk.

She removed her slippers and tossed them out the window, lifted the hem of her gown, and then with as much care as she could muster, she lifted up her leg and slung it over the side of the window frame. She sat straddling the frame for a moment gathering her courage. She could to do this; she had to find her way back to Dylan. She drew in a steadying breath and swung her other leg around, then on the count of three she dropped to the ground below. Claire made a concerted effort to land on the front part of her feet in hopes of sparing her ankles the burden of her full weight. She landed surprisingly easy and was pleased to realize that the drop had only been about ten feet. She scrambled around in the dark for her slippers, and once she found them both, she quickly put them on and set about finding a safe place to go until daylight. She was grateful to see that the sun was quickly coming up so she could make out shapes of buildings now. She thought she could make out a steeple of a church up ahead and quickly made her way in that direction.

Perhaps there was a parson on the premises, and he would offer her shelter until she could figure out what to do. She wondered how long it would be before Mr. Ensley realized that she was gone and set out in search of her. She hoped that he wouldn't go back to the room until much later today, but she suspected that he would return with the intention of sleeping, if nothing else. He had looked tired and worn out from the night before, whereas she was quite rested, having slept for what must have been hours. The closer she got to the church, the quicker she walked. When she reached the outside of it she saw that a candle was burning inside, and her heart leapt with relief. She walked up to the door, took in a few steadying breaths and knocked. After a moment, she heard a male voice say that he was coming. He opened the door and gaped at her, and she realized that this must be something quite out of the ordinary for the elderly man.

"Forgive me sir, but I am lost, and I need your help," she implored him.

"Lost ye say?" he asked incredulously.

"Yes sir. I was abducted from a ball in London by a madman, and I have escaped him, and now I am lost and have no idea how to get home," she told him.

He chuckled and opened the door all the way and allowed her to come in.

"That's quite a story you have there, missy," he chided with a warm, friendly voice.

"I assure you sir that it is quite true. My name is Claire Melville, and I am an American, and I have only been in your country for a little under two months. I am engaged to be married to the Marquess of Wentworth, and his grandfather the Duke of Blackstone honored us with a ball to celebrate our wedding last night, but I was abducted from there by Mr. Ensley, who is the Marquess of Kenwick," she rushed out as she followed him through the church.

He led her to the kitchen and she watched as he

put a pot of water on to the stove to boil.

"How did you get yourself in such a fine pickle lass?" he asked her with a huge grin.

"I wish I knew sir," she told him with a blush.

"I don't know how I can help you, but you are welcome to stay here until you contact someone to come and fetch you," he told her.

"I have no money to pay you for your kindness sir, and I don't even know the address of where I was staying in Mayfair," she told him, then began to sob at the futility of her situation.

"There, there lass, don't cry. Everything will be alright. It won't be hard to have a message delivered even without an address, and your money would be no good here," he assured her with a pat on the back.

Claire looked up with tears rolling down her cheeks.

"Do you mean it sir?" she asked.

"Of course child; this is a house of God, and we help those in need, and you my dear are definitely in need," he said with a comforting smile.

"I can do some chores for you to earn my keep in the event that it takes more than a day or two for someone to arrive for me," she offered.

"Now, that I will accept," he said beaming.

"I should probably warn you that I escaped Mr. Ensley from the inn up the road, and he could come searching for me at any minute. I do not wish for him to find me, of course, because the man is trying to force me to marry him. He even lied to my fiancé and told him that we were lovers, and Dylan believed him and sent me away with him," she said sobbing again.

"Oh come now dear; dry those eyes. I'm sure that it can all be cleared up once you have an opportunity to speak with your fiancé. And rest your mind; I shall not let this Mr. Ensley find you," he told her.

Claire rushed at him, threw her arms about his neck and kissed him on the cheek.

"Thank you so much, kind sir; I was quite sure I would be lost forever," she told him.

The old man laughed and patted her on the back.

"That's enough of that now; let's have some tea," he told her.

*****

Claire wasn't sure who she should contact for assistance. She didn't think that Dylan would read her missive, so she thought perhaps she should write to the duke or maybe Adeline and explain to them what had happened. She hoped that he too hadn't cast her off, because if he didn't come, she wasn't sure what to do next. She supposed she could try and contact Luther or maybe the Duchess of Windhaven, but being friends of Dylan's they may sympathize with him and ignore her plea for help. She decided that she would try the duke first, and with the paper and ink that the parson provided she set about writing. It was difficult to put what had happened into words as the whole story seemed quite incredible, even to her.

She wasn't sure how she would ever convince

Dylan that Mr. Ensley lied to him, given that she did inadvertently admit to some wrongdoing. She hadn't meant what he thought she did, but she wasn't given time to explain before Dylan thrust her away and left. She couldn't believe that he had so little faith in her that he would have taken Mr. Ensley's word for it the way that he did, and she decided she wouldn't dwell on that now as it made her very angry. What was important now was getting back to London so she could confront him and tell him her side of the story. She finished her letter and sealed it up, then went in search of the parson so he could have it posted. She hoped that she would hear word by tomorrow one way or the other, so she would know what to do next.

*****

Dylan was in fine form as he swaggered away from the Dirty Knave Inn. He was stinking drunk and bleeding from his nose from the fight that he had just got in with a pickpocket. It felt good to be drunk, and he had been able to vent his anger quite nicely on the bloody arse who had tried to steal his purse. He was drunk, yes, but not so much that he hadn't noticed when the man stuck his hand inside his coat pocket. He supposed he shouldn't have made such a mess inside the taproom as now he didn't have a place to bed down for the night. He was drunk, and he hadn't slept at all the night before because he wanted to put as many miles between him and London as he could.

At least he was no longer sexually frustrated

thanks to the very accommodating red-headed wench at the inn. She worked him over good with her luscious lips and drained every last drop from his cock. It felt good to have a release, and he would have stayed and shagged her had he not gotten in the fight with the pickpocket and gotten himself thrown out. It was just as well, she probably had a disease, he inwardly grumbled. He didn't suppose he would catch anything from simply having his knob polished, but he had been beyond caring at the time. There would be other whores to sample, and he fully intended to do so, diseases, be damned. He no longer cared if he remained celibate; what was the point? It had caused him nothing but trouble so far, and he was through trying to be honorable.

He was simply Dylan Stanford now, Stanford being his mother's maiden name, and he would be a commoner from this day forward, living as they did right down to the lowborn immoral behavior. Never again would he be responsible for tenants or be forced to circulate with the ridiculous ton. He had never belonged there anyway, and if it wasn't for his friends, he would have never had anything to do with it at all. He would miss his friends, but they would have to be a casualty of this war he had decided to wage against his lot in life. He felt bad about his grandfather too, but he couldn't let that stop him. He would just have to seek out another heir for his title.

Dylan never wanted any of it, and now he would simply walk away from it all never looking back. He wasn't sure where he would go, but the farther away from London he could get, the better. Perhaps he would go into Wales or maybe take a ship and go to the West Indies. There was the war going on though and traveling the seas wouldn't be a good idea unless ... perhaps he should join up with the Royal Navy and help annihilate all those blasted Americans. The thought made him smile sardonically. Perhaps that bitch would take a ship home, and he could blast it out of the water and watch as the sea swallowed her up into the abyss. He couldn't believe he had been so taken in by the harlot but he had. He had become besotted with her, much to his shame; she certainly opened his eyes to the ways of women. They were all deceitful whores, and they were only good for one thing.

He staggered around to the stables and sought out his horse, and after two failed attempts, he finally mounted him up and slowly made his way out of the village. He hoped there would be another inn up ahead because he was really drunk. It was dark now, but the night was still fairly young. Perhaps once he got to the next village he would get a second wind, and there would be more accommodating wenches; perhaps he would even have two at the same time; he hadn't done that in years. He smiled at the thought and kicked his horse, shooting off into the darkness like a man hell-bent for destruction.

About thirty minutes later, he was in luck as there was an inn that looked to have just what he was looking for. He handed his horse to the stable boy and flipped him a coin before swaggering inside. He walked up to the bar and ordered a bottle of whiskey and a room. The innkeeper, who was a shrewd businessman, asked if he would need any other accommodations. Dylan smiled and told him what he required. The innkeeper handed him his key and signaled to a woman, and the next thing he knew, two black haired wenches came up beside him and escorted him to his room. It was going to be a good night.

*****

Claire lay in her bed and tried to sleep, but the tears wouldn't stop coming. She had sent her message early this morning and had hoped that she would have had a return message, but the runner never came back. She missed Dylan terribly and wondered what he was doing right now, and her heart sank as she realized that he was probably in his room drinking his life away. She knew in her heart that he would turn to drink after what had happened, and the knowledge of it distressed her. She hated to think that he would go back to those awful habits when he had come so far, but she knew that he felt betrayed and would seek solace in the bottle. Poor Dylan! Well, she would convince him of her innocence and help him quit again if he had been seized by the demon.

At least she hadn't heard any more from Mr. Ensley, and for that she was grateful. Perhaps he left town when he discovered that she was gone and wouldn't be a problem. She sighed deeply and turned over, making a frustrated attempt to fluff up her flat pillow as best she could, and then there was

a terrible ruckus outside as the dogs began to bark
ferociously. Perhaps she had been too hasty
thinking she had heard the last of Mr. Ensley. She
jumped up from the bed, put her wrap on and
looked out the window. There were two men
outside on horseback, and oh it couldn't be, could
it? Luther and Jasper had arrived; she was saved.

Chapter Twenty

Claire ran through the church, flung the door open wide and ran straight into Luther's arms, crying uncontrollably.

"It's alright now Claire, we've got you," he crooned as he held her.

She pulled herself away from him and threw herself into Jasper's arms and continued to sob. She was so relieved that they had come for her and that she was safe now. Jasper pulled her off of him and rubbed her arm.

"Tell us everything Claire and leave nothing out," he commanded her.

"You all better come inside before that crazy man sees ye," the parson called out from behind them.

Claire jerked in response to that and grabbed Jasper and Luther's hands, dragging them behind her into the church. Once inside, the parson directed them to the kitchen, and he put on a pot of water for some tea. Everyone sat down at the table, and Claire proceeded to tell her tale, starting from the night of the dinner party when Mr. Ensley had thrown rocks at her window. When she was through telling her story, Jasper took her by the chin, and a look of terrible anger crossed his face.

"Did he do this to you?" he demanded.

Claire had forgotten about the bruise on her chin and jaw but nodded her head that he had.

"He's a dead man," Luther growled.

"To be fair, I was attacking him, and he did it

in self defense," she told them.

"You would defend him after what he has done?" Jasper asked incredulously.

"No, I am not going to defend him, but I wanted you to know that it wasn't done out of cruelty. He has really been quite kind in his own peculiar way," she explained.

"He is a dead man, anyway," Luther grumbled.

"What of Dylan?" she asked.

Jasper and Luther looked at each other and had some kind of silent communication with their eyes, and her heart fell in her stomach. She had a bad sense of foreboding about what they were about to tell her. Jasper looked back at her and took her hands in his.

"He's gone," he told her.

"Gone?" she barked in alarm.

"We don't know where he has gone. He left his house with a bag full of coin and a suitcase and told Simmons he didn't know if he would ever return," he told her with sympathy in his eyes.

"Oh this is terrible," she said, then laid her head on the table and cried.

What was she going to do now? He had left and would never return, and no one even knew where he was.

"We will find him for you Claire, but first we have to get you home," Luther told her.

"I cannot go back there. He said it was no longer my home," she told them with a hiccup.

"We will take you to the duke's house," Jasper told her.

"May we leave Claire here for a little while

longer? We want to go over to the inn and see if Kenwick lacked the sense to leave," Luther asked the parson.

"She is welcome to stay as long as she likes. She has been good as gold to me and cleaned this church from top to bottom without so much as one complaint," he said with a big smile.

"Thank you," Jasper said and the two men stood up.

"What will you do to him?" she asked them.

"That is not for you to worry about, Claire. It is in our hands now," Jasper told her.

Claire had a twinge of pity for Mr. Ensley and hoped that the two men wouldn't actually kill him. She didn't think he was a bad man, but he was certainly misguided and had ruined her life with his determination to rescue her.

"Try not to kill him," she allowed.

The two men took their bow and quickly left.

*****

"Look Jasper, the fool is still here," Luther said as they entered the tap room of the inn.

The two men walked straight over to him and Luther hoisted him out of his chair then dragged him kicking and screaming out of the inn as he took him around by the stables.

"You will stay away from Claire, Kenwick," Luther said, and commenced to pummeling him.

"Claire doesn't want him dead, Luther; perhaps you should only thrash him a little while longer," Jasper said casually after a few minutes of watching his friend work the poor bastard over.

"I want him to remember why he is to stay away from her," Luther grunted as he delivered another rib cracking blow to the man's side.

"All the same, perhaps you should avoid his ribs, you wouldn't want to puncture a lung and have the bloody sod cock up his toes. Claire wouldn't like that," Jasper advised.

"I suppose you're right," Luther grunted as he delivered a nose breaking blow to his face.

That one sent him flying backwards into unconsciousness, and the two men picked him up and took him over to the horse trough and dunked his head below the water.

"That ought to do it," Jasper advised after about thirty seconds.

Luther lifted his head out by the hair and looked to see if he was still alive, and once satisfied, he dropped him on the ground and kicked him in the arse for good measure. Kenwick lay on the ground, a groaning bloody mess, and Jasper squatted down beside him to look him over to see if he had any fatal wounds.

"Did you get the message, Kenwick or are we going to have to pay you another visit down the road?" he asked.

"I got the message," he slurred.

"Good, shall we call someone for you?" Jasper asked.

"My valet is in the inn, somewhere. His name is Daniel," he said with strained effort.

"Luther go and fetch Daniel and tell him his master is in need of his assistance," Jasper commanded.

"Why do I have to do all the work?" he complained.

"Just do it, man," Jasper barked.

Luther growled and stomped off toward the inn and returned shortly dragging the valet by the hair and threw him on the ground beside Kenwick.

"Take care of the bloody arse," he ordered, and with that, he and Jasper left the two bewildered men and went back to retrieve Claire.

*****

Claire couldn't believe that Dylan had left his home because of her. The more she thought about it, the more distressed she became. What if he was laid out somewhere, drunk in a strange place, and someone harmed him? She was sure that under normal circumstances he could defend himself, but if he had returned to the bottle as she suspected he had, he could be set upon by ruffians and harmed or worse. She supposed that she shouldn't care whether or not he came to any harm as he obviously hadn't given her well-being a single thought when he'd thrown her away like so much rubbish. But she did care; she cared because she loved him with all her heart, and she knew deep down that he loved her too.

"Where do you suppose he went?" she asked the duke.

Claire had arrived back in London early that morning, and Jasper and Luther had already left in search of Dylan.

"Dylan never wanted to be an earl, and he certainly never wanted to be a marquess and ultimately a duke. He is using this as an excuse to escape his fate, and there is no telling where he would have gone. It is my hope that he is still in England, but I suspect that he will leave the country sooner rather than later," the duke said with great sadness in his eyes.

Claire didn't like the sound of that. If Dylan left England, they may never find him.

"I am so sorry that this has happened," Claire said with a sob.

She thought she was through crying as she had been crying off and on for two days now and didn't think she had a single tear left to cry.

"You must stay strong Claire," the duke admonished gently.

"I know what you say is true, but it's so hard. He could be lying drunk in a ditch somewhere; I'm so afraid for him," she cried.

"I suspect that he has returned to his old habits, in which case he will be easier to find," he told her with a pitiful smile.

Claire hadn't thought of that. If he had started drinking again, then it would slow him down and give them a chance to find him. She gave a trembling smile at the prospect and dried her eyes.

"I will try to think positive," she said with a sniff.

"You really love him, don't you?" the duke asked.

"I do, more than you know," she told him.

"It is my belief that he loves you too, and love

will conquer all in this, I swear," he assured her.

"I believe he hates me now," she said, and fresh tears streamed down her face at the thought.

"No my dear, you mustn't think that. He is hurt to be sure, but if he didn't love you, he wouldn't have reacted as he did," the duke told her.

The thought didn't offer much comfort, but it would have to serve. Even if Jasper and Luther found Dylan, there was no guaranteeing that he would come home. He would probably never believe that she was innocent of any wrongdoing.

"He will never believe that … that I am innocent," Claire said.

"But you are, and when you marry the proof will be there, will it not?" the duke asked.

Claire blushed and nodded her head. That was the only saving grace that she had now. The fact that she was still a virgin proved her innocence, but if Dylan refused to marry her, how would he ever know?

"What if he comes back but still refuses to have me?" she cried.

"My dear, all we can do is to take this one day at a time. Do not stress yourself just now. You need to get some rest, and perhaps by morning we will have word from Jasper and Luther," he told her.

"I suppose I should get some rest; I am very tired, but I don't know how I will ever sleep," she said as she stood up to take her leave.

"You will sleep," he commanded gently.

Claire hugged him, kissed his cheek, and then took her leave. She would try to put her mind at rest so she could sleep, but her heart was broken, and she was worried out of her mind. She dragged herself up the stairs feeling defeated and utterly despairing that she and Dylan would ever be together again. Once in her room, she stripped off her clothes down to her shift, sat on the edge of the bed and wept anew.

*****

The duke watched Claire leave with sadness in his heart. He hadn't wanted to tell the poor girl that it was likely that Dylan would never be found as he didn't want to be found. Dylan was a stubborn man, and once he set himself upon a course, he was determined to see it through. He suspected that he would be using an assumed name so as not to make it known who he really was, which would make it impossible for Luther and Jasper to track him. He wouldn't put it past the scamp to join up with some pirates in the West Indies. Dylan had always had a fascination with such things, and as a boy he often pretended to be a Barbary Corsair. He hoped that he was wrong as he needed Dylan to come home as soon as possible.

He hadn't told Dylan yet, but he was very ill and probably wouldn't be around much longer. His heart was failing him now, and it was getting harder to ignore. He often felt weak, and at times he had an awful aching in his left arm and pains in his chest. He refused to give up on Dylan though as he was his last remaining heir. If Dylan couldn't be found, his titles and estates would revert to the crown as there were no other Crenshaw males to assume them after his death. He had lived a good long life, far longer than many of his peers and felt fortunate to have lived to such a ripe old age. He had always had good health until recently, but the strain of his son's long illness and his recent death, along with Dylan's depression and now this, had finally taken their toll.

For a long time, he had despaired that Dylan would ever be able to stand up to the responsibilities of a dukedom, but when Claire came into his life and he quit drinking and seemed to pull out of his depression, he began to hope. This trouble between them was a huge setback, and if Dylan couldn't be found and soon, he could lose it all. He couldn't understand why Dylan had been so quick to believe that rapscallion Kenwick, instead of holding fast to his faith in Claire. Perhaps he had been looking for an excuse to end the relationship and run away, but he didn't think that was the case. Dylan had seemed genuinely happy for the first time in several years with Claire.

He believed that Claire was innocent, and it was clear that she fought valiantly for her virtue before escaping. The poor child had been left to defend herself because Dylan had cast her aside without so much as a second thought for her innocence. If he were a younger man, he would thrash Dylan within an inch of his life for the hurt that he had caused the girl. She didn't deserve what was done to her, and he suspected that Dylan was at this very moment doing the things he accused her of doing, and then some. He hoped that wasn't the case, but Dylan was too much like himself at that age, and he knew from his own experiences when he had fought with Joanna before their wedding, what Dylan would be doing now.

It was critical that Jasper and Luther located him before too much harm could be done. The last thing they needed was for Dylan to end up killed or diseased from his exploits, and he hoped that Claire would never have to know the pain of such things. Joanna had learned of his proclivities, and it had nearly destroyed any chance of reconciliation for them. Claire seemed like a forgiving sort, but a woman could only take so much before she would protect herself and leave a scoundrel to his own fate.

The duke walked over to the table, blew out the lamp and decided that he had better turn in for the night. There was nothing more that he could do until he heard from Jasper and Luther, and he was feeling particularly bad at the moment. He left the drawing room and headed for the stairs, and just as he reached the staircase he was seized with a tremendous pain in his chest that sent him to his knees. He tried to call out for help, but the words would not come, and then he collapsed into darkness at the foot of the stairs.

Chapter Twenty-one

Nearly a month had passed since Dylan had left, and there had been no word; not even a whisper of his whereabouts. The Duke of Windhaven had hired Bow Street to assist with locating him, but so far it appeared that he had simply fallen off the face of the earth. Jasper and Luther had hunted tirelessly for him and had begun to suspect that he was no longer in England. They had begun to search the ports of all the coastal towns asking people if they had seen a man matching Dylan's description, but so far nothing had turned up.

The Duke of Blackstone was near death and not expected to live much longer as he had suffered an apoplexy that had rendered him very weak and confined him to his bed. He could no longer speak, nor could he do such ordinary tasks as feed himself, and Claire didn't understand how he had lasted as long as he had. Claire suspected that he was stubbornly hanging on until Dylan returned, but she despaired that he ever would. She missed him dearly, but she had stopped crying over him long ago and devoted herself to the care of the duke. She had remained vigilant at his bedside and personally cared for many of his needs. He tried desperately to communicate with her, and she could sense his frustration and felt a deep sense of helplessness that she could not provide more comfort to him.

She had started reading to him daily, which seemed to soothe him considerably when he became agitated. And often times she would sing to him, and he would smile crookedly and nod his head in approval. Claire had begun to love the old man and would miss him sorely when he was gone. *Why do we always have to lose the ones we love*? She didn't have an answer to that, but she had seen so much loss of late that she was starting to feel empty inside. She had lost her mother and then her father as well as Dylan. Now she would lose the duke, and when that happened, she didn't know what she would do.

Poor Adeline was beside herself with grief and had reverted to drinking again to deal with it. When she wasn't sleeping in a drunken stupor, she was crying her eyes out for her brother and worrying over Dylan. Claire had given up on her writing as it didn't seem to have the same fulfillment for her that it had before. Perhaps, one day, she would pick it back up, but for now there was no point in trying. It was a silly dream anyway and probably would have never amounted to much, so she didn't consider it a great loss.

The Duchess of Windhaven had taken to calling on her often as her husband had joined in the search for Dylan, and she and the babe were lonely. The child was adorable and growing like a bad weed and would have a sister or a brother before long as the duchess had just learned that she was with child again. Claire hoped that one day she would have a child, but wondered now if the father she had planned on having them with would be the same. She had decided that whether she and Dylan ever married or not, she would one day marry someone. She inwardly giggled and thought perhaps she might even marry Mr. Ensley, but of course, she wouldn't.

The poor man would probably run from her if she were to ever see her again after the thrashing that Luther gave him. She had felt bad about that because he really hadn't been cruel to her when all was said and done. She wasn't even sure she wanted to marry Dylan now after all that had transpired between them. She had lots of time to consider how harshly he had treated her and had reached the decision that she deserved much better than she had received. Maybe Dylan never really loved her after all; how could he have thrown her away so completely if he did? She wanted to believe what the duke had said, but so much time had gone by now that she found it hard to cling to the notion. One thing she had decided was that if he didn't return before the duke passed on, she would simply go back to America. Without Dylan or the duke, there was really nothing here for her. True, there was nothing for her in America either, but at least it was home.

The duke's secretary had shown her the paperwork that the duke had prepared for her to receive her dowry, and since Dylan had abandoned her, he had planned to give it to her for fulfilling her end of their bargain. Of course, he hadn't had time to tell her of it because the solicitor had not finished preparing them before the duke was struck down. She was hesitant to take the money that had been set up in an account for her because as it turned out the money was from the duke's own fortune as it had been impossible to go against the terms of her father's will. So for now, the money sat untouched and would remain so until she decided what she would do after he passed.

Dylan was still her appointed guardian, so if she did marry she would have to wait until her twenty-first birthday unless she eloped to Gretna Green where she wouldn't require permission to wed. Since she didn't have any immediate plans to wed, the point was moot. The duke was sleeping now, so Claire quietly got up and decided to stretch her legs with a walk in the garden. It was a beautiful day, and she wanted to enjoy a bit of it before the sun went down.

*****

"Aye, there be a bloke here matching that description, but he goes by a different name," the innkeeper of the Fox and Hare Inn in Stratton told Jasper.

"What name is he going by?" he asked.

The old man checked his register and said, "Dylan Stanford."

Jasper elbowed Luther in the ribs.

"We've got him," he said.

"Isn't Stanford his mother's maiden name?" Luther asked with excitement.

"It's him," Jasper said, nodding his head.

"The bloke is a drunken sod and stays holed up in his room with two or three wenches at a time," the innkeeper grumbled.

"Yep, that's him," Luther beamed.

"How long has he been here?" Jasper asked.

"Been here about a fortnight, I'd say; says he is

going to get on a ship next week and go to the West Indies and become a pirate," the old man said with a snicker.

"Is he in his room now?" Luther asked.

"Aye, he's there, and he has two whores with him; been in there with him since yesterday," he told them.

"May we have the key?" Jasper said holding out his hand that contained two guineas.

The innkeeper scooped up the coins and handed them the key.

"Is he all settled up with you?" Jasper asked.

"Aye, he paid in advance; throws coin around like a drunken sailor, he does," the innkeeper said.

Jasper and Luther thanked him for the information and went upstairs to find their friend.

"He won't come along willingly Luther, so be prepared to wrestle him down," Jasper warned.

"I plan on giving him a sound thrashing for what he's put us through," Luther promised.

"Don't bruise him up too much; Claire wouldn't like that," he advised.

"I bet she would appreciate giving him a few bruises of her own," Luther snickered.

"Yes, so leave a few spots available," Jasper said with a cheeky grin.

They located the room, and Jasper put an ear to the door, but didn't hear anything so he inserted the key in the door and opened it. Dylan lay sprawled naked between two equally naked whores, and they were all sound asleep. Jasper put his finger to his mouth to indicate silence and advanced to the bed. He tapped on one of the women's shoulder and she quickly sat up. He once again indicated silence, and she scurried out of the bed and began dressing while he woke the other woman the same way. Once they had removed themselves from the room, he motioned for Luther to come forward. He picked up the pitcher of water on the sideboard and signaled Luther to hold him down, and poured the water on his face. Dylan jerked his eyes open and sputtered briefly before growling like an animal when he realized that he was being restrained. He started thrashing about trying to free himself, but Luther had a firm hold on his wrists, keeping them pinned at the sides of his head.

"Get hold of yourself man!" Jasper shouted.

Dylan froze then as he realized who it was that had him, and he let his body sag back against the bed.

"Get out!" Dylan told them with hostility.

"Oh, we shall be leaving this dive, but you will be going with us," Jasper taunted.

"I will do nothing of the kind," he said insolently.

"Oh, yes you will; get up and get dressed or Luther will thrash you," Jasper threatened.

Dylan looked at them both with a snarl. "Luther will have to release me," he said snidely.

"Oh, right!" Luther said backing away.

Dylan jumped up, swinging, and threw a punch at Jasper, sending him flying across the room. He tried to swing at Luther, but he swung wide and missed. Luther tackled him then, and the two men wrestled on the floor until Luther pinned him down with a knee to his back and a chokehold around his neck.

"Get off of me, you big ox!" Dylan growled.

"What has gotten into you, Dylan?" Jasper asked as he rubbed his jaw.

"Nothing has gotten into me," he grunted.

"Why are you acting like a savage?" Luther barked.

"You two attacked me," he reminded them.

"We have come to take you home Dylan. Claire misses you and …" Jasper's words were cut off.

"That bitch can go to hell for all I care," he shouted.

Luther slugged him in the side of the head.

"Shut up you bastard; don't you dare talk about her like that," he shouted.

Dylan dropped his head as he was no doubt seeing stars from the punch Luther had delivered.

"If you had taken the time to listen to Claire, you would have learned that she was quite innocent of any wrongdoing," Jasper told him.

"Whores are never innocent," he grumbled and was punished for his words by another savage blow.

"Would you please stop that Luther," Dylan grumbled.

"Did you know that Kenwick tried to rape her that day in the garden, and that's why I found her heaped on the floor unconscious?" Luther yelled at him.

When Dylan didn't respond, Luther tightened his hold around his neck.

"I should kill you for what you did to that poor girl. You threw her away like she was rubbish and put her in the hands of a man bent on raping her, based on a lie that he told you. She had to fight to escape him, and when we found her she was covered in bruises. But she still loves you, and even now she keeps vigil over the duke at his deathbed and cares for him in your stead while you have been shagging every whore you can slip your cock into," Luther told him.

Dylan froze at Luther's words.

"Yes the duke is dying," Jasper said softly.

Luther released Dylan then, and he laid his head down on the floor and closed his eyes.

"Get up and get dressed," Luther told him.

"I can't go back," he said quietly.

"You can, and you will," Luther told him.

"I don't want to be a duke, and I don't want Claire," he said.

"If you don't want her, I will take her, but you are going back one way or the other," Luther said.

"I always knew you were in love with her. I suppose you are disappointed to have found me, but worry not, I won't stand in your way," he said as he stood up.

"You disgust me," Luther told him, then turned and left the room.

Jasper stood there looking at his friend, and he hardly recognized him either physically or by his bitter behavior. He had changed fundamentally, and he wondered if he would ever be the same again. He hadn't shaved, giving him a full beard, and he had even gotten a tattoo on his arse, and his attitude was extremely hateful.

"You look like shite, and that tattoo is

hideous," Jasper told him.

Dylan laughed bitterly.

"Rosaline is learning the trade, and I let her practice on me," he said without an ounce of shame.

"Is Rosaline one of the whores that I found you with?" Jasper asked.

"Yes, the one with red hair," he said as he pulled on his trousers.

"What is it supposed to be?" Jasper asked.

"I haven't a clue," Dylan said with a snicker.

"Claire is innocent," Jasper blurted out.

"I know," Dylan said quietly.

"Then why don't you want her?"

"She deserves better," he said as he shrugged into his shirt.

"I agree, but it's you she loves," Jasper told him.

"She will get over it."

"You didn't see her cry her eyes out, or the bruises on her beautiful face from what that man did to her," he told him.

Dylan made a pained sound in his throat.

"Did he rape her?" he growled.

"No, she fought like a tiger for her virtue, which is more than you did for her," Jasper said with anger laced in his voice.

Dylan dropped down to his knees and wept mournfully.

"I should have listened to her, but it's too late now," he sobbed.

"I don't think it's too late yet. She has said that she will stay as long as the duke needs her, so you still have time," he told him.

"I can never face her now," he said.

"Get up off the floor and finish dressing so we can leave this cursed place. The duke needs you and whether or not you still want Claire can be settled later," Jasper advised.

Jasper turned and left the room. He had to put some distance between him and Dylan because he wanted to thrash him for his stupidity. He was right about one thing; Claire deserved better, and it probably was too late to salvage anything between them. He made his way down the stairs and to the taproom, where he ordered ale for him and Luther, and they sat at a table and waited for their friend.

*****

Dylan knew now that he had been a fool. He had thrown away the best thing that ever happened in his life. He was a worthless sack of shite, and she was a goddess who deserved far better than him. Why had he done it? Why had he been so quick to throw her away? Why had he believed what Kenwick had said? Because he was a coward; he knew that now. He didn't have the courage to take what she had offered and took the first opportunity he could to cast her aside with a clear conscience.

"What a bastard I am!" he said to the empty room.

There was a knock on the door, and he thought maybe his friends had returned so he commanded them to enter.

"Are you leaving me?" Rosaline asked.

"Yes," he said.

"But we were just starting to have fun," she purred as she walked slowly up to him, untying the drawstring of her blouse.

"Don't," he said, reaching out to stop her.

"Are you going back to that woman?" she asked.

"I have told you nothing of a woman," he said, a bit surprised.

"Sugar, you talk about how much you love that woman in your sleep," she said with a sad smile.

Dylan hadn't known that and found it surprising. He had tried to exorcize her from his heart and mind and thought he had been successful.

"She will not have me now," he said quietly.

"She would be fool not to," she told him.

"Can I ask you something?" he asked her.

"Anything."

"What is that tattoo supposed to be?" he said with a grin.

She giggled.

"It's a heart, and on the inside it says, 'My Beloved Claire',"

Dylan smiled; so he had talked quite a bit in his sleep.

"Thank you Rosaline, for everything," he said giving her a kiss on the forehead. He walked over to his bag, fished out his coin purse and handed it to her.

"Take it and share it with Emma," he told her.

Rosaline opened the bag and gasped.

"There must be a hundred guineas in here," she blurted out.

"You both earned it."

"Thank you Dylan; I shall never forget you," she said with tears in her eyes.

"You should, because I intend to forget you," he said with a crooked smile and a wink.

Chapter Twenty-two

"You know you are welcome to come and stay with us," Alyssa said as she placed her tea cup down on the table.

"Thank you, that is very kind. I don't want to leave until … I want to stay as long as the duke has a need of me," she said.

Claire didn't want to leave the duke, but neither did she want to be here when Dylan returned. Jasper had sent her a message saying that he had located Dylan and that they were in route to London and would be returning on the morrow. She was glad that he had been found, but she wasn't sure what would happen now. She supposed that if Dylan wanted to communicate with her, he would have sent the missive himself, but it was Jasper who had.

"What will you do when Dylan comes home?" Alyssa asked.

"Well, I won't beg him to take me back, that's for sure," Claire said with a twinge of anger in her voice.

"I think the way he has treated you is deplorable. You should forget about him and find someone else. I could assist you with that," Alyssa said.

"You know, I think you're right. Why should I sit here pining away for a man that could care less about me to the extent that he would abandon me without a single thought to my well-being?"

"Exactly dear; what we need to do is give you a come out here in London; that way you can be introduced to all the eligible bachelors," Alyssa said, warming to the idea.

"Oh, but I can't do a thing with the duke suffering so," Claire said.

"I don't think the duke will last much longer," Alyssa suggested sadly.

"True, I think he is only holding on until Dylan returns; it's so sad to see. He tries desperately to communicate with me, and I know that he wants to say something about Dylan, but he simply cannot say the words," Claire said with tears welling in her eyes.

"I don't think he would want you to sit here wasting away over Dylan. There is nothing stopping you from going to a ball or two," Alyssa prodded.

"Perhaps, you're right. Dylan will probably send me away when he returns anyway, so I had better have a plan in motion."

"He cannot send you away from the duke's home," Alyssa said with anger sparking in her eyes.

"I suppose I will know soon enough what I should do next. It wouldn't hurt to have my things packed and ready to go. Are you sure I can stay with you; your husband won't mind?" Claire asked.

"Lud, it was his idea," she said with a smile.

"It's good to know that I have such good friends, but I can't help but feel like an interloper. Dylan wouldn't like the fact that his friends have become mine," she ventured.

"You listen to me, Claire; Dylan made his choice. He chose to abandon you, all his friends and his family. What happens now is none of his concern. You are a stranger in a strange land, and you need all the support you can get, and I intend to provide that support," Alyssa said sternly.

"I should have known that you would feel that way considering all of your good works for women; you are a such a good woman, and I thank you from the bottom of my heart," Claire said with tears rolling down her cheeks.

"You must dry your eyes now, Claire; you have much to be thankful for, and I have a good feeling about your future," Alyssa said with a wink.

"I hope you're right. I will wait and see what Dylan plans to do about the duke, and then I will make my plans. Dylan has shown that he has no concern for anyone but himself, and he might not be as attentive to the duke as he should, and I would hate to leave him without proper care," Claire told her.

"The duke has plenty of caretakers Claire. Are you sure you aren't using the duke as an excuse to stay about in hopes of reconciling with Dylan?" Alyssa asked with a suspicious expression.

Claire laughed but not joyfully.

"You may be on to something. Perhaps I should plan to leave in the morning," Claire allowed.

"I think you should plan to leave today," Alyssa argued.

"Oh I couldn't; could I?"

Claire wouldn't feel right about it, but she supposed she really had no justification for staying. It would appear to Dylan that she had hung on waiting for him, and she didn't want him to think such a thing because it would make her appear pathetic. She sighed deeply.

"I will have Lucy pack my things and leave

with you. She will need at least an hour to get everything prepared," she said without much conviction.

"Excellent!" Alyssa said clapping her hands.

"You have just freed yourself from the bondage that Dylan has kept you in for the last month. You are making real progress," she added.

"I must go and make my farewells to the duke and speak with Lucy. Will you be alright here for about a half an hour?"

"Go on and take care of it, and I shall keep myself company," Alyssa said with a smile.

*****

Claire entered the duke's room and was pleased to see that he was awake. She didn't want to say goodbye to him because she knew she would never see him again, and the thought was heartbreaking. He had been so kind to her, and she would forever be grateful to him.

"Mr. Crenshaw? I have something to tell you, and it pains me to do it," she ventured.

She took his hand in hers, kissed the back and rubbed it fondly on her cheek. A tear escaped her eye and rolled down her cheek at the thought of what she was about to do.

"I am leaving to go and live with the Duchess of Windhaven. She has invited me to stay with her and wants to help me be introduced to society. Dylan will be returning tomorrow, as you know, and I just don't feel right about staying on as he clearly has no wish to see me, and I don't want him to feel pressured in any way with regard to me," she told him, sniffing back more tears.

The duke lifted a trembling hand and stroked her hair, smiled and nodded his head. She squeezed his hand in hers and kissed it again.

"I will always love you for all that you have done for me, and I will never forget you," she told him.

He tried to form words and made a frustrating groan.

"Shhh ... don't strain yourself sir. I know that you care a great deal for me and wish me the very best. I know that you still hope that Dylan and I may reconcile, and perhaps we might, but I have to go and leave it to him now. If he wants me, he will know where to find me, but he will have to grovel on his hands and knees before I take him back," she told him with a wink.

He laughed and nodded his head that he agreed.

Claire leaned forward and kissed him on the forehead. She wished it wasn't so hard to say goodbye, but she had grown very fond of him over the last couple of months. She had no idea what would have become of her had he not helped her as he did. She stood and squeezed his hand one last time.

"Goodbye sir. I shall never forget you," she said, then quickly took her leave, fearing that if she didn't go now, she never would. She went back to her room to help Lucy with the packing. Lucy was smart and had already begun the packing as soon as the message was sent about Dylan. She must have anticipated that she wouldn't want to stay here once he returned.

"Lucy, you are a marvel of a woman, and I wish I could take you with me," Claire told her when she saw that the trunk was all packed and awaiting a footman.

"The duchess 'as already instructed me to pack my things and come along," Lucy said beaming.

Claire laughed and threw her arms around her. She had grown very fond of her maid.

"When did she do that?" Claire asked bewildered.

"She sent a note with the butler when she arrived. She 'ad no intentions of leaving without you, it seems," Lucy told her.

"She is rather sneaky, isn't she? Then if we are all packed, I suppose there is nothing left to do but call the footmen to carry our things to the carriage," Claire said with a smile.

"Already done; they will be 'ere in just a moment," Lucy said preening.

*****

Claire gasped when she saw her new apartments; she had never seen such splendor in all her life. She had thought her room at the duke's was beautiful, but this was fit for a queen. It had wallpaper with roses and ivy, and the bed was huge, decked out with an abundance of lush pillows to match. There was a velvet sofa and chairs arranged around a table, and a huge wardrobe and vanity that seemed to flirt with the beholder. There was a water closet with a huge copper bathing tub that had hot water piped straight to it. She had never seen anything to equal it. Why, she even had gas lighting, so she didn't have to fool with candles. Her dressing room was big enough to hold two good-sized beds, and there was a very nice sized room that connected to hers for Lucy. Why, I must have died and gone to heaven.

"Lucy, have you ever seen such splendor?" she marveled.

"Aye it's beautiful," Lucy agreed as she looked around.

"I don't know about you, but I can't wait to get in that tub and have a good long soak," Claire beamed.

"Should I prepare one for you now?" Lucy asked.

"Oh no, I shall wait until this evening after dinner; it's much too early to bathe now," Claire told her.

"With a tub like that you could bathe anytime you like," she told her.

"Don't tempt me, Lucy," Claire giggled.

"You never know, but the duchess might 'ave guests for dinner," she prodded.

"Oh, alright Lucy, you have quite talked me into it," Claire told her, kicking off her slippers.

Lucy laughed and bounded into the water closet and turned on the water, then returned to help her with her buttons.

"You should probably wear something nice, just in case, too," Lucy told her.

"Yes, this house is rather grand, and I'm sure their dinners are very formal," Claire agreed.

Lucy stripped her down to her shift, and she went to the water closet and watched as the tub filled itself. Amazing! What would they think of next? Claire quickly took off her shift then stepped into the tub, and sitting down in the water, she watched as the water poured out of the faucet.

"I find that a rather soothing sound, I think," she said more to herself than to Lucy.

"Just lay back and let the water rise over you and enjoy yourself. I will come back in a little bit and turn the water off and wash your 'air and scrub your back," Lucy told her.

Claire really was in heaven. The only thing missing now was … him.

*****

The closer they got to London, the more Dylan was filled with dread. What would he say to Claire? What if she wouldn't even speak to him? He sighed deeply and turned to Jasper.

"Do you think Luther will ever speak to me again?" he asked him.

Luther was up ahead of them by several paces, and so far he had refused to speak a word to him since they left the inn in Stratton a few days before. He knew that he had been an arse, but at the time, he had been angry and half drunk. He didn't mean to say the things he had, but he did, and now he couldn't take them back. He realized that he didn't deserve such good friends as Jasper and Luther, and he certainly didn't deserve Claire. He had accused her of being a whore when he himself had been that, and worse. Yes, he had behaved deplorably and slept with countless women over the last month. Most nights, he would have two, but there were plenty of nights that he had three and sometimes four women in his room.

He had done it to try and purge Claire from his heart and mind, but as the tattoo on his arse testified, he had failed miserably. He still loved her desperately, but his behavior had guaranteed that he would never have her. How could he look her in the eye knowing what he had done? All those women he had lain with in an attempt to forget about her had literally left their mark. She would see his sins written on him, and the shame he would suffer from it would be too much. Perhaps, he should just stand aside and allow Luther a chance to court her. Luther would be good to her, like a loyal dog, and that's what she deserved.

"Just give him time," Jasper said after a moment.

"What about you? Can you ever forgive me?" he asked.

"You are my brother, of course I forgive you," Jasper said with a crooked grin.

"I wish we had all been born brothers," Dylan mused aloud.

"That would be far too much lunacy in one family, don't you think?" Jasper teased.

"I suppose it would have. What will I say to Claire?" he asked.

"That is up to you Dylan. Only you can make it right with her."

"She will probably never speak to me again,

and why should she?" he said.

"You did her a great unkindness, and if I were her I would cut off your bollocks and feed them to you," Jasper told him.

"I don't think I could eat my bollocks unless they were well seasoned, and I had plenty of ale to wash it down with," he mused.

"Then perhaps you should avoid her for awhile," Jasper teased.

"I truly believed that she had taken Kenwick as a lover, and I even suspected that she had been with Luther too. Did I tell you that I accused her of being with child the first day I met her?"

"You have a very suspicious mind, Dylan. You should work on that because it will continue to cause you pain," Jasper told him.

"It has already ruined my life," Dylan admitted.

"Claire is a very forgiving soul. You can make it right with her Dylan, but it will take time, and if you really want her, you will do whatever it takes."

"I should probably leave well enough alone and allow her to find happiness elsewhere. I am no good for her," he said with sadness in his voice.

"Don't wait too long to decide because I do believe that Luther is quite smitten with her. It wouldn't be fair to continue to dally with her emotions when someone else would make her a good husband."

"Call me a selfish bastard, but I don't want Luther to have her," he growled.

"And she doesn't want him, she wants you, so what are you going to do?"

"So much time has passed, she may not love

me anymore," he choked out the words.

"A woman like that never stops loving," Jasper said quietly.

"How can I face her with what I've done?"

"Are you talking about abandoning her, or all the whores you shagged?" Jasper asked.

"Both!"

"She needn't know about the women, but abandoning her was a terrible thing, Dylan, and you will have to beg and plead to get back in her good graces, but you can if you will quit being such a self-absorbed arse," he told him.

"I found out what the tattoo was supposed to be," he said.

"Oh? Do tell."

"It's a heart, and on the inside it says, 'My Beloved Claire'. Apparently I talked quite a bit about her in my sleep, and Rosaline thought to remind me of what was important to me," he said with a crooked smile.

Jasper threw back his head and roared with laughter.

"Wait until the others find out. You will never hear the end of it," he said.

"I can hardly wait," he said sarcastically.

"She didn't do a very good job," Jasper said casually.

"It was done just a few hours before you arrived, so it's still a bloody mess, I would imagine. I will have to see how it looks after it heals; it itches like the Devil."

"Good, you deserve a little discomfort," Jasper chided.

Chapter Twenty-three

Dylan arrived at the duke's home and was disappointed to learn that Claire had left the day before and was now currently residing with Gabriel and Alyssa. She must have wanted to avoid him, and he really didn't blame her. He hadn't decided what he would say to her in any event. He took a deep breath as he prepared to enter his grandfather's chamber; he felt shame for abandoning him as well. Whether he wanted to or not, he was about to become a duke, and the method by which he would obtain the title sat like a stone inside his heart. He knew that he would never measure up as his grandfather's footsteps would be impossible to follow. He had accepted his fate over the last few days and knew now that he could never escape it. His grandfather was counting on him, and he couldn't let him down again.

He turned the knob and entered the chamber that was darkened except for a lamp beside his bed. A nurse sat nearby in a chair, and he indicated to her that she should leave. He waited for her to exit the room before quietly approaching the bedside. The duke appeared to be sleeping, and Dylan had a brief moment of doubt that he should disturb his slumber, and just as he was about to turn away and go sit in the chair that the nurse had been sitting in, his grandfather's eyes came open, and he smiled. It was a smile of forgiveness, and Dylan's heart lightened as he gingerly sat on the side of the bed and took his hand in his own.

"I'm sorry that I failed you," he murmured.

The duke furiously shook his head and grunted his protest at Dylan's admission, and he gathered that the old man would tell him that he had not failed. But he knew the truth.

"I have, but I will not fail you now," he assured him.

"I have been a fool and nearly lost everything including you," he added.

The old man squeezed his hand with feeble strength and smiled warmly at him.

"Can you forgive me?" Dylan asked.

The duke nodded his head and grunted.

"I will try very hard to fill your shoes, but I fear I shall never measure up," Dylan confessed.

His grandfather squeezed his hand again and a tear escaped his eye.

"Do you think she will forgive me?" he asked him.

The duke nodded his head and tried desperately to speak, and if Dylan knew his grandfather, he was trying to tell him to go after her. He would go after her, but he didn't know when the courage to do so would come.

"I'm afraid," he told him.

The duke furiously shook his head and continued to try and speak.

"Please don't stress yourself, grandfather. Just relax and try and go back to sleep, I will not leave you," he told him.

The duke shook his head and pointed across the room in the direction of his desk.

"You want something from your desk?" Dylan

asked.

The duke nodded and made a gesture with his hand that indicated something in writing.

"Is there a letter there that you want me to read?" Dylan asked.

The duke shook his head.

"Do you want to write something?"

The duke nodded his head that he did. Dylan got up and went to the desk and brought back his journal and a quill and ink. He placed the journal on a blank page and propped it up so the duke could write easily and dipped the quill in the ink before handing it to him. The duke scrawled on the page with considerable effort, and Dylan hoped that he would be able to read the message when he was through. He wrote a sentence then handed the quill to Dylan, and he dipped it back in the ink and handed it to him again. He scrawled some more, and when he was finished, he shoved the journal toward Dylan. Dylan took the journal and read the message, and tears rolled down his cheeks, and he laughed softly. The message said, 'Claire is innocent, and she loves you very much. Go after her, or I will haunt you from my grave for the rest of your days, and for God's sake, shave.'

Dylan smiled, "I know she is innocent; I have been an irrational fool. I was afraid to trust that someone as wonderful as she, could actually love a wretch like me, but she did, and I tried to destroy it; but no more. Rest assured; I will go after her so you can enjoy the hereafter in peace. I only hope that she will still have me," Dylan told him.

The duke patted him on the hand and nodded

his head.

"I hope she will have me because I got her name tattooed on my arse," Dylan said with a smile.

The duke chuckled and then began to cough violently. Dylan immediately felt bad about making the jest and causing his grandfather to have a coughing fit. He got up and poured him a glass of water and lifted his head and shoulders so he could drink. He took a sip of the water, and Dylan gently laid him back down.

"Better?" Dylan asked.

The duke nodded that he was, and Dylan was relieved.

"You should rest," he told him.

The duke nodded that he needed to rest and closed his eyes. Dylan sat there on the side of the bed and watched the motion of his grandfather's chest as it rose and fell laboriously, and then it slowed down, and then ... there was nothing. The duke was gone.

Dylan took his hand in his and brought it to his lips and kissed his knuckles, then wept as he never had before.

*****

Dylan sent for his grandfather's secretary, told him to contact the solicitors and make the preparations for the funeral, and then he left his grandfather's house. He went to his home and was greeted by a very happy Simmons until he relayed that the duke had died.

"I'm very sorry to hear of your grandfather's

passing, your grace," Simmons said.

The term sent a ripple of fear through Dylan's body as he realized that he was now the Duke of Blackstone.

"I am not ready for that, Simmons. Please refrain from the use of it until I have accustomed myself," Dylan said.

Simmons nodded his head that he understood, and Dylan went upstairs so he could shave and bathe. He still had the road dust on his body, and he probably smelled horrific, not to mention he probably looked like a pirate with his beard. He couldn't go to Claire looking like that ... but go to her he would. He had been given his marching orders by his grandfather, and he would fulfill the mission. He would do whatever it took to get Claire back, if he had to beg, borrow or steal, he would have her.

"Simmons, I need a shave and a haircut, and then a nice hot bathe to clean the stench of England's whorehouses off of my body," he said with a smile.

Simmons eagerly started preparing by retrieving his grooming implements, and Dylan took a seat in the chair inside his dressing room.

"Are you going to go after the girl?" Simmons ventured while he was mixing up the lather.

"If she will have me back," he told him.

"I didn't like her when she first arrived, but the effect she had on you was miraculous my lord and I would hate to see you lose her," he said as he began dabbing the lather on Dylan's beard.

"Then you had better work some miracles of

your own, Simmons, because I will need all the help I can get," he told him.

"I will have you so handsome that there is no way she can deny you, my lord," he said as he continued his work.

"I think I would like to have one of those Brutus cuts, Simmons," he told him.

"Are you sure you want to cut it so short my lord?" he asked.

"It's almost to my arse, Simmons; it's time to look civilized, don't you think?" he asked.

"I agree my lord; a Brutus cut you shall have. Would you like muttonchops?" he asked.

"No, just regular sideburns will do," he told him.

"A wise choice my lord," Simmons said as he worked.

Simmons worked diligently, and before long Dylan had a whole new look. He marveled that he was even the same man as he looked at himself in the mirror.

"Your bath is prepared my lord," Simmons said, breaking into his concentration.

He stood up, placed the mirror on the sideboard and began undressing for his bath. He stripped off his trousers and small clothes, and he jerked his head around at the gasping sound that Simmons made.

"My lord something is wrong with your arse," he blurted out.

Dylan laughed.

"It's a tattoo, Simmons; have you never seen one?" he asked.

"It looks awful," Simmons said shaking his head.

"That's just dried blood. It's fairly fresh, and I haven't bathed in awhile," he told him.

"I'm not sure a bath will help," Simmons said as he poked at it.

Dylan ignored him, climbed down in the tub and sighed at the feel of the hot water on his body.

"You really shouldn't drink my lord," Simmons mused aloud as he began scrubbing Dylan's back.

"Yes, I was quite drunk when I allowed that to happen," he told him.

"You should stand up and let me clean it for you, my lord," Simmons said when he was finished with Dylan's back.

Dylan grunted in agreement and reluctantly pulled himself up so Simmons could clean off the dried blood.

Simmons scrubbed away the blood and made another gasping sound.

"What is it?" Dylan asked in alarm.

"You have her named tattooed on your arse, my lord," Simmons said incredulously.

"Yes, apparently I had a hard time forgetting her," he told him.

"It doesn't look so bad now my lord; it's quite nice actually," Simmons said.

"Alright, quit admiring my arse, and let's get this bath over with. I would like to get over to Windhaven's sometime this afternoon," Dylan grumbled.

"You had better hope that she will take you

back now that you have her name written all over your bum my lord," Simmons stated.

"It would be tragic if she turned me down wouldn't it?" Dylan said with a half-hearted chuckle as he sat back down in the tub.

"I can't imagine what possessed you to do that my lord," Simmons grumbled as he began lathering up Dylan's hair.

"I had little to do with it; it's a long story, one I wish to forget."

*****

With butterflies in his stomach, Dylan awaited Claire in the drawing room of Gabriel's home. His friend greeted him with warm affection and told him that he was glad that he had been found and was sad to hear about his grandfather. Gabriel cautioned him not to get his hopes up with regard to Claire as she had been deeply hurt, and it would take time and a lot of effort on his part before she could forgive him. The fact that she had agreed to see him at all gave him hope that all was not lost. He stood before the window looking out at the lawn beyond and didn't hear the door when it opened.

"Hello Mr. Crenshaw," her sweet voice called to him.

Dylan spun around, and the sight before him took his breath away. She was even more beautiful than he remembered.

"Hello, Miss Melville," he said after he collected himself.

"I'm glad to see that you have decided to come

home; your grandfather has missed you sorely," she told him.

He realized then that Claire didn't know yet that he had passed on, so with sadness he said, "I'm afraid that I have some bad news."

"Oh no," she said, shaking her head and beginning to weep.

He walked over to her and was about to embrace her, but he didn't think she would welcome his touch, so he clenched his fists at his sides to control the ach that his hands felt with the need to touch her.

"He passed quietly a couple of hours ago. His last thoughts were of you," he told her softly.

She sobbed harder then, and he did reach out this time and touched her on the arm. When she didn't flinch, he tugged her into an embrace and was relieved when she didn't pull away. He held her thusly while she cried, and all he could think about was how wonderful it felt to have her in his arms again. After a moment, he placed his hand under her chin and lifted her face to his. Her beautiful eyes were full of tears, and her nose was red from crying. She never looked more beautiful than she did at that moment, and he was overcome, so he leaned forward to kiss her. Her lips were warm and salty with tears, and for a brief moment she allowed the contact. Then as if she suddenly remembered that she hated him, she stiffened in his arms and pulled away.

"I am sorry for your loss Mr. Crenshaw. Please let me know if there is anything I can do for you," she said with formal indifference.

Dylan's heart plunged into his gut, and he closed his eyes tight in response to the chill in her voice. He shook his head and made a groaning sound before opening his eyes again to look at her. He was going about this all wrong but didn't know how to fix it. He knew she still loved him, but she no longer trusted him; of that he was sure.

"I don't deserve it Claire, but I hope you can forgive me some day," he ventured.

"I don't know that I can," she said softly.

Dylan didn't know what to do or say next. He felt like a fish out of water. The woman he loved was standing before him, and yet she was so far away. Her eyes were full of accusation and pain, but they still held love. He felt intense shame standing there before her, knowing all he had done and if he lived to be a thousand, he could never make it up to her ... never.

"I'm sorry," he choked out, then he quickly quit the room, fearing he was about to break down and cry.

He knew it was going to be hard to get her back, but he wasn't sure he was strong enough to endure the pain of seeing how much he had hurt her.

Chapter Twenty-four

Dylan was almost to the foyer when Claire called to him. He stopped in his tracks but didn't turn around to face her. He held his breath while he waited for her to approach from behind.

"Mr. Crenshaw, I should like to be released from our betrothal," she told him.

Dylan felt as though a knife had just sliced his heart in two. He slowly turned around and faced her then. She still had tears welled in her eyes, and the sight of them did something to him on a primordial level. Without a thought for what he would do, he rushed at her and pulled her to him, delivering a punishing kiss to her soft lips. She didn't fight, and he reveled in it as he deepened the kiss. He knew then that she loved him just as much as he loved her, and he was not about to let her get away from him again. With great reluctance, he broke the kiss.

"I will never release you Claire," he told her with fire in his eyes.

"You have no choice sir," she said defiantly.

"We will marry Claire, and that kiss just confirmed it. You can't possibly stand there and tell me that you felt nothing and wish to marry another," he argued.

"I shall not marry you sir, and the kiss proved nothing but that you are still the same overbearing brute that you have always been," she said with squared shoulders.

He smiled at her. This was the woman he fell in love with; his mighty American warrior. He grabbed her by the wrist, dragged her back to the drawing room, forced her inside and slammed the door shut behind them. He jerked her back toward the door and pinned her there with his body.

"Say that you hate me Claire," he demanded.

"I do," she said hotly.

"I say that you're a liar," he said lunging forward to take her lips in another bruising kiss.

She tore her lips away and shoved at his chest, but he was immoveable.

"I shall never have you," she growled as she tried to get away from him.

He took her by the chin with one hand and forced her to look at him as he began to unbutton her bodice with the other. Her chest was heaving with her anger, yet she did nothing to stop him, their eyes never breaking contact. He slid his hand inside and felt her soft silky flesh, beginning a slow sensual caress of her breast as he leaned forward and kissed her lips again with a desperate hunger. She hit him in the chest with her fists several times then wrapped her arms around his neck, and with a whimper of defeat she began to kiss him back. Stimulated as never before, he began lifting up her skirt and found his way to her woman's mound and slowly massaged her sensitive nub until she was moaning and writhing in ecstasy. Encouraged by her ardor, he unbuttoned his trousers, pulled out his throbbing erection and rubbed it against her hot flesh.

He broke the kiss and looked into her eyes, and what he saw there convinced him that she wouldn't deny him, so he lifted her up, wrapped her legs around him and started a slow penetration of her tight sheath. She was so hot and slick as he inched his way in until he reached her barrier of innocence. He halted and leaned forward to whisper in her ear.

"This will hurt," he told her.

She shook her head.

"I hate you," she said, then lunged forward and kissed him savagely just as he thrust home.

She cried out, but he swallowed the sound and held himself still until she became accustomed to the intrusion.

"You love me, Claire, admit it," he murmured hot in her mouth.

"No, you're a pig and a brute," she said back into his mouth without ever breaking the kiss that she now controlled.

"You love me," he said again.

Again, she shook her head and growled into his mouth and bit down on his lip. He bit her lip back, and once he was sure she no longer felt pain he began a slow thrusting in and out of her passage; the feeling was such as he had never known. He closed his eyes in an attempt to keep from being unmanned as the feeling was pure bliss, and he wasn't sure how long he could last. All of those women he had been with over the last month couldn't even come close to comparing with her. He wanted to go deeper, so he clamped his hands on her hips to hold her in place and slid down to his knees, bringing her with him, then gingerly shifted them on the floor at the base of the door, all the while encouraging her to keep her legs wrapped around him so he could stay seated in her passage.

Once he had her on her back, he put his hand

under her bottom and lifted her then he thrust deep into her womb. She cried out again, but this time it wasn't from pain, and the sound of it was nearly his undoing. She began to buck and grind to meet his thrusts as he rammed himself deep inside her with a fierce, desperate urgency.

"Say you love me Claire," he commanded.

She shook her head and closed her eyes tight.

He dove forward and took her lips in a hungry kiss, and after a few more deep thrusts he felt her stiffen then shudder and her sheath started pulsing around his shaft. He was undone then and climaxed so hard that he had to strain in order to hold back the roar that had built up in his throat. When the last pulse of his orgasm ceased, he collapsed atop her breathing raggedly.

"Get off of me," she grunted.

He quickly rolled off of her, and she quickly jumped up and started putting her clothing back to right. He was stunned that she could act as though nothing had happened after such a momentous loving that left him completely drained and weak as a newborn pup. He slowly stood up and began to fix his clothing too and saw her virgin's blood on his member. He tucked himself inside his trousers and took out his handkerchief and wiped the blood off of his hand.

"We shall marry now, Claire," he told her.

"No," she said.

"How can you say no after that?" he asked incredulously.

"I only did it so you would know the wrong that you have done to me Dylan. You accused me of terrible things and believed Mr. Ensley over me," she said with cold conviction.

"What are you saying?" he demanded.

"You thought I was a whore," she shouted.

"So you gave me your virtue to prove that you aren't?" he asked with barely contained rage.

"It's done now so you may go," she said tilting up her chin.

Dylan couldn't believe what he was hearing. Why was she doing this?

"What if I have gotten you with child?" he demanded.

"It will not be your concern; just leave," she said.

"I'll leave for now, Claire, but we are not finished," he vowed.

"We were finished the moment you threw me away."

"You belong to me Claire, and I will have you."

"That's what Mr. Ensley said after he tried to rape me; I belong to no man, Mr. Crenshaw. Please leave now."

Dylan stood there glaring at her. How could she be so cold and indifferent after what they had just shared? This was not the woman he had fallen in love with; he didn't even recognize her. He could see now that there was nothing he could do; she had made her decision, and to stand here and argue with her would serve no purpose.

*****

Claire watched Dylan go, and once she was sure he was gone, she ran up the stairs to her room. She couldn't believe what she had just done. She hadn't intended to make love with him, but she had been quite unable to resist him. He had looked so handsome with his hair cut, and he was looking at her as though she were the very air that he breathed. She had lied to him just then. She hadn't done it because she wanted to prove her innocence. She had simply wanted him and decided that she would have him no matter the cost. *Why couldn't I have just told him that? Why did I have to be cruel?* She barged into her room and closed and locked the door behind her. She walked over to the bed and threw herself down on it and began to cry with deep heaving sobs. She loved him, but she had treated him with such cold indifference, and for what?

Was it foolish pride that drove me to such stupidity? she asked herself. It must have been because if she had been a little bit kinder to him she would still be his fiancée, and they could have been married at any time. Instead, she had probably lost him for good. She grabbed a pillow and tucked it under her breast and cradled it tight in her arms. She felt lost and alone now; more than she had when he left her a month ago. Somehow, this seemed more final; it must really be over between them; how could they recover from this? What if he had gotten her with child? What would she do then? Oh, what a tangle! She closed her eyes and held the pillow close against herself, trying to satisfy the aching in her arms that wanted to hold him. She could still feel the ache between her legs from the power of his body thrusting inside her. She had never imagined that lovemaking would have been so wonderful, and now she would probably never know the wonder of it again.

*****

Dylan was in a foul mood on his way back to his home. He was angry and confused, and he felt used. He simply couldn't understand why she had done it. How could she have made love to him and not be as affected by it as he had been. She had to have felt something in her heart for him; her body had certainly responded. It had been the most incredible experience of his life, and she had acted as though nothing out of the ordinary had happened. What was he to do now? He couldn't give her up, but apparently it was her wish; or was it? Perhaps she was trying to teach him a lesson of some sort. She must have wanted to punish him for his crimes against her. He certainly deserved it, but was it all really lost between them? He refused to accept that; especially after what just occurred between them. He would get her back, but how?

Perhaps he should start from scratch and court her properly; he had never done that because of the unusual nature of their relationship. Aye, that's what he would do. He tapped on the roof of his carriage to get the driver to stop. The driver pulled the carriage over, hopped down and came to the window.

"Go by a florist, Buckley, and after that, a jeweler," he instructed.

"Very good your grace," the driver said then

scurried back to the driver's bench.

He cringed at the driver's words; he would never get used to the title, and it would be meaningless without Claire by his side.

*****

Claire must have fallen asleep after Dylan left, because the next thing she knew, Lucy was waking her up to get dressed for dinner.

"Are ye ill, Claire?" she asked with concern in her eyes.

Claire sat up and shifted her legs over the side and sat there bewildered.

"Sick at heart Lucy, that's all," she said and then began to weep.

"Aye tis sad about the duke," she murmured.

"Oh, it's so much more than that Lucy. Dylan came by, and I treated him deplorably," she sobbed.

"I'm sure 'e deserved it, and then some," she said with a huff.

"I did a terrible thing," she told her.

"What could ye 'ave done that was so terrible?"

Claire hung her head in shame.

"I gave him my virginity right there in the drawing room when he came to visit," she mumbled.

"Why?" she asked with a gasp.

"Oh, I don't know Lucy, but when it was over, I told him it was so he would know the terrible wrong he had done to me when he accused me of being a whore, and then I sent him away," she cried.

"Child, ye must marry him now," Lucy

declared.

"It is over now Lucy. I'm sure I killed whatever was left between us. The look on his face when I said the words was so awful," she told her.

"Ye gave 'im a taste of 'is own medicine is all but ye must find a way to repair the damage. Ye could be with child now," she admonished.

"Surely, I couldn't be with child after only one time," Claire said with fear in her eyes.

"It only takes one time, Claire."

"Oh this is terrible, Lucy. Whatever shall I do?"

"Ye will 'ave to get 'im back. I don't think that will be too 'ard seeing as 'ow a messenger arrived just a few minutes ago with some flowers and a package addressed to ye. It must be from 'im," she told her.

"Oh Lucy, why did no one wake me?" she cried out.

Lucy laughed.

"I just did," she told her with a twinkle in her eye.

Claire jumped up from the bed.

"I must hurry and change so I can go and see," she told her.

"I brought them with me; they're over there on the sideboard," she said with a chuckle.

Claire dashed over to the sideboard and gasped when she saw the roses; there had to have been at least three dozen of the most beautiful red roses she had ever seen in her life.

"They're gorgeous," she sighed and then put her nose in the bouquet.

"Oh, and they smell divine," she said, then grabbed the card and quickly flipped it over.

'Please don't forsake me, my beloved Claire, Dylan' the note said.

"I wonder if he sent them before or after he was here?" she wondered aloud.

"They were a late delivery so I would imagine it was after," Lucy said with a smile.

Claire hoped that Lucy was correct because that meant that he still loved her, even after what had happened. She looked at the small package sitting next to the roses and hesitantly picked it up and began to unwrap it. She gasped at the sight within the small box. A diamond and emerald bracelet that must have cost a king's ransom lay within.

"Oh, I couldn't possibly accept this," she said regretfully.

"Ye can, and ye will," Lucy commanded her.

"We are not yet wed," she defended.

"Ye weren't wed when he gave ye the other jewels," Lucy pointed out.

"Yes, but we were betrothed then, and our wedding was just days away; this is different and besides, I returned those to the duke," Claire insisted.

"Ye are still betrothed and ye will still wed. Ye just 'ave to set a new date," Lucy pointed out.

Claire couldn't argue with that, but she still felt that there was a principle that should be adhered to.

"I will keep the roses but return the bracelet. I cannot make it too easy for him," she decided.

Lucy clucked her tongue but said nothing.

"Well, I can't very well send the message that I

would accept such expensive gifts after what happened. I am not his mistress, after all," she said defensively.

"I suppose ye 'ave a point; now let's get you out of that gown so I can clean that spot of blood off of it," Lucy huffed.

Claire blushed and put the bracelet on the sideboard beside the roses and presented her back to Lucy so she could unbutton her gown. She was glad she hadn't been walking around like that. Lucy undressed her down to her shift and went to start her bath water. Claire realized then that she was very sore between her legs and couldn't wait to sit in the warm water.

"My goodness 'e must have torn ye to pieces," Lucy proclaimed when she returned.

"I am rather sore," she admitted with a blush.

"Ye go get into that tub; that should soothe ye. Shall I call for a doctor?" Lucy asked.

"Heaven's no!" Claire said with alarm.

Lucy urged her toward the water closet, and once there, she removed her shift and looked at the stain.

"I never seen so much virgin's blood; do ye suppose ye are 'aving your courses?" she asked.

"It isn't time for that yet," Claire said as she stepped into the bath.

She gingerly sat down in the warm water and sighed at the pleasure of it.

"I 'ave some salve we can put on ye when ye are done with your bath," Lucy told her.

"Thank you Lucy; I'm sure there was no real harm done. It doesn't hurt too much," Claire told her.

"Ye had better give it some time afore ye bed 'im again," she instructed.

"Oh I will Lucy; rest assured about that," Claire told her then sank back in the tub.

Claire wouldn't make such a mistake again. The next time she and Dylan joined it would be in the marriage bed. She only hoped that it would be soon and that he hadn't gotten her with child. She closed her eyes and thought about what had happened and shivered at the memory. He hadn't really hurt her too bad, so she couldn't account for all the blood. *Perhaps some women bleed more than others.* He had been surprisingly gentle all things considered, and he had seen to her pleasure before he achieved his own. She wished that it hadn't been such a hasty coupling as she would have loved to feel him skin to skin when they made love.

"I don't need to wash my hair Lucy. I will just have a soak this time," she told her.

"As ye will; I'll go and fetch that salve and ready your dinner gown," Lucy said as she left the water closet.

After Lucy left, Claire gingerly felt between her legs to see if anything was different there and was relieved that everything was still intact. There didn't appear to be any tearing, and for that, she was grateful. She took a cloth and cleaned the dried blood off of her thighs, gently cleansed herself below and then lay back in the tub again and thought about what she should do next.

Gina Rose

Chapter Twenty-five

Dylan arrived early the next day to call on her and offered to take her for a ride in his curricle. Claire declined on the basis that it wouldn't be proper since they were in mourning. Dylan reluctantly agreed with her and, instead, they sat in the drawing room in awkward silence for several minutes.

"I cannot accept the gift that you sent last evening," she said to break the silence.

Her words sparked his temper as he was already in a foul mood because she refused to go riding with him.

"You cannot accept the gift, or you cannot accept me? Which is it?" he demanded.

"We are no longer betrothed," she argued.

"I have not released you from our betrothal," he retorted.

Claire didn't have an answer to that and said nothing in response.

"When is your grandfather's funeral to be held?" she asked, obviously wanting to change the subject.

"On the morrow at two o'clock," he grumbled.

"I should like to attend," she told him.

"You shall attend by my side as my betrothed should; I shall pick you up at ten o'clock as Blackstone Manor is about a three-hour ride by carriage. Prepare to stay overnight," he stated.

"What will people say?" she asked in alarm.

"I don't give a damn what people will say," he growled.

"If you are going to be so grumpy, perhaps you

should leave," she snapped.

"Forgive me," he said with a sigh.

"I'm trying," she retorted.

"It doesn't seem as though you want to," he said with sadness in his eyes.

"You hurt me Dylan, and I cannot easily forget it," she returned.

He got up and dropped to his knees before her, taking her hand in his.

"Please forgive me Claire; I cannot bear this," he pleaded.

Claire stiffened and pulled her hand away. The action wounded him to the core, but he was not about to give up.

"I cannot promise anything Dylan," she told him.

"Marry me at week's end," he blurted.

"I couldn't possibly do that," she replied.

"When then?" he demanded.

"Why are you pressuring me?" she demanded in return.

"What if I have gotten you with child?" he asked.

"Is that the only reason for your urgency?" she asked incredulously.

"No of course not, but it is a very important reason. Marry me!" he demanded again.

"I need time to think about this Dylan."

Dylan dropped his forehead to her knee and remained there for several seconds trying to think of what to say next. Finally, he looked up at her with his heart and soul in his eyes.

"I know that I have treated you unfairly, Claire.

I was a fool, and I realize that now; I am trying desperately to make amends. I love you so much that it hurts, and I need you with me. Please say that you will have me back," he pleaded.

Claire reached up and touched him on the cheek.

"It will take time to trust you again," she told him.

He gave a pained expression and stood up and walked toward the window. He stood there with his back to her, looking out over the lawn. She wasn't going to make this easy for him at all, he could see that plainly. He was fully prepared to take the abuse as long as it took to win her back, but he was growing increasingly frustrated.

"I will give you two weeks," he said as he continued to look out the window.

When she didn't respond, he turned and looked at her, and she gasped when she saw his face. He knew that his pain was written there for all to see, but he could do nothing about it.

"Let's take it one day at a time," she offered.

"Two weeks Claire!" he reiterated.

"That may not be long enough. The duchess is going to give me a season to introduce me to society," she told him with her chin tilting up.

"So you can meet other gentlemen," he stated.

"What of it?" she demanded.

"I will not give you up to another," he growled.

"You may not have a choice," she growled back.

"Two weeks!" he stated, and then he quickly quit the room without so much as a fare-thee-well.

He had to remove himself from her presence before more harm could be done. It was all he could do not to grab her and repeat what happened the day before, and that he could not allow.

*****

The following morning, Dylan arrived to pick her up for the funeral. The carriage ride was long and awkward as they barely had two words to speak to one another. He was still angry with her, but he didn't want to say anything that would cause another argument. After he left her yesterday, he wanted to throttle someone in his frustration. The woman was being stubborn, and he was forced to go along with it. He shouldn't have issued the ultimatum, but he was feeling desperate, and now that he knew that she planned on having a season that desperation was ten-fold. The idea that she could meet someone else was like a knife to his heart, and he simply couldn't stand for it. He was hopeful, however, as she hadn't refused to see him when he came to call and she had stopped calling him 'Mr. Crenshaw', and though she said she couldn't accept the bracelet, she had yet to return it, and she still wore the betrothal ring. He knew that she wanted him as much as he wanted her, but the trust had been severely damaged. The only way he could make it up to her was by being a devoted husband, but she would have to consent to marry him first.

"We should be there in about a quarter of an hour," he said to break the silence.

"It's beautiful here," she said conversationally.

He smiled at her attempts to be congenial.

"Yes, it is lovely. Perhaps, after we are married, we could live at Blackstone," he suggested.

She blushed and looked out the window but didn't say anything one way or the other. The minx was playing hard to get; he could see that now. He inwardly smiled, and they traveled the remainder of the trip in comfortable silence, and he was glad that he would have the whole day and night as well as most of tomorrow to press his suit; he would need all the time he could get.

*****

There had been a fairly large turnout for the duke's funeral, and he was buried beside his wife at the local parsonage. Afterwards, there was a luncheon inside the church to celebrate his life. The duke had been loved and respected by his tenants as well as his peers, and Claire was touched by all the warm sentiments that had been spoken about the man she had known so briefly. Dylan had been so attentive to her all day that she found herself forgetting that she was angry at him. Well, she wasn't really angry per say, but she didn't want to appear to be too eager to take him back. She tried very hard to remain indifferent to his ploys, but it was growing harder by the minute.

She was a little anxious about the night to come, knowing that she would be alone with him at Blackstone. She had hoped that Gabriel and Alyssa would stay, but they had left their child with the nurse, and she was eager to return to her. She couldn't help but notice that there seemed to be a great deal of tension between Dylan and Luther, but Jasper put himself between them as a buffer and things went along rather peacefully. It was curious behavior between the friends, and she couldn't help but wonder if she were the cause of it. Dylan made sure she was never alone with Luther, but he didn't seem to mind when she was alone with Jasper. She had tried to pry information out of Jasper at one point, but he simply told her that it was best to let the matter work itself out without interference. Still it bothered her to see them at odds with one another, and since she felt that it had something to do with her, she felt a certain obligation to try and help them patch things up.

She was waiting for Dylan to finish saying goodbye to all the attendants of the funeral, and then he promised her a tour of the grounds at Blackstone. She saw Luther standing off to the side, and every now and then he would cast her a look that she couldn't fathom. Was it possible that Luther had developed feelings for her? She hoped not because she really liked him and had started to view him as a brother, and she didn't want that to change. She decided to have a walk about the cemetery to have a look around at the grave markers and statuary while she waited and quietly eased away from Dylan's side. She silently marveled at some of the dates on the headstones and wondered what kind of lives the people had led; of course, many of the graves were from the Crenshaw family.

"Claire?" a male voice said softly from behind her.

She turned around and saw Luther standing there, and she quickly looked around to see if anyone could see them. Dylan had his back turned and was speaking with a group of people, and she hoped that he wouldn't grow angry if he were to turn and see them.

"Luther, how are you?" she asked politely.

"I am fine, but how are you?" he asked solemnly.

"I shall be fine, don't worry about me," she told him with a soft smile.

"I can't help but worry for you Claire; you see, I have grown very fond of you, and it pains me to see you suffering," he told her.

"That is very kind of you Luther, and I am very fond of you as well," she said with a blush.

"Will you marry him?" he asked her.

"I haven't made up my mind yet," she fibbed.

"If you decide against it, I would be honored if you would consider … I would like it very much if you would … Oh, I don't know how to say this Claire," he said frustrated.

She touched him on the forearm.

"Don't say it Luther, please. I cannot bear to think that I could be the cause of a rift between you and Dylan," she said softly.

"He doesn't deserve you, but I could make you happy," he vowed.

"Luther, you will no doubt make a wonderful husband, but not to me. If things don't work out for me and Dylan, I suspect that I will return to America," she told him as kindly as she could.

"I would go with you; all you have to do is ask," he persisted.

"Luther please; do not do this. I do not wish to cause you pain, but I must insist that you forget the idea," she said uncomfortably.

"Just think about it, Claire; that's all I ask," he said with defeat in his voice.

She reached up and touched him on the cheek and shook her head.

"You are a good friend, Luther, but nothing more," she said.

She looked over at Dylan, and her heart thudded in her chest when she saw the look on his face as he observed what had just taken place between her and Luther.

"Please Luther, Dylan is watching us, and I don't want to be the cause of any more trouble between you. I must go now," she told him and started walking away.

"Claire," he called after her.

She stopped but did not turn around.

"If he ever hurts you again, I will thrash him within an inch of his life," he promised.

She squared her shoulders and started walking again with a sense of dread as she approached Dylan. As she suspected, Dylan was livid, but he said nothing. Instead, he took her by the arm in a firm grip and kept her close to him until all the funeral attendants had vacated the churchyard. She suspected that he was barely containing his anger, and her palms were beginning to sweat from nerves as he assisted her into the curricle. They rode in silence until they reached Blackstone, and instead of the tour he had promised, he went straight up the drive of the huge imposing structure.

"I thought we were going to take a tour of the grounds," she asked nervously.

"I've changed my mind," he grunted.

He jumped down from the curricle, assisted her down and led her inside the great estate. She had been so nervous that she didn't really take in all of the scenery, and if she had to tell anyone what the exterior was like she wouldn't be able to as she hadn't a clue; she only knew that it was huge.

"Why did you change your mind?" she asked as he ushered her inside, bypassing the butler as if he hadn't been there at all.

"I'm sure you wouldn't have enjoyed it as I am nowhere near as entertaining as Luther," he growled as he was practically dragging her up the stairs.

They reached the landing, and he took the hall going west, and when they reached a door near the end of the hall, he stopped and opened it.

"Your quarters," he stated with cold indifference.

She stood there dumbfounded, and he prodded her into the room. She stepped inside and turned to ask him why he was being so hostile, but she was met with a closing door; he had gone and left her alone. She opened the door, looked out and saw him walking briskly away toward the stairs and thought to call after him, but decided against it. Now was not a good time to try and have a discussion with him as he looked like he was fit for violence. She shivered at the thought and hoped that Luther was well on his way back to London.

Gina Rose

Chapter Twenty-six

Dylan mounted his horse and left Blackstone in a fury in pursuit of Luther and Jasper. It was time that he confronted Luther to let him know that he was to stay away from Claire if he knew what was good for him. Jasper and Luther had a good half an hour start ahead of him, but it was his belief that he could catch up to them quickly as he pressed his horse to give it all he had. Anger was coursing through his body like hot needles at the thought that his friend and brother would try and move in on his territory. The four friends had always had an unwritten code not to poach on one another's women, but Luther had apparently cast all that aside and decided to pursue Claire for himself. Claire belonged to him, and he wasn't about to let any man, especially one of his so-called friends have her. He had made the mistake of casting her aside to another man before, but never again. This time he would fight for her, even if it meant the death of his friend.

Up ahead, he saw two figures on horseback in the middle of the road, and it appeared that they were just sitting there. As he moved closer, he could see that Jasper and Luther had apparently anticipated such a meeting and decided to wait for him. "Very accommodating of them," he grumbled.

As he neared, he saw Luther dismount and start walking toward him, his arms cocked and fists tightened in a battle stance. When he was within two yards, he jumped down from his horse, and the two men met one another and the punches started flying. They fought viciously, pummeling one another with savage blows, and neither man gave an inch to the other. Luther was a big man, but Dylan had one thing on his side and that was desperate determination, and it drove him like a machine as he delivered blow after blow, finally sending Luther to the ground on his back. Dylan towered over him with his chest heaving, and he knew that his own face was just as bloody as Luther's because he could feel the blood trickling from his eyes and nose.

"Stay away from Claire," he growled at him.

"Hurt her again, and I will kill you," Luther retorted.

Dylan stood there and blinked his eyes at Luther's threat, and he realized then that his friend must be in love with her. He turned on his heel and started pacing back and forth while Luther pealed himself up from the ground.

"I hope the two of you have gotten it out of your systems," Jasper chided from atop his horse.

Dylan stomped back up to Luther, and the two men stood chest to chest.

"Do you love her?" Dylan asked.

"Yes, I love her, and if she wasn't so in love with you, she might have accepted my proposal," he told him.

"You proposed to her?" he asked incredulously.

"Aye, and I would do it again," he gritted out through clenched teeth.

"She belongs to me Luther," he shouted.

"That's a crying shame," Luther retorted.

"I think it's more a case of Dylan belonging to

Claire," Jasper said with a snicker.

Dylan shot his friend a look; he knew what he was about to say.

"You keep quiet," he told him.

"Well, it's true, isn't it?" Jasper asked with a raised eyebrow.

"What are you talking about?" Luther demanded.

"Dylan had himself branded," Jasper said, clearly enjoying the taunt.

"I told you to keep quiet," Dylan shouted.

"Branded?" Luther asked perplexed.

"Show him!" Jasper prodded.

"I will not," Dylan said indignantly.

"Show me what?" Luther demanded.

"Dylan, if you don't willingly drop your trousers and show Luther your tattoo, he will hold you down, and I will do it for you," Jasper threatened.

"You wouldn't," Dylan said defensively.

Jasper dismounted from his horse and started advancing toward Dylan. Luther fell in beside him, and the two men had a look of absolute determination in their eyes.

"I will not bare my arse on a public road," Dylan declared futilely.

"Get him Luther," Jasper commanded.

Luther launched himself at Dylan, tackled him to the ground and quickly pinned him down with his signature chokehold, knee in the back combination, and Dylan was helpless as Jasper grabbed his trousers and pried them over his hips to expose his arse. There was silence for a moment as the two men looked at his arse, and then Luther released him and roared with laughter.

"You can pull your trousers back up now, Dylan, and by the by, the tattoo looks much nicer now," he said casually.

Dylan lay there, completely humiliated. Luther continued laughing so hard that he fell to his knees and rolled around on the ground, carrying on like a lunatic

"That's the funniest thing I've ever seen," he said in between bouts of laughter.

Dylan rolled over on his back, looked up at the sky and wondered when his life would ever get back to normal.

"Come now, the two of you will get fleas lying on the ground like a couple of dogs," Jasper said as he extended an arm to help Dylan to his feet.

Dylan took his assistance as his trousers were still down around his thighs, and once on his feet, he unbuttoned them, pulled them up and started putting himself back to rights. Luther finally quieted and heaved himself up off the ground, and the three men stood there in the middle of the road in awkward silence.

"I can't believe that you proposed to her," Dylan said breaking the silence.

"If you cast her aside again, I will do whatever it takes to convince her to marry me," Luther promised.

"I will never cast her aside again, so perhaps you should find someone else," Dylan said sarcastically.

"Relax brother; I love her, but I'm not in love

with her. I only wanted to offer protection; she is all alone in this world, you know?" Luther told him.

Dylan realized that he was directing anger at his friend, when Luther's heart was pure, and his intentions were noble.

"I'm sorry that we fought," Dylan told him.

"Make sure you treat her right or it will happen again," Luther promised.

"If she will have me," he mumbled.

"I don't think that is going to be a problem; have you told her about the tattoo?" Jasper put in.

Dylan shot him a look and shook his head.

"I wonder what she will think of it," Jasper mused aloud.

"That depends on whether she ever learns how I came about it," Dylan grumbled.

"She won't learn it from me," Jasper promised.

"How did you come about it?" Luther prodded.

"Never mind," Dylan barked.

"How come I'm always left out of the juicy gossip?" Luther complained.

"One of those wenches we found him with did it because he always talked about Claire in his sleep," Jasper said with a toothy grin.

Without thinking, Dylan slugged Jasper in the nose, sending him on his back.

"What the hell did you do that for?" Jasper demanded.

"Because it felt good," Dylan said with a chuckle.

"I suppose I will have to blackmail you now," Jasper said casually as he rubbed his nose.

Dylan groaned and went to his horse and

mounted.

"Go home," he shouted over his shoulder as he turned his horse toward Blackstone.

*****

When Dylan returned to Blackstone and cleaned himself up he went in search of Claire and found her walking in the garden, and he knew that he had some explaining to do. His face was a mess; it was obvious that he had had an altercation, so there was no getting around explaining what happened.

"Claire?" he called to her.

She twirled around and gasped at the sight of him, and then she started laughing.

"I'm sorry, I don't mean to laugh, but I have been sitting here worrying about Luther, and it looks as though he took care of himself quite handily," she said, then laughed some more.

That wasn't what Dylan had expected from her, and he was slightly offended.

"So it was Luther that you worried about and not me?" he asked.

Claire sobered and straightened her shoulders, prepared to do battle, and he realized that he was about to make matters worse. He hadn't come out here with the intention of quarreling with her as he wanted to avoid that at all cost if they were to ever mend the rift between them.

"The way you left here sir, I feared that you would shoot your friend first and ask questions later," she stated boldly.

Dylan smiled and winced as the action hurt his

split lip.

"In a manner of speaking, that's exactly what I did," he admitted.

"It looks as though Luther was prepared for you," she chided.

"Oh, that he was," he said, trying to smile again.

"Luther is a big man," she said and started advancing toward him.

"Yes he is, and he looks just as handsome as I do right now," Dylan told her, taking steps to meet her.

"When will you learn Dylan?" she asked.

"I'm learning as I go, Claire," he admitted taking her hand in his and bringing it to his lips.

He gingerly kissed her palm and closed his eyes, basking in the pleasure of the contact as he held her hand there for a suspended moment. She didn't pull away, and when he opened his eyes the look in her own took his breath away.

"I love you Claire," he told her.

"And I you, Dylan, but you are an ass," she told him with a sardonic smile.

"I know that now, believe me I do. When I saw you touching Luther as you did, I lost all reason and wanted to thrash him within an inch of his life," he admitted.

"Luther loves you Dylan," she admonished.

"He loves you too Claire; did you know that?"

Claire dropped her head and sighed.

"I don't think he really does," she told him softly.

"He doesn't love you as much as I do, no one

could. I know that you find that hard to believe, but it's true. My soul cries out for you Claire, so much so that you haunt me in my sleep," he told her.

She glanced up at him and looked deep into his eyes as if she were trying to see inside him.

"Then why do you act this way? Why can you not trust me Dylan? You always think the worst and jump to conclusions," she complained.

He put his hand under her chin and gently put his lips to hers. He tried to kiss her with passion, but the pain in his lips would not allow it. He winced and pulled back with a soft chuckle.

"I am a desperate man, Claire. I am so afraid that I have lost you and it makes me an irrational fool," he confessed.

She was going to speak, but he placed a finger on her lips.

"Wait; hear me out before you speak," he told her.

Dylan knew that he had to say this right or he could lose her, so he proceeded cautiously.

"You came into my life at a time when I cared about nothing or no one, and I had set out to kill myself, but I found that I lacked the courage to do it with any finality, so I became a worthless drunkard, hoping that one day I would simply cease to exist.

"Then you came along, and it was like a thunderbolt from the heavens and you shocked me back to life, and I resisted it with every ounce of strength I had but found I could not.

"I couldn't understand how a woman as wonderful as you would want someone like me, and I became very distrustful of it. I didn't think that I deserved love, and I certainly didn't deserve you, but despite all that, I wanted you with a hunger such as I have never known.

"Then that son of a ... Kenwick lied to me and because I didn't think I was deserving of you, I believed him, and then I made the mistake of my life and abandoned you to him.

"I ran away then like a coward, and I behaved ... deplorably while I was away. Claire, I don't want to tell you this, but I must if I am to fully make amends, but I did the very thing I accused you of and much worse."

Claire gasped and spun around so she didn't have to look at him. He reached out and touched her shoulder, and she didn't pull away, so he continued.

"Night after night, there were women upon women in my bed; most of whom I cannot remember their faces because I was so deep in my cups that they were just a blur. I tried to purge you from my heart and soul and thought that if I slept with enough women I could.

"I couldn't you see, because you live so deep within me, so deep that even when I sleep, I'm thinking of you."

She turned back around to him and tears were flowing from her eyes. She stood there for a moment just looking at him as if she didn't know who he was. His heart fell, and he knew that his confession sealed his fate, and she would never have him now."

"Why are you telling me this?" she demanded.

"Because I love you, and I want to come to you with a clear conscience. I cannot live a lie; I want you to see me for what I really am, and if you decide that you can forgive me, then perhaps I can move forward without all this jealously and distrust. I will know that you really love me … me, Claire and not the man you thought I was."

"I don't know what to say to you Dylan," she told him.

"I promise you that I will be a faithful husband. I will never stray, and there will never be another," he told her.

"How can I ever believe that now?" she asked.

"You will have to have the kind of faith in me that I refused to have in you, until now. I will never again accuse you of any wrongdoing because I believe in you Claire, and I am asking you to believe in me too, even though I don't deserve it."

"How many women were there, Dylan?" she asked.

"Honestly, I don't know," he told her with shame in his eyes.

She chewed on her lip while she pondered his confession. Then she squared her shoulders and tilted her chin.

"I would like to court other men to decide if you are right for me, Dylan. I am not discounting you completely, but I have not had an opportunity to meet anyone else, and I don't want to make a mistake and marry a lecherous drunkard," she said.

Dylan closed his eyes and absorbed the blow of her words. He should never have told her about the other women. He looked at her and decided that he couldn't leave it like this.

"I have something to show you," he told her.

He began unbuttoning his trousers, and she gave a look of absolute shock.

"Relax, it's not what you think," he told her before turning his back to her, dropping his trousers and presenting her with the proof of his love.

She gasped at the sight, and then she studied it closely and poked it with her finger.

"What is that?" she demanded.

"It is proof that I love you even when I'm sleeping in a drunken stupor," he told her pulling up his trousers.

He buttoned them, turned to face her and nearly laughed at her expression and the color of her skin. She was red all over from her hairline to the neckline of her gown.

"Are you trying to tell me that … that … thing just materialized while you were sleeping?" she asked incredulously.

"In a manner of speaking," he told her.

"You had better explain it in a manner that I understand, Dylan. My name is branded on your backside for crying out loud; I think I deserve an explanation!" she huffed.

"You will hate me for sure when I tell you how I came about it," he told her.

"It surely can't be any worse than anything else you have told me," she retorted.

"There was a woman … a whore, that insisted on tattooing me. I didn't care because I was so drunk, and I didn't even know what she did until later when I asked her what it was. She said that I talked about you in my sleep, and I guess that was her way of reminding me what was important to me," he explained.

"A whore wrote my name on your buttocks?" she asked, her eyes blinking rapidly.

"Yes," he admitted with shame.

"This beats all I have ever heard, Dylan Crenshaw," she declared. "I should like to go inside now and retire for the evening," she said as she began walking quickly to the house.

Dylan followed behind her feeling like the biggest fool in all of England. But at least she knew it all now, and if she decided to forgive him, he could go to her with a clean slate.

Chapter Twenty-seven

The ride back to London had been horribly quiet as Claire rode back alone in the carriage. Dylan rode his horse out of respect for her after what had occurred the day before. She was glad that she didn't have to be cooped up in the carriage with him because she didn't know what to think or do now about him, but one constant remained; she loved him deeply. Many times, she had thought about that brand upon his bottom, and every time she had a different emotion about it. Sometimes she was insulted, and other times she was even flattered, and once she had even laughed at the absurdity of it, and once she had been touched that he had been so in love with her that he talked about her in his sleep to whores.

Then she would imagine him with all those women, and any tender feelings she had quickly evaporated. He had a lot of nerve accusing her of anything after what he had done, and when she thought about the courage it took to confess it all to her, she found that she couldn't stay mad about it. He risked everything with his confession, yet he had done it anyway so he could come to her with no secrets; completely open and honest. She had to admire that in him, but she was still hurt by it. She wished she could talk to someone about this, but it was so humiliating that she didn't dare. She would simply have to work this one out alone.

Alyssa informed her that there was to be a ball tonight, and she thought it would be a good thing for her to attend. She wasn't really in the mood for it because her mind was so confused and she didn't see how she could possibly enjoy herself, but maybe it was just the thing she needed. She could forget her troubles for a few hours and dance and meet new people. She hadn't really enjoyed anything London had to offer since her arrival, and it was time for her to do so. She wished that Dylan could escort her, but she was determined to keep him at arm's length until she decided that she could forgive him and move forward. She wanted to desperately, but after his confession, she wasn't sure she ever could. She sat at her vanity and looked at her reflection in the mirror as if the woman there would have all the answers. She didn't, of course, but it would be wonderful if she did, she thought as she twisted her betrothal ring around and around on her finger. There was a knock on her door, and she called out for them to enter.

A footman entered with a bouquet of flowers and a message.

"Thank you," she said accepting the delivery.

It was a lovely mixed bouquet with lilies and roses and some other flowers she had never seen before. They looked exotic and very costly. She took the card off and saw that it was from Dylan.

'I hope these flowers find you well, your devoted servant, Dylan' was all it said.

She put the card aside and smelled the flowers one more time before opening the letter that accompanied them.

My dearest Claire,

I release you from our betrothal with regret in my heart, and I cannot begin to tell you how sorry I am for all the hurt that I have caused you. If it is your will to someday marry another, I will endeavor to wish you all the happiness in the world, though it will pain me to do so.

Enjoy London and all it has to offer, and if you would be so kind as to allow me to call upon you from time to time, it would please me immensely.

It is my hope that you will find it in your heart to forgive me, though I understand how difficult it will be.

Know that I love you more with each passing moment and will wait for your forgiveness as long as it takes.

If ever you have need of me, I will be there with love and devotion,

Dylan

That was not at all what Claire had expected. She folded the letter up and held it close to her heart and hot tears streamed from her eyes.

*****

Two weeks had gone by since Dylan had released Claire from their betrothal, and as she sat at the Huntington ball with a group of admirers vying for attention, she was miserable. None of the gentlemen she had been introduced to over the last two weeks held any appeal for her, and she missed Dylan with a deep aching in her heart. She was getting tired of smiling and pretending to be happy when all she wanted to do was go home and crawl into her bed so she could dream of Dylan again. She hadn't seen even a glimpse of him since her return from Blackstone, though he sent the occasional bouquet of flowers with a card attached that simply said his name. He had made no effort to call upon her, nor had she seen him at any of the functions she had attended. She supposed that he wouldn't attend any balls, particularly since he was in mourning for not only the duke, but his father as well, so she was not surprised that she had not encountered him.

Jasper and Luther had been her escorts on many a night, but when she tried to get information out of them about Dylan's well-being they were very tight lipped and gave her nothing to go on other than he was doing well. She hoped that he wasn't wasting his life away with drink as he had before, and everyday that went by without seeing him caused her more distress. Luther hadn't made any more overtures toward her, and for that she was grateful, but he had taken the stance of her protector and kept rakehells at bay. She appreciated that as well but wished that Dylan were here to do it.

Her dance card was full most nights, and she was starting to feel fatigued from such a rigorous schedule, and she couldn't seem to get enough sleep lately. She promised herself that after tonight, she would take a night or two off from society and catch up on her rest; otherwise, she feared that she would pass out in a heap on the dance floor.

"You don't appear to be enjoying yourself," a familiar voice said from behind her.

She snapped her head around and found herself looking at Mr. Ensley.

"Whatever are you doing here sir?" she asked.

"I am doing what everyone else is doing; searching for a mate. It is the season whereby all the eligible bachelors and debutants come together in hopes of finding a suitable match," he told her with mischief glinting in his eyes.

"I had a suitable match until you destroyed it," she retorted.

"He was unworthy of you, princess," he responded.

"That was for me to decide, sir," she said hotly.

"It was not my wish to cause you pain, Claire," he told her softly.

"I have not given you leave to use my Christian name," she told him.

"Forgive me; I seem to do everything all wrong when it comes to you," he said repentantly.

Claire didn't respond.

"May I have the next dance?" he asked.

"I had not planned to dance as my feet are killing me," she told him.

"I could rub them for you," he suggested in her ear.

"I think not sir; you overstep yourself!" she admonished with a hiss.

"I thought I told you to stay away from her," Luther said as he walked up seemingly from out of nowhere.

Mr. Ensley looked at Luther with loathing then he made her a courtly bow and removed himself from her presence.

"Thank you Luther," she told him.

"Think nothing of it; it is my pleasure to look after you," he told her kindly.

"I am ready to go home, I think," she told him.

He extended his arm, she took it, and he led her away from the ballroom.

"I am very tired lately Luther so I think I should like to stay home tomorrow night, if that is alright with you," she told him as they waited for their carriage.

"Are you unwell?" he asked with concern.

"Just tired," she told him.

Claire felt faint and weak, and when the carriage pulled up, her knees buckled and she nearly swooned. Luther was quick to prevent her from falling, took her firmly in his grasp and helped her inside the carriage.

"Are you sure you are not ill? You are very pale, Claire," he told her.

"I just need some rest," she assured him.

"Perhaps you should rest for a few days. Are you eating well?" he asked.

"I haven't been eating as well as I should," she admitted.

"Is it because of him?" he prodded.

"Oh Luther, I miss him so," she said and began to weep.

He put his big strong arm around her and pulled her into the crook of his shoulder in a brotherly fashion, and her weeping turned into a full sobbing.

"He misses you too, Claire," he assured her.

"I don't think so, Luther," she said with a hiccup.

"He asks about you every day," he told her.

"Then why has he not come to call?" she asked with another hiccup.

"He is giving you the time you need," he told her.

"I don't need time; I need him," she cried.

"Tell him Claire; it would only take one word from you, I'm sure of it," he told her.

"If he wants me, he can call; he said he would call, but he hasn't," she insisted.

"The two of you are letting foolish pride stand in the way of your happiness," he chided.

"How can I forgive him for all of those women?" she demanded.

"I think you can Claire, if you will allow yourself to do so," he said softly.

"Oh, I don't even care about all that now; I don't even know why I mentioned it," she pouted.

"Then you have forgiven him," he stated.

"Have I?" she asked.

"I think you have," he said with a nod.

"Is he still … drinking?" she ventured.

"Not to my knowledge," he told her.

If that was true then perhaps he had changed. Maybe she could forgive him, and they could marry; but what of women?

"Has he … has there been …"

"Not a one," he assured her, cutting off her words.

She renewed her sobbing, and Luther rubbed her arm in a soothing manner.

"I love him so much, Luther," she cried.

"And he loves you, so what's the problem?" he asked.

She didn't have time to answer as the carriage arrived at the Windhaven's home in Mayfair where she currently resided.

"Luther ... will you ... never mind," she said as the footman opened the carriage door to assist her down.

Luther stepped out behind her, and she turned to him and hugged him.

"Goodnight Luther," she said, patting him on the chest.

"Get some rest Claire," he commanded.

"I will," she promised over her shoulder as she went inside.

*****

The next morning, Claire didn't feel well at all. She was sick at her stomach, and she was very weak as though she hadn't slept a wink.

"I don't want anything for breakfast Lucy. I think I will just stay in bed. I think I may be coming down with something," she told her.

"Ye 'ave come down with something and ye will be sick with it for the next eight and a 'alf months," Lucy told her in a matter-of-fact fashion.

Claire sat up with alarm.

"What are you talking about?" she demanded.

"It is plain as the nose on your face Claire. Ye missed your courses and ye are sick and tired all the time and ye 'ave no appetite; ye are with child dear," she explained.

"No Lucy, please don't say that; it cannot be," she said with a groan.

"I suppose it's possible that ye 'ave come down with something else, but what about your courses?

Ye should 'ave had them a week ago and ye didn't. That's a sure sign that ye are with child," she said shaking her finger in a motherly fashion.

Could it be true? Claire flopped back down on her pillows, pulled the covers over her head and groaned in exasperation.

"It's not something ye can 'ide from dear," she heard Lucy chide.

Claire turned to her side, balled herself up, and closed her eyes tight. She didn't want to think about this right now. All she wanted to do was sleep.

*****

A week later, the morning sickness had a firm grip on Claire as she hovered over a chamber pot, heaving and straining to empty her stomach.

"Ye 'ave to tell 'im, Claire; ye don't want the poor mite to be born a bastard," Lucy admonished.

"No," Claire growled between the heaving.

"Lord what will I do with ye?" Lucy complained.

"I will not tell him. He will think that is the only reason that I want him back," she said.

Lucy handed her a wet cloth, and she wiped her eyes and then her mouth. She stood up and walked back to the bed and threw herself upon it in a very unladylike fashion, then pulled the covers over her head, balled herself up, and went back to sleep.

*****

Another week went by, the morning sickness began

to ease up, and Claire was feeling much better. She felt rested and decided that it was time to pull herself up and rejoin the world. For the first time in nearly two weeks, she dressed for breakfast and dined with the duke and duchess.

"Feeling better?" Alyssa asked as she entered the breakfast room.

Claire blushed.

"Much better, thank you," she told her with a nervous smile.

Gabriel put down his newspaper, looked her over from head to toe, and shook his head.

"You have to tell him Claire," he told her.

Claire was mortified; how did he know?

"I'm sure that I don't know what you mean," she said as she fixed her plate at the sideboard.

"It is my estimation that you are about a month along," he prodded.

Claire stiffened so she wouldn't drop her plate as her whole body was quaking with fear.

"You are upsetting her Gabriel," Alyssa admonished.

"What of Dylan; doesn't he have a right to know that she is carrying his child?" he asked.

"I'm sure when the time is right, she will tell him," she told him.

Claire felt her gorge begin to rise in her chest. She turned and looked at them and wanted to excuse herself but was afraid she would humiliate herself if she opened her mouth. Instead, she ran as fast as she could up the stairs and to her room, heading straight for the chamber pot and didn't have even a second to spare as she began emptying the practically non-existent contents of her stomach.

Chapter Twenty-eight

The next afternoon, Dylan came to call. Claire quickly got dressed and hurried down to the drawing room. She halted at the sight of him and tried to collect herself as she was out of breath, but her heart was soaring.

"Hello Claire," he said with a smile.

"Hello Dylan," she said, smiling in return.

"It's good to see you," he told her as he advanced toward her.

He took her hand in his and gently kissed her knuckles. Claire's heart was pounding in her chest, and her palms started to sweat. She continued to get her breathing under control and noticed that he was still holding her hand. She gently tugged it away and wiped away phantom wrinkles on her skirt.

"Please sit down, and I will ring for tea," she told him.

"Don't trouble yourself; I won't be staying long," he said softly, taking a seat on one of the sofas.

Claire sat across from him and nervously put her hands in her lap. She couldn't believe he was here after all this time, and the sight of him was wonderful.

"How are things with you Dylan?" she asked.

He bit his lower lip and sighed.

"I am well," he said simply.

"I am glad to hear it," she said awkwardly.

"It is my understanding that you have been ill for the last couple of weeks and haven't been attending any balls or parties; I thought that I should call and see about you," he told her.

Claire's nerves felt like razors scraping in her veins.

"There isn't very much appeal to me for those sorts of things," she fibbed.

He looked away for a moment and his jaw tightened.

"Have you had any more trouble with Kenwick since that night a couple of weeks ago?" he asked, turning back to look at her.

"No, not a single bit of trouble," she said.

"I wondered if perhaps he was the reason you had stopped going out," he said.

"Oh no, I just have no desire to go is all," she fibbed.

"Luther said he thought that you were ill that night, and Gabriel said that you had been ill for the last two weeks. What's going on Claire?" he prodded.

Claire looked away this time, and she was fidgeting with her skirt.

"Tell me," he insisted.

"There is nothing going on," she snapped.

"Are you with child?" he asked.

She looked at him and felt a rush of blood through her veins, and she shook her head violently.

"You are with child aren't you?" he demanded.

She jumped up and went to the window, refusing to answer.

"Were you not going to tell me?" he asked from behind her.

She stiffened but said nothing.

He placed his hand on her shoulder and turned

her to him.

"I have a right to know," he insisted.

"Yes damn you, I am with child!" she blurted out.

He grabbed her by the upper arms and gave her a stern shake.

"My child Claire; you are having my child," he told her with fire blazing in his eyes.

"Yes it's your child," she cried out.

He let go of her then.

"We will marry tomorrow," he commanded.

Claire dropped to her knees and cried.

He stood there for a moment, and then he reached down and pulled her to her feet.

"I will not marry you if that is the only reason Dylan," she told him with a sob.

"You know as well as I do that it is not the only reason," he told her.

He handed her his handkerchief, and she dried her eyes and tried to sniff back her tears.

"I will not marry you unless it is what we really want," she said.

"I know what I want Claire; what do you want?" he asked.

"I want you Dylan, but I am scared," she told him.

"Scared of what?" he demanded.

Claire didn't know what she was scared of, but she was apprehensive. So much had happened between them and most of it bad. How could they build a future together for their child when they were always at odds with one another?

"We fight too much," she said.

"Couples fight sometimes, Claire," he told her.

"But we always fight," she retorted.

"There was a time when we didn't, and it was beautiful," he said softly.

She looked at him with troubled eyes and trembling lips; she remembered that too. When she was sick, he had stayed by her side and treated her as though she were the most important thing in his world. They were so happy then. How did it all go so terribly wrong?

"What if we never find that again?" she asked.

Dylan sighed, brought her into his embrace and spoke softly into her ear.

"I can't promise that we will always be happy, but I can promise to love you until my dying breath; marry me Claire."

She nodded her head.

"Is that a yes?" he asked, pulling back so he could look at her.

"Yes, I will marry you," she confirmed.

Dylan lifted her off the ground and spun her around before gently placing her back on her feet and kissed her soundly.

"Tomorrow," he told her.

She nodded her head in agreement. He took her left hand in his and smiled.

"You still wear the ring," he said.

Claire laughed and fresh tears rolled down her cheeks.

"In my heart, I have always belonged to you, Dylan," she told him.

"We could marry today; I still have our license," he suggested casually.

Today; could they really marry today?

"Yes, yes, yes … let's do it today before anything else goes wrong," she said with a nervous chuckle.

"Go and tell Lucy to prepare your things to be sent home, and then we shall go to the parson," he said with a smile.

Claire rushed to the drawing room door and flung it open and was met by a smiling duke and duchess.

"We shall go and be your witnesses," Gabriel said.

Claire threw herself in his arms and hugged him, then she threw herself in Alyssa's arms and kissed her on the cheek.

"I must hurry and tell Lucy," she said.

"I will have Mr. Connelly take care of it," Gabriel said.

Claire turned to Dylan.

"Well then, what are you waiting for; let's go!" she commanded.

*****

Claire and Dylan were wed at three in the afternoon with Gabriel and Alyssa as witness. Claire nearly lost her breath when the parson referred to her as 'your grace' as she had not considered that before. She was a duchess now, and the idea was mind boggling. Claire Elizabeth Crenshaw sounded wonderful to her ears, but the addition of 'the Duchess of Blackstone' was terrifying. She knew absolutely nothing about the English aristocracy and now she was a part of it. How in the world would she possibly manage? What would be expected of her? She didn't know, and she wasn't sure she wanted to know, but it was not something she would be able to ignore. She had been raised to believe that all men were created equal, and now she was part of a system that set her above others. She wasn't sure she was going to like this at all. They stood outside the church saying their goodbyes to Gabriel and Alyssa, and Claire was deep in contemplation and hadn't realized that a long stretch of silence had prevailed.

"Claire?" Dylan prompted.

Claire shook her head and looked at Dylan.

"I'm sorry I was woolgathering," she said.

"You looked frightened," Dylan said.

"I am," she admitted.

Dylan looked at her as if trying to determine the problem, and then turned to his friend and his wife.

"We shall be off now; thank you for coming," he told them.

They departed, and when Dylan and Claire were ensconced in the carriage he took her hand in his and brought it to his lips.

"Everything will be alright, I promise," he said with concern.

"I don't know what to do," she said with trepidation in her voice.

"Tell me what concerns you," he prodded.

Claire didn't know how to go about explaining her concerns, and she didn't want to say anything that could cause an argument.

"It is nothing to worry about," she told him.

Claire hoped that Dylan would let the matter go, but she could see that he was contemplating her words.

"I will be faithful to you Claire; you need not fear that you have made a mistake by trusting me," he said after a moment.

Claire realized that she was going to have to explain the nature of her concerns; otherwise, he would think that she was unhappy to have married him.

"It's not that Dylan … it's … I am a duchess now, and I don't know what is expected of me," she told him.

"Nothing is expected of you beyond loving me," he told her warmly.

"But look at Alyssa; she is involved with many great works, and she is a pillar of society. I know nothing of your society Dylan; what if I fail?" she argued.

Dylan laughed, wrapped his arm around her and pulled her close.

"Let us get through the honeymoon before you start planning great works of charity, my love," he told her.

"This is not a laughing matter, Dylan," she admonished.

"You are upsetting yourself for nothing. We don't have to have anything to do with society if you do not wish. If you will recall … I have always had an aversion to it myself. I never wanted to be a duke, but by an accident of birth and a few cruel twists of fate, here I am, the Duke of Blackstone.

This is new for both of us, and we will get through it together," he said in a soothing voice.

Claire thought about that. Dylan never wanted it either so in that, they were alike. Perhaps it wouldn't be so bad really, but she didn't think she would ever get used to the title.

"When the parson called me 'your grace', it all came home to me that I was different now," she explained.

"You are still Claire, and I am still Dylan, nothing has changed," he assured her.

"I suppose you're right," she said unconvinced.

"I am right, and I don't wish to dwell on what I cannot change. I want to think about my future with you, particularly the immediate future," he said waggling his eyebrows.

Claire blushed and dipped her head down. This was her wedding day, and there would be a wedding night. Tonight, she would finally make love to Dylan, skin to skin as she had dreamed of for so many weeks. Dylan put a finger under her chin and lifted her face up to his. They looked into one another's eyes, and her whole body responded. She felt warm and tingly and wondered if she would be able to last until tonight without … he kissed her, and all thought fled her mind as she wrapped her arm around his neck, pulling herself closer to him. He put his hands around her waist and pulled her into his lap, leaned her back, and then deepened the kiss. He licked his tongue across her lower lip, and she gasped in response, giving him the opening he wanted to thrust his tongue inside her mouth. Their tongues mingled in a sensual manner that mimicked a sexual joining, and Claire was in absolute bliss. Claire groaned, and Dylan moaned in response and started a slow soothing massage of her breast. He lovingly rubbed and stroked her fleshy mounds, then gently pinched at her sensitive nipple through the fabric of her gown, and sparks coursed through her blood like blazing fire. She reached up and started massaging his chest, and it was then that Dylan broke the kiss.

"I will not take my wife in a carriage on her wedding day," he said breathlessly.

"You can do it in a carriage?" Claire asked with surprise.

Dylan laughed quietly, shifted her off of his lap and sat her back down beside him.

"My love, I have many things to teach you about lovemaking. It can be done in many ways in all manner of places," he said with a crooked smile.

Claire remembered how he had taken her up against the door, and she blushed.

"I want to learn them all," she said boldly.

"I shall enjoy the teaching," he assured her.

Claire had a spark of jealousy then as she thought about all the women Dylan had learned his skill with and stiffened in response.

This didn't go unnoticed by Dylan.

"What is it?" he asked.

"Nothing," she snapped.

"Tell me Claire," he insisted.

"I do not wish to quarrel on our wedding day," she said stiffly.

Dylan sighed.

"Claire, you are the woman I love, and all the

other women that have come and gone are meaningless," he told her.

Claire knew that wasn't true. There had been Wishy and her death had caused Dylan a great deal of pain.

"What about her?" she found herself asking.

Dylan stiffened this time and looked out the carriage window.

"I only knew her for a day, Claire. I had a tryst with her in a stable at an inn, and then she died. I didn't love her, but her death impacted me profoundly for a multitude of reasons. The primary one being, that I could do absolutely nothing to protect her from those two men, even though I was armed with two pistols, and I am a superb marksman," he said.

Claire felt like a jackass for even bringing it up now.

"I'm sorry to have mentioned it; please forgive me," she told him, reaching out to place a hand over his.

He placed his other hand over hers and squeezed gently.

"She was a terrible mistake, Claire. I should never have allowed myself to partake of what she so freely offered. She was young and sweet, and she was infatuated with me, and I being a man was attracted to her body. It had been so very long since I had lain with a woman that I was quite unable to abstain when she ... persisted. I hated myself for it, even as I coupled with her, and had she not been killed so soon after, I probably would have felt compelled to marry her. She was only seven and ten, and far too innocent for what I had done to her. Honor, not love would have governed our marriage, and I know now that I could never have been happy that way," he explained further.

He looked at her with unfathomable eyes, and Claire understood.

"Love will govern our marriage," she told him.

"You are the only woman I have ever loved," he admitted.

"I am honored that you have chosen me Dylan," she said with a smile.

"Is that what happened? I'm not so sure, but I think you were sent to me Claire, and I found that I couldn't help but love you; choice was never part of it."

Chapter Twenty-nine

Claire was happy to be home; it was really her home now and upon arrival she had been surprised to see that Mr. Simmons was actually smiling at her. She returned the smile and wondered at the strange change in his attitude toward her.

"Your grace, my lord welcome home," he told them with a bow.

Claire was confused by the greeting; why was he calling Dylan my lord? Her confusion must have been written on her face because Dylan leaned over and whispered an explanation in her ear.

"I told him not to call me your grace until I was used to the title."

"Mr. Simmons, please call me Claire or Mrs. Crenshaw ... until I too am used to the title," she said with an awkward smile.

Simmons rolled his eyes heavenward and grumbled something she couldn't quite make out.

"She is an American Simmons," Dylan said as if that would explain it all.

Apparently it did because Mr. Simmons smiled, bowed and said, "Welcome home, Mrs. Crenshaw."

Claire beamed and nodded her head in appreciation, and Dylan started guiding her up the stairs to his chambers. He reached his door and opened it, and then whisked her up in his arms and carried her over the threshold. Once inside, he carried her over to his bed and placed her down gently.

"We shall share a room now Claire; we shall never be apart again," he told her smiling.

Claire blushed and looked around the room. Her trunk was already there, and she wondered where Lucy would be staying.

"Where will Lucy stay now?" she voiced the thought.

"Simmons will have put her in the room down the hall next to his. It's very spacious, and I think she will be quite comfortable there," he told her.

"Oh!" was her simple reply.

"Do you have need of her?" he probed.

"Yes," she admitted.

"Come," he said tugging her to her feet.

He led her through a dressing room and beyond, where a huge water closet with a copper tub sat.

"Does it have its own hot water?" she asked mystified.

"It does," he told her with a crooked grin.

"All the time that I lived here, the servants had to bring in a hip bath and buckets filled with hot water, and you had a tub like this all along?" she asked incredulously.

"I'm afraid that the modernization didn't extend throughout the entire house; it was a bachelor's residence, and I didn't have a lot of overnight guests," he admitted.

Dylan leaned over, put the plug in the drain and turned on the tap. He straightened up, took her by the shoulder, spun her around and started taking the pins out of her hair.

"What are you doing?" she asked.

"I am being your ladies maid," he said.

Claire shivered from the warmth of his touch

and stood still as he began unbuttoning her gown.

"The tub is big enough for two," he whispered in her ear as he began sliding her gown off her shoulders.

A rippling current traveled from her ear to her private center as he continued to undress her. He ran a finger down the length of her back and up again, then leaned his head forward and kissed her shoulder.

"Shall I join you?" he asked with a sultry voice.

Claire couldn't speak, so she nodded her head. He bent down and slid her gown over her hips, and then took her by the hand and assisted her as she stepped out of it. She stood there in her shift, slippers and stockings and listened as he began removing his clothing. After a moment, he pressed himself against her from behind, reaching down to gather the hem of her shift and drew the garment up and over her head. He turned her to him then and went down on one knee and removed her slippers. He looked up at her from his kneeling position and slowly moved his face forward until his lips were touching her woman's flesh. Claire jerked in response as his tongue touched the sensitive spot nestled in her folds, and she grabbed a handful of his hair and tried to pull him away. Dylan chuckled and continued with his naughty kiss, and Claire shivered and soon realized that she was actually holding him in place while he administered to her. Just when she felt as though she were starting to reach for something, he pulled away and shook his head.

"Not yet my love," he told her and then began

removing her stockings.

He stood then and took her by the hand and turned her to the tub.

She stepped into it and lowered herself within, and he followed and positioned himself behind her and brought her back up against his chest. He reached for the soap and a cloth and began to bathe her breasts with a slow circular motion before working his way down her belly, where he rested his hand on the flat surface.

"Soon, you will be swollen with my child," he said softly in her ear.

She nodded her head and closed her eyes, relishing in the moment of their intimacy.

"Your breasts have already started to grow with the life giving sustenance he will need, and I find that I am already jealous thinking about him suckling you," he said as he lowered his hand and caressed the flesh between her legs with the soap.

Claire arched her back, and he took his other hand and started caressing her full breasts, and her nipples stood up demanding their fair share of his touch. Dylan noticed this and took mercy on them and began to lightly tug and pinch them.

"Do you suppose the little mite will share with his papa?" he asked with a husky voice.

Claire nodded her head, and he chuckled at her speechlessness. He was working magic on her body with his touch, and she was experiencing pure ecstasy. He knew this and increased the pressure on the sensitive nub of flesh, and she groaned and bucked against his hand in response.

"You have a lovely body, Claire," he said as he

continued his ministrations, and soon she found herself on the verge of release.

"Don't stop," she gritted out with a strained voice.

Dylan didn't stop and within seconds she broke beneath his hand in hard trembling waves, and she was unable to contain a loud moan of appreciation.

"That's my girl," he purred as he pressed his hand more firmly where she was still pulsing.

When the tremors stopped, she sagged against him, and he leaned forward and kissed her neck beneath her earlobe. She turned toward him and straddled his lap and started kissing him with an ardor that she hadn't known she possessed. Dylan shifted his hips and guided her onto his erection, and Claire slid down until he was fully seated within her and began a slow undulation with her hips.

Dylan groaned and held her hips still.

"I have to turn off the water," he panted.

Claire laughed as she reached back behind herself to turn the faucet off, and then turned back to him resuming the motion. Dylan reached up and splashed water over her breasts to remove the soap suds, and then lowered his lips to her breast and began to suckle her. Claire placed her hands on his shoulders and threw her head back while Dylan continued to lave and kiss at her nipples. She had never experienced such a feeling in her life, and she basked in the wonder of it like a flower reaching for the sun. She could feel his shaft deep in her womb, and she wanted to swallow him up so he could reside there forever. He grabbed her by the hips and thrust harder into her, and she increased the motion of her hips to match his movements while he continued to feast upon her breasts. He growled in appreciation and squeezed her buttocks so he could grind her hard against him. They were so lost in one another that they didn't care that water was spilling out of the sides of the tub as their bodies crashing together made splashing waves that could not be contained. All they knew was the hunger they had for each other that must be quenched at all cost. Dylan fisted a handful of her hair at the base of her head, pulled her face toward his and thrust his tongue deep into her mouth. He kissed her with a savage need, and she thought that he would consume her completely.

"Come to me, Claire," he breathed into her mouth.

Claire whimpered in response and ground herself against him with a fierce urgency until she felt the tightening of the muscles inside her sheath followed by pulsating ripples that she felt all over her body.

"Yes, just like that," he said, and then he followed with a shout of ecstasy.

Claire collapsed against him, and they held tight to one another as they rode the waves of their mutual release. Claire could feel Dylan's heart pounding beneath her breast, and his breath was ragged against her neck.

"That was wonderful," Claire proclaimed.

"That was just one way; I have much more to show you," he told her with a tender kiss.

"Do you think we will ever make love in a

bed?" she asked teasingly.

"Oh I think it's safe to say that we will," he said with another kiss.

"I like your copper tub," she purred.

"We shall turn into a prune soon," he remarked.

Claire made a pouting expression, pulled out of his arms and started looking around on the floor.

"We made a mess," she told him.

"Stay right there, and let me get out first. I don't want you to slip and fall," he told her.

Dylan got out of the tub, went to the linen closet, brought back a stack of towels and began wiping up the mess on the floor. Once satisfied, he toweled himself off, then wrapped the towel around his waist, offered her his hand and helped her out of the tub. He wrapped her up in a towel and carried her to the safety of his bed, sat her down on the edge and dried her off more completely with another towel.

"I think that will do," he said with a sexy smile.

"You will spoil me," Claire observed.

"A duchess should be spoiled on her wedding day," he responded.

"That still sounds strange to my ears," she told him.

"When I met you, I still had not gotten used to being an earl, and then I became a marquess and now I am a duke. It will take time for both of us, but we will get used to it," he said crawling into the bed with her.

Dylan pulled the covers over them both so Claire wouldn't take a chill and snuggled her close to his side and sighed deeply in contentment. All the tension over the last few years seemed to slide out of his body and was replaced with absolute peace.

"I love you Claire," he said after a few moments of silence.

His wife answered him with a light snoring, and he smiled widely in response.

*****

Hours later Dylan was awakened by his wife as she kissed her way down his body. He held himself still to see what she would do and was surprised when she placed her lips on his aroused member. He flinched in response, and she giggled and then ran her tongue along the length of him.

"What are you up to minx?" he asked.

"I wanted to see if you responded to a naughty kiss the way I did," she said playfully.

"Oh, I'm responding; please do continue," he softly commanded.

She continued to explore him with her mouth, and after a torturous moment she took him inside and began to mimic the act of copulation with her mouth. He groaned aloud, and she stopped.

"Am I hurting you?" she asked with concern.

He couldn't form the words to speak, so he shook his head, and she gingerly started working her magic on him again. This was heaven and Dylan was king. Dylan basked in the pleasure of it until he felt close to release and grabbed her by the arms and pulled her up, then flipped her onto her back and nudged his way between her legs with his knee.

"You were courting danger," he breathed as he plunged his shaft deeply into her sheath.

Claire gasped and wrapped her legs around his buttocks, and he took her with fierce pounding thrusts. He knew he wouldn't last long, and he wanted to bring her with him, so he slid his hand between them and started massaging her sensitive spot. She moaned and bucked against him, and the motion excited him, and he began plunging fast and hard into her passage. He could feel her body reaching and it took all of his concentration to hold back until she reached her plateau, then with a final stroke he followed in a mind-numbing orgasm unlike any he had ever experienced.

"I'm famished," she said gasping for air.

Dylan laughed, rolled off of her and drew her into his embrace.

"I should keep you starved from now on," he teased.

Claire giggled and nuzzled closer to him.

Dylan wasn't sure what time it was, but it was late, and he was sure that they had missed dinner.

"We will have to go to the kitchen and forage for sustenance," he told her.

"I can make an omelet," she boasted.

"That sounds delicious. Get dressed, and you can demonstrate your culinary skills for your new husband," he told her.

Dylan tossed back the covers, got out of the bed and went to retrieve his trousers from the water closet. When he returned to the bedroom, he found Claire lying on the floor. He ran over to her and lifted her into his arms, and that's when he noticed the pool of blood. He lifted her, put her in the bed and tried to wake her. Her eyes fluttered open and then rolled back in their sockets, and his heart thudded in his chest.

"Claire!" he shouted.

When she didn't open her eyes again, he ran to the bedroom door, jerked it open and shouted for Simmons. Simmons and Lucy both answered his desperate summons.

"Simmons, go and fetch a surgeon quickly. My wife is losing the babe," he ordered.

Lucy ran over to the bed and started fussing over Claire.

"It's my fault," Dylan said over her shoulder as he watched her tending to his wife.

"No your grace, tis simply the will of God," she said.

"We made love twice, and the second time was … it's my fault," he reiterated.

"Your grace, it 'appens all the time. Tis no one's fault, and I never once 'eard of a woman losing 'er child because she made love with 'er 'usband," she assured him.

"Are you sure?" he asked, desperately wanting to believe her.

"I lost two babes, your grace but I 'ad four 'ealthy ones that lived to be fine adults," she assured him.

"I'm sorry that you had to suffer so Lucy, but I thank you for easing my mind; she will be alright then?" he asked.

"Right as rain your grace; fear not, there will be

other babes," she told him.

Dylan went to fill a bowl with some water and washcloth and brought it to Lucy, who started wiping Claire's forehead with the cool water. Claire opened her eyes and smiled at them, and then quickly gave a look of concern.

"It's alright love," Dylan quickly told her.

"What happened?" she asked.

Dylan and Lucy looked at one another, and he was the one that told her.

"I think you have lost the babe, my love," he told her with his heart in his eyes.

Claire looked horrified and cried out at the news, and then turned on her side, drew her knees to her chest and sobbed. Lucy started patting and rubbing her shoulder, but Claire was inconsolable. Dylan slid into the bed beside her and gathered her in his arms.

"Shhh my love; it just wasn't meant to be this time," he told her.

"I failed," Claire cried.

"No love, don't say that," he crooned.

Claire was wracked with heaving sobs, and Dylan was beside himself about what to do for her other than to hold her and allow her to grieve. A half an hour later the surgeon came and confirmed that she had lost the child and explained to them both that no one was to blame, and that it was quite normal to lose a child in the first trimester, especially for someone with Claire's recent medical history. He assured them both that there was no reason that she shouldn't be able to try again after a few weeks, and that she would need to get plenty of bed rest for the next few days. His words didn't offer comfort to Claire as it had Dylan, and when she continued to cry uncontrollably, he provided some laudanum for her with instructions to administer it carefully over the next three days and on the fourth to cut it off entirely; this was to keep her calm and allow her to get the rest she would need to quickly recover.

Once the surgeon left and Claire was sleeping, Dylan went to his library, sat at his desk and brooded. He was angry that this dark cloud had formed over their attempt at happiness and hoped that it wasn't a harbinger of things to come for their marriage.

Chapter Thirty

Claire woke up the next morning, and she remembered what had happened with a sharp pain in her gut. She looked over, expecting to see Dylan there, but he wasn't. She carefully sat up and did a mental inventory of her body to see if everything was in order, and once she was convinced that all was right, she slid out of bed. She put on her robe, went to the vanity, sat down before it and looked at her reflection as she often did when she was troubled. Why had it happened? Why now when they were trying so hard to find happiness? It didn't seem fair that God would do this to them after all they had suffered thus far, and she couldn't help but feel a little resentful. What if Dylan blamed her for this? What if he never wanted to touch her again? Tears streamed down her cheeks, and she put her head on her arm on the table and wept. That was how Dylan found her a few minutes later.

"What are you doing out of bed?" he barked at her.

She jerked her head up and looked at him, and as she feared, he appeared to be angry at her.

"When I woke up you were gone, and I didn't know where you were," she said.

Dylan advanced toward her, took her by the hand and drew her to her feet. He whisked her up in his arms and took her back to the bed without saying a word. He crawled in beside her and drew her into his arms in the fashion of two spoons in a drawer.

"You are to stay in bed for three days," he said

solemnly.

Claire didn't want to stay in bed; she felt fine and didn't think that it was necessary.

"I am not tired," she grumbled.

"It matters not; you will stay in bed," he commanded.

"I want to be with you; not lying about in bed," she complained.

"I will stay with you then," he assured her.

Claire felt like a selfish brat, but it mollified her and she closed her eyes in contentment.

"Are you in pain?" he asked after a moment.

"No pain," she said

"The doctor said you should have laudanum three times a day while you take bed rest," he told her.

"I do not want it," she said obstinately.

"If you experience any pain at all, you will tell me, and I will give it to you," he stated.

Claire couldn't help but notice his mood seemed dark and wondered at it.

"Are you mad at me?" she ventured.

"Why would I be mad at you?" he asked with a hint of sharpness in his tone.

"Because I lost your baby," she said pathetically.

Dylan squeezed her closer to him and kissed her cheek.

"Silly goose," he said in an attempt to lighten his tone.

"So you are not mad at me?" she asked.

"No, and I was worried that you might blame me for it," he told her.

"How could I blame you?" she asked with a gasp.

He was quiet for a moment.

"Because I was a bit aggressive with you when we made love that second time," he finally admitted.

Claire thought about that, but she didn't think he had hurt her.

"I didn't feel any pain or discomfort from it; in fact, I enjoyed it immensely," she told him.

He squeezed her tight and kissed her cheek again.

"I shall have to be more careful of you the next time you are with child," he told her.

"The doctor said you didn't cause it Dylan, so I don't want to hear that kind of talk; do you hear me?" she admonished.

Claire understood then that he must have sat up all night blaming himself, and she felt bad for him. He hadn't hurt her, and she hated to think that he would hold himself back from her during their lovemaking.

"We shall just wait and see how it goes next time," he allowed.

Claire pulled away from him and sat up.

"Listen to me you stubborn jackass! I will not have you withholding yourself from me out of an irrational fear born out of unfounded guilt. When you make love to me, you will give me your all or nothing," she demanded.

Dylan sighed and tugged her back into his arms.

"Hush my mighty warrior; we both need to

rest," he told her.

Claire snuggled up against him and closed her eyes. She didn't like the way he was acting and couldn't help but feel trouble brewing.

*****

Dylan stayed with her in bed for the next three days and was very attentive to her needs. He was gentle and kind, but he still seemed to be holding himself back. Claire couldn't imagine what was going on in his mind, and the distance that she felt between them was starting to concern her. On the morning of the fourth day, she was ready to get up and move about as she was sick and tired of lying around, so she woke Dylan up and told him she was ready to get bathed and dressed. He grumbled, but got up with her and assisted her with her bath. He didn't climb in with her as he had the other day, and it kind of hurt her feelings, but she kept her complaints to herself. She could see that he was trying very hard to act normal and not show his bad mood, but she could see it nonetheless. It was more of a feeling actually; a sort of vibration in the atmosphere around him. She could feel it deep in her bones, and it quite unsettled her.

"I should like to go for a walk in the garden after we break our fast," Claire told him casually while he was getting dressed.

Dylan grunted in response, and she sighed in frustration. He seemed to be going through the motions with her, but he just wasn't putting anything behind it.

"What?" she demanded.

He looked at her with a perplexed expression.

"I didn't say anything," he said.

"Yes I know," she said sarcastically.

"Then why did you say 'what'?" he asked calmly.

"What is wrong with you, Dylan?"

"Nothing is wrong with me? Are you trying to pick a fight?" he asked with a crooked smile.

"A fight would be better than this … this … whatever this is," she stated with a frustrated wave of her hand.

Dylan finished buttoning his shirt and walked over to her, drew her into his arms and kissed her on the forehead.

"Forgive me, I have much on my mind," he told her.

"Such as," she prodded.

"I am concerned about you primarily, and secondly, I have much to attend to with my stewards now that I have inherited both my father's and grandfather's estates," he explained.

"There is no need to worry about me; I shall be fine," she softened.

"I trust that you will, but I don't want you to try to do too much too soon," he told her.

"So you are opposed to my going out in the garden?" she asked.

"A short walk but not too far, should be alright," he allowed.

"I just need to stretch my legs a bit," she complained.

"I understand, but after the exercise, I insist

that you take it easy the rest of the day," he told her.

"I suppose that's a fair compromise," she consented.

He leaned forward and kissed her on the forehead again, pulled out of the embrace and went back to his dressing. Claire wasn't sure that he was completely honest just now, but at least it was something.

"So you will be busy all day?" she asked.

"Most of it, yes, and I suspect late into the evening, as well," he told her.

"Are things that bad?" she prodded.

Dylan sighed and slipped into his jacket.

"I have been very neglectful of my estates, and now I have the others to contend with, so yes, it's really that bad," he snapped.

"You don't have to be so testy," she snapped back.

"Are you sure you aren't trying to pick a fight?" he chided with a sardonic smile.

Was she trying to pick a fight? Was everything fine and she was just trying to find something wrong?

"I don't know what I'm doing," she admitted.

"I think perhaps you are trying to find problems where there are none," he told her.

"Perhaps," she allowed.

"Let's go down and break our fast, and perhaps you will feel better," he told her.

"Yes, I think you're right," she said taking his extended arm.

Perhaps Dylan was right, and she was just being over sensitive. She did feel a little edgy and restless, so maybe it was her and nothing was really wrong with them. Still, things didn't feel quite right.

*****

Dylan sat in his library brooding. Something wasn't right with Claire, and he didn't know what to make of it. She seemed to be in the mood to quarrel and normally he would enjoy it, but he didn't want to upset her unnecessarily. Perhaps he should speak with the doctor about it to see if this kind of behavior was normal. Perhaps she was depressed due to the miscarriage. An idea occurred to him and he got up and called for Simmons.

"Simmons, I want you to go and fetch Lucy, have her come to the library please, and if you can avoid it, don't let my wife hear you make the summons, if you please," he instructed.

A few minutes later, Lucy knocked on the door.

"Enter," he called.

"Ye called for me, your grace?" she asked timidly.

"Yes Lucy, I am concerned about Claire's … morale, and I wanted to ask you a few questions if I might," he ventured.

"Ye may your grace," she told him.

Dylan didn't like hearing her say 'your grace' and was going to say something but decided he had better start getting used to hearing it, so he let it go.

"Is it normal for a woman to become irritable after a miscarriage?" he asked.

"Aye tis most normal your grace; sometimes all they want to do is cry. My sister sat in 'er room for three weeks without saying a word after 'ers, and I wanted to commit murder on my lecherous 'usband after mine," she said with a blush.

"How long did it last?" he asked.

"It depends on the person, your grace," she told him.

Dylan was relieved to hear that Claire was behaving normally and that a bigger problem wasn't brewing.

"Is there anything to help bring them out of it?" he asked.

"Get 'er with child again as soon as possible, and she will be right as rain," she said with a cheeky grin.

"The doctor said it would be alright to try again in a few weeks, but I'm not so sure that it's wise to do it so soon," he said mostly to himself.

"My Billy jumped on me bones as soon as my courses stopped," she offered.

Dylan blushed at her frankness and cleared his throat uncomfortably.

"It wasn't harmful to you?" he probed.

"Women are not so delicate, your grace," she told him.

"Still, I think it would be wise to wait the three weeks the doctor recommended," he mused aloud.

Lucy sighed exasperatedly.

Dylan looked up at her and saw that she had a somewhat impatient look on her face.

"You may speak freely," he offered.

"The longer ye wait the more 'er mind will conjure up all kinds of trouble. She will think ye don't want 'er anymore, and then ye will 'ave a real problem on your 'ands," she warned.

"So I should romance her along the way?" he asked with a smile.

"If ye know what's good for ye," she said with a nod.

Dylan chuckled.

"I thank you for your indispensable advice, Lucy," he told her.

"I love 'er like my own your grace, and I want to see 'er 'appy," she told him.

"Forgive me, but I have no idea what my grandfather was paying you, Lucy, but I shall see to it that you have an increase in your pay. You can expect to see it with next month's wages," he told her.

"Ye are too kind, your grace," she said with a big smile.

"Not at all; you are a jewel, and I intend to keep you happy," he told her.

"Thank you, your grace,"

"You're welcome Lucy; that will be all," he told her.

Lucy curtsied and left the library with an extra pep in her step, and Dylan felt immeasurably better.

*****

Dylan ducked just as a glass went flying over his head by the madwoman who was his wife. She was in a tirade and was throwing everything within reach at him.

"You ass … you lout … you lecherous dog," she shouted as she hurled a hairbrush at his groin.

He hadn't been able to miss that projectile and it found its mark, and Dylan went to his knees with a groan. His wife had accused him of having a mistress because he hadn't come to bed since the night before. He had been working late in his library and hadn't wanted to disturb her rest, so he slept on the sofa. It had been a week since Claire was up and about again, and she had been near impossible to deal with. Dylan was just about at the end of his rope. He could understand that she might be irritable, but this was beyond the pale. She marched over and stood glaring at him.

"I shall be moving back to my own room," she informed him.

"You will do no such thing," he gritted out between clenched teeth.

His bollocks were throbbing, and he felt like he was going to pass out from the pain.

"You just watch me sir; I refuse to spend another night in your bed after you have been lying with your whores," she informed him.

"Woman, I told you that I fell asleep on the sofa in my library," he told her with a groan.

"That's a likely story," she huffed.

"It's the only story I have, because it's the truth," he said trying to get to his feet.

She spun around on her heel, went to the bell-pull and nearly yanked it down trying to summon Lucy. Dylan was on his feet now, and he felt like he was about to cast up his accounts so he leaned against her vanity for support. A moment later, Lucy came into the room and stopped in her tracks at the mess Claire had made.

"Lucy, I want all my things moved to my old room this morning," she commanded.

"You shall not move her things, Lucy," Dylan countermanded.

Claire growled and spun around looking for something else to throw, so Dylan quickly left the room, and just in time too because something crashed against the door just as he shut it.

The woman has gone mad!

Chapter Thirty-one

That evening at supper, Claire was seemingly in a better temper. Dylan was glad to see that her mood had improved, but he certainly didn't trust it.

"I am glad to see you in better spirits, my love," he ventured.

"Yes, I am much improved, thank you," she said with a smile that Dylan thought seemed to be a little cool

"How did you spend your day?" he asked conversationally.

"I did a little writing on my manuscript," she told him.

"I'm glad to hear that you have started writing again," he told her.

"Are you really?" she asked a little sarcastically.

"Of course," he said.

"You have never expressed any real interest in my writing before," she told him.

Warning bells started going off in Dylan's head.

"I should have been more attentive on the matter," he said cautiously.

"Yes, you should have," she said in a flat tone.

Dylan sighed and resigned himself to another quarrel with his wife as he did a mental calculation of the number of days that it had been since the miscarriage, trying to decide when it would be safe to make love to her again. He had been so busy with his estates that he hadn't been able to romance her properly as Lucy had advised, and he could plainly see the repercussions of his neglect.

"How would you like to go to the theatre tonight?" he asked.

"I don't think I'm up to it," she said with chilly indifference.

So much for romance, Dylan inwardly grumbled.

"I thought you might enjoy getting out, and going to the theatre wouldn't be too taxing," he prodded.

"Perhaps another time," she allowed.

Dylan searched his mind for something to entice her out of her mood, but nothing came to him. He was beginning to think that he had married a shrew.

"Perhaps you could read some of your manuscript to me after supper," he said animatedly as the idea suddenly occurred.

"I never give readings of my manuscripts," she said again with a cutting bite.

"Did you not just tell me that I should have been more attentive with regard to your writing," he said with sarcasm slipping through.

"Far be it for me to force you to do anything," she hissed.

"What is that supposed to mean?" he demanded.

"You have no interest in my writing. You are probably waiting with baited breath for me to go to bed so you can slip out and go to your whore," she snapped.

Dylan threw his napkin on the table and got up so fast his chair fell over backwards.

"Damn you, woman," he shouted, and then he quit the room.

Dylan had enough; he wasn't going to stay and be abused by her another minute. He needed a drink, and by God, he intended to have one. He went into the foyer and ordered Simmons to have his horse brought around. If she was going to accuse him of wrongdoing, then by God, he could at least have the pleasure of committing the crime.

*****

Dylan didn't go to the brothel as he had set out to do. He went there but couldn't bring himself to go inside, so instead he went to Whites and drank some ale alone.

"Marriage trouble already?" asked a familiar voice.

Dylan looked up and found himself looking at the Marquess of Kenwick. Dylan said nothing to his snide comment and inwardly groaned as he took an open seat at the table.

"You don't mind if I join you, I hope," he said beckoning the waiter with a raised hand.

"I can't imagine why you would want to," Dylan said sardonically.

"Come now Blackstone, we used to be friends," he said.

"I wouldn't go that far," Dylan quipped.

"Can we not put the past behind us?" he asked, but the question lacked sincerity.

"What do you want?" Dylan asked calmly.

"Oh, I should think that would be apparent," he

said snidely.

"I'm afraid you will have to spell it out," Dylan retorted.

"I want her," Kenwick said boldly.

Dylan stood up then, and Kenwick quickly followed.

"If you go near my wife, I won't think twice before killing you," Dylan told him.

"Like you killed those other men and that girl?" Kenwick said tauntingly.

"I didn't kill the girl," Dylan said a little too defensively.

"That's not what Diana said," Kenwick chided.

"Diana is a lunatic," Dylan snapped.

"That is beside the point; I want Claire and I will have her," Kenwick taunted.

"Over my dead body," Dylan told him.

"I told you before that it could be arranged," Kenwick told him.

"Name the time and the place, and I shall be glad to give you the chance to try," Dylan said in a menacing voice.

"The north side of the park in an hour should do nicely," Kenwick responded.

"We will need lighting," Dylan offered.

"Bring a lantern if you're afraid of the dark," Kenwick said with a sinister chuckle, then made for the door.

Dylan watched him leave and wondered what had possessed him to agree to a duel without benefit of seconds. An hour didn't give him much time to prepare, so he quickly left in search of Luther and Jasper. He needed to let one of them know what was going on in the event that he was killed, so they could look after Claire. He went to Annabelle's and hoped that they were true to form and would be there chasing after the notorious twins. When he arrived, Annabelle said that they had not been there yet, but that she expected them within the hour as was their usual habit. He asked her for some parchment and ink and quickly wrote a note for Jasper detailing what had occurred. He left instructions with her to tell them to come to the north side of the park as soon as they arrived. He told her it was a matter of life and death and that they should not delay, and then he quickly set off to the park so he could scout around to see what Kenwick might have planned for him.

He didn't trust him to actually fight him with any kind of honor and suspected that he might try to lay some kind of trap to take him unawares. Kenwick was a clever man, so he would be foolish to underestimate him. He got to the park with twenty minutes to spare and was grateful for the full moon that lit the park adequately enough for him to see with a limited amount of clarity. He didn't see anything amiss, so he walked his horse to a wooded area and tied him to a tree within, and hunkered down so he could wait unseen.

*****

Claire felt like a harridan for the way she had treated Dylan. She didn't understand what had come over her, but she couldn't help herself from trying to provoke him. Just the sight of the man irritated her, and she wanted to rip his head off. She didn't really believe that he had gone to a brothel or had a mistress, but the accusation had come out multiple times, quite beyond her control, and now she had probably driven him away. She was an emotional wreck, and when she wasn't brooding over him she would cry about the loss of the baby. She wanted to take back all the hateful things she had said and done, but she had done so much damage now she wasn't sure he would ever forgive her. All she wanted to do was hold him and tell him how much she loved him, but he had stormed out and went God knows where.

He had been gone a couple of hours now, and she was tired and decided that she wouldn't wait up for him. If and when he came back she would tell him how she really felt and apologize, but in the meantime, she was exhausted. She climbed up the stairs feeling a bit defeated and only wanted to curl up in a ball and go to sleep. Dylan's big bed was so lonely and cold without him that the idea of sleeping in it was depressing. She decided not to call for Lucy as she was still embarrassed about the mess she had caused earlier and thought she could manage alone and spare Lucy the extra work. She opened the door to their chambers and looked longingly at the bed, then started to disrobe. Just as she finished pulling her nightgown over her head, she thought she heard a shuffling sound coming from the dressing room and wondered what Lucy could be doing.

"Lucy?" she called out.

There was no answer, so she approached the

dressing room and stuck her head inside, but she saw nothing there. She thought perhaps she had imagined it and let the matter drop. She climbed into the bed with a weary heart and turned down the lamp beside the bed. What would she do if Dylan wouldn't forgive her?

*****

Dylan heard a snapping twig behind him and turned around quickly to ascertain what it was and was rewarded with a blow to the face by an unseen assailant. He struggled to his feet, realized that there were two men advancing toward him, and he came up swinging. He landed a solid blow to one of the men and heard a grunt and a corresponding thud as the man fell backward, but when the other man launched himself at him, he found that he was very strong and armed with a knife. He swung the knife wildly at Dylan's head and he barely managed to dodge it as it arched down and sliced his shoulder. He cried out at the shock of the wound and tried to reach for his pistol but was quickly overcome when the second assailant recovered and joined his companion in the fray. The second man had a club of some sort and swung it at Dylan's knees, making contact and knocking his legs out from under him. He was quickly subdued then, and the one with the knife straddled his torso and held the weapon to his throat.

"Kenwick said to tell you that he would be fucking your wife as you lay dying," he said with a sinister voice.

Dylan froze at his words, and his veins were filled with ice. Kenwick had tricked him and hired these two blaggards to kill him, so he could go after Claire. He was a fool to have believed that Kenwick had an ounce of honor and would have actually met him here.

"How much did he pay you to kill me?" Dylan growled.

"Two hundred pounds," the smelly cut throat told him with a snicker.

"I will triple it if you spare me," Dylan told him as he used stealth to reach for his pistol.

"Did you hear that Ollie? The duke said he will triple our reward if we spare his worthless hide," he said laughing.

Dylan slid his pistol out of his holster and carefully raised it to the man's chest and cocked it.

"You should have taken the money," he said with cold calculation, then fired the weapon.

The man slumped forward and landed on Dylan. He shoved him out of the way and quickly grabbed his other pistol, but Ollie had been fast and knocked it out of his hand with his club. Dylan tried to scramble to his feet, but the man swung his club again making contact with the side of Dylan's head. The impact was stunning, but it wasn't a killing blow and Dylan rolled away, once again trying to scramble to his feet. The man advanced on him, raised his club high and suddenly froze. He looked down, and Dylan could barely make out a knife lodged in his chest.

"Blast and damn," Ollie grumbled then

collapsed in a heap on the ground.

"Dylan," Luther shouted.

"I'm alright," he grunted.

He had never been so glad to hear Luther's voice in all his life as he made his way to his feet. He was dizzy from the blow to the head, and his right knee was hurt badly.

Luther came closer and looked at the two dead men.

"Who were they?" he asked.

"Kenwick hired them to kill me. I have to get home; he has gone after Claire, and I may already be too late," he said trying to mount his horse.

Luther saw his struggle and came over to assist so he was able to sit atop his mount.

"Where is Jasper?" he asked.

"I don't know; Annabelle said you had left a message for Jasper and that it was a matter of life and death, so I read the message and came as quickly as I could," he told him.

"We had better be hurry then," Dylan said, prodding his horse to proceed.

Dylan was worried sick about Claire and hoped he would be on time before … God, he had to hurry.

Chapter Thirty-two

Claire had just fallen asleep when Dylan slipped into the bed beside her. She opened her eyes when she felt his hands moving over her breasts as his touch didn't feel quite right.

"Dylan?" she spoke his name.

He didn't answer but continued to massage her breast, and then he covered her with his body and kissed her on the mouth. Claire knew instantly that it wasn't Dylan and began to struggle under the weight of the man.

"Shhh … don't fight it, my love," a familiar voice crooned.

Claire went still and her mind was reeling, trying to understand what was happening. Was this a nightmare? She didn't think so because it seemed all too real. He moved his hand lower and started lifting her nightgown and began to kiss her again. Claire cried out, and he quickly placed a hand over her mouth to silence her.

"I have waited a long time for you Claire, and I will wait no more," he told her.

Claire shook her head and tried to buck him off of her, but he was heavy and she was unable to budge his weight. She realized then that he was nude from the waist up, but she was relieved that he was still wearing his trousers. Her relief was short-lived, however, when he nudged her thighs apart with his knee and moved his hand between them to unbutton his pants. Claire cried out again and struggled with all her might when his intentions became clear.

"You can make this hard, or you can lie back and enjoy it; either way I will have you," he grunted as he struggled to position himself at her entrance.

Claire felt his shaft touch her entrance and bucked him wildly then, and she actually managed to slide out from under him. She tried to jump from the bed, but he grabbed her from behind, flung her back down on her back and slapped her hard across the face. The blow left her ears ringing and stunned, and it took her a moment to realize that he had ripped her gown and exposed her breasts to his view. She was about to scream, but he lunged forward and covered her mouth with his hand and started kissing her breasts frantically. She quickly started thrashing wildly, but her efforts were futile when he subdued her with a blow to the side of the head that left her somewhat disoriented.

"You belong to me now Claire as it should have been. There are no longer any obstacles to our union as I have made sure that murdering husband of yours will no longer plague us," he taunted.

Claire's mind was foggy, and his words hadn't made sense. She wanted to fight against him, but her head was ringing, and she felt on the verge of blacking out from the savage blow to her head. She lay there in a blank stupor and seemed unaware of his actions as he continued to grope at her body. He ran a hand down her throat and moved downward to her breasts and pinched her nipple hard to make it peak. He moaned and dipped his head lower to suckle her as he positioned his body between her thighs again. Claire knew she should be resisting him, but she was quite unable to move. What had he said about Dylan?

"I'm glad to see that you have decided to be cooperative," he told her as he ground his hard member against her woman's flesh.

Claire came alive then and began to fight him like a wildcat. She growled and bucked and thrashed with all her strength and raked her nails across his face just barely missing his eyes. He howled in pain, grabbed her by the hair, slapped her hard across the face and then wrapped his hands around her throat and squeezed.

"You stupid bitch; can you not see that you belong to me?" he said in a harsh tone.

Claire could feel herself losing consciousness after a moment, and then he was gone. She gasped for air and slowly became aware of a struggle across the room. She scrambled to the bedside table, turned up the lamp and cried out at the sight before her. Dylan and Mr. Ensley were engaged in a brutal battle, and Dylan was bleeding and looked to be losing the fight. Mr. Ensley had his hands wrapped around Dylan's throat, and he was struggling to remove his grip. She heard bones crunching as Dylan peeled his fingers back, and Mr. Ensley howled in pain and released his hold. Dylan got the break he needed then and landed a forceful blow to his nose, sending him falling over backwards. Dylan jumped up and straddled him, and it was then that Luther appeared in the doorway and took in the sight before him. Luther pulled out his pistol and handed it to Dylan, and he placed it at the side of Mr. Ensley's head.

"Tell me why I shouldn't kill you now

Kenwick," Dylan asked him in a menacing voice.

Claire gasped and cried out.

"Please Dylan, he isn't worth it," she begged.

"Did he rape you?" he asked without looking back at her.

"He tried but ..." her words were cut off as Mr. Ensley started laughing.

"She lies," he taunted.

Claire gasped.

"Don't listen to him Dylan; he did not rape me," she told him adamantly.

"My cock touched her sweet quivering honey-pot, and my lips were wrapped around her luscious nipples," he continued his taunt.

Dylan roared and slammed the pistol into the side of his head, knocking him unconscious.

Dylan got off of him and turned to glare at Claire. "Luther, please leave the room," he said with an ice cold voice.

"What about this worthless sack of shite," he said, kicking Mr. Ensley in the leg.

"He is harmless for the moment," Dylan said never taking his eyes off of Claire.

Claire felt more fear now than she had with Mr. Ensley as the look in Dylan's eyes was murderous. Luther left the room and Claire shrunk back as Dylan advanced toward the bed. She moved to the far side of the bed to keep distance between them.

"Is what he said true?" he calmly asked.

Claire was afraid to answer, and her body was trembling.

"He ... he ... d-didn't rape m-me," she stammered.

"But he touched you … there … with his …?" he prodded, unable to finish the question.

Claire lowered her head in shame because Mr. Ensley had touched her there with his privates, but she didn't want to admit it.

"Claire? I need to know if he … harmed you," he insisted.

Claire looked up and screamed as Mr. Ensley was standing behind Dylan with a knife raised high. Dylan quickly turned around and fired the pistol at him, killing him instantly. Luther burst back into the room and stopped cold when he saw that Mr. Ensley was dead. He looked up at Dylan, then over at Claire and back at Mr. Ensley. Just then, Simmons who was bleeding from a nasty head wound came to the door, followed by a hysterical Lucy.

"I'm sorry your grace, but I was caught unawares by the blaggard and he struck me with a candle holder," Simmons explained.

Lucy ran into the dressing room and came back with a robe for Claire, and she gratefully put it on, having just realized that she had been exposed for all to see.

"Luther, get a couple of footman together and remove this rubbish from my wife's presence," Dylan said calmly.

"Simmons if you are well enough, send for the magistrate and a surgeon, and Lucy please tend to my wife," he said before collapsing to the floor with a grunt.

Claire rushed over to him and lifted his head into her arms.

"You're hurt," she exclaimed.

Claire moved his jacket off of his shoulder and gasped at all the blood on his shirt.

"Please someone help me get him to the bed," she cried out.

Luther was there quickly, picking him up in his strong arms, carrying him to the bed, and gently laying him down.

"Please, Mr. Simmons, hurry and fetch the surgeon; my husband is dying," she cried.

Dylan's eyes fluttered open.

"I have no plans for dying," he grunted.

Claire wiped his brow with a cloth that Lucy handed her.

"Shhh my love, don't talk now," she told him.

"Did he ..." Claire cut his words off with a hand over his mouth.

She shook her head and kissed his forehead.

"You came in time, my love," she told him with a trembling smile.

Dylan looked at her with tears in his eyes, and then he swooned into unconsciousness. Claire held him tight and wept.

*****

Dylan came around an hour later as the surgeon was stitching up his wound. He groaned and gritted his teeth against the stinging pain, and felt a gentle squeeze on his hand.

He looked over and saw Claire there with concern in her eyes, and he could clearly see the bruises on her face and neck that he hadn't noticed earlier.

"Did you see to my wife?" he asked the doctor.

"Your wife will be fine; it is you who is bleeding like a slaughtered pig," the man grumbled as he continued his sewing.

Dylan looked at his wife and was grateful that she hadn't been ... he shook his head at the thought. He didn't want to think about what could have happened had he not arrived when he did. When he saw the man strangling her, he lost all sense of reasoning and tried to kill him with his bare hands. It was foolish to try, considering his wounds, but he had been beyond rational thought. Things could have gone a lot worse had Luther not been there tonight, and he would never be able to thank him enough for what he had done. Claire was safe and that was all that mattered.

"Where is Luther?" he asked.

"Explaining things to the magistrate," Claire told him.

Dylan sighed; he supposed there would be an inquest into what had transpired. A peer of the realm had died here and that was not something easily swept away.

"There we are; all done," the doctor said admiring his work with a smile.

"I must insist that you see to my wife," Dylan told him.

"Of course, your grace, but there is little I can do about the bruising," he told him.

"He tried to rape her, and I want to be sure ... I need to know that she is unharmed," he told him.

Claire felt a ripple of anger course through her. He didn't believe that Mr. Ensley hadn't raped her.

"Dylan, I told you that I am unharmed," she told him firmly.

"Humor me," he told her.

Claire sighed and stood up beside the bed.

"Follow me," she told the doctor.

Claire led him out of the room and into the bedroom that was joined to the master chamber. She was angry and humiliated that she would have to suffer through an examination because Dylan couldn't take her word that she was unmolested. She lay down on the bed with a huff and assumed the position, and the doctor made his examination without further ado. Once it was over, she got up from the bed and marched back into the master chambers with the doctor following in her wake. She walked over to her vanity and started running a brush angrily through her hair while the doctor quietly conferred with Dylan. She strained her ears to hear what was being said, but she was unable to make anything out. After a few moments of intense discussion between Dylan and the doctor, he gave instructions to Dylan on how to attend his wounds and promised to call again on the morrow. When he left, Claire hurled her hairbrush at Dylan, missing him by just inches.

"You couldn't have just taken my word for it?" she demanded.

"That is not why I had him examine you," he told her with a look of mischief in his eyes.

"Then why would you have humiliated me in such a way?" she asked.

"Because I wanted to know if I could make love to my wife without harming her," he shouted as he struggled to his feet.

Claire gasped.

"Yes, I want to make love to my wife; is that so horrible?" he demanded.

"But you are injured," she said incredulously.

"I m not dead," he said as he limped toward her.

Claire jumped up from her chair and ran over to him.

"You get back in that bed this instant," she admonished.

"Only if you come with me," he grunted.

Claire groaned with exasperation and started leading him back to the bed.

"I will lay down with you Dylan, but you couldn't possibly make love in your condition," she insisted.

Dylan grabbed her by the wrist.

"I need to make love to you Claire," he insisted.

"But ..." she tried to protest, but he pulled her onto the bed.

"Now," he insisted.

"But ..." again her words were cut off.

"Woman, you will allow your husband to make love to you," he demanded.

"How dare ..." again he cut her off.

"You have been a horror to live with Claire, and the only thing that is going to change it is for me to show you how much I love you, and I desperately need to make love to you," he told her.

"I have not been a horror," she retorted.

"Oh, you have been a living nightmare my

love," he told her, untying her robe and baring her breasts.

"You haven't been a prince yourself," she told him.

"I think I have handled myself quite gallantly, considering you were trying to kill me," he said as he ran his hand between her breasts and then moved it lower until he found her woman's flesh.

"I need this; you need this," he said, taking her firmly in his hand, kneading her flesh.

Claire felt herself heating up, and she lifted her hips in invitation.

"I'm afraid you will have to do most of the work," he said with a pained expression.

He lay on his back and tugged her wrist.

"Ride me Claire," he told her.

Chapter Thirty-three

Claire collapsed in exhaustion on Dylan's chest and marveled at his endurance when he surely must have been in agony. She hadn't been as gentle as she should have been because she had been so swept away by the blissful pleasure he gave her that she hadn't given his wounds much thought.

"Do you feel better now?" he asked softly in her ear as he stroked her back.

"Mmmm," she said.

"There will be no more tantrums and bouts of madness?" he asked with a chuckle.

"I was bad wasn't I?" she asked.

"Terrifying," he told her with a kiss on her cheek.

Claire gingerly sat up and slid off of him and nestled closely at his uninjured side.

"I'm sorry Dylan," she told him.

"Don't be; you were reacting to the miscarriage," he told her.

"Yes, but I treated you deplorably," she said rubbing her nose on his chest.

"I can take it," he told her with a gentle squeeze on her bottom.

"I was angry because I lost our baby," she told him.

"I know but we will have others," he said softly.

"I wanted that one," she pouted.

"So did I," he murmured.

"I hope I am with child again," she told him.

"I kind of like the idea of having you all to

myself for awhile," he told her.

"I suppose that would be nice too," she agreed.

"I love you Claire," he said almost inaudibly.

"I love you too Dylan," she said softly.

She was answered by a light snore, and she smiled. The poor man was exhausted and wounded, and all he cared about was pleasing her. She felt shame that she had behaved so badly and would endeavor to make it up to him with every waking moment for the rest of her life. She closed her eyes, and soon she followed him into a peaceful sleep.

*****

Dylan was awakened, pleasantly aroused during the night as Claire was exploring his body with her soft delicate hands. When she realized that he was awake, she leaned forward and kissed him passionately, and with a groan and great effort, he flipped her over on her back, nudging her legs apart before taking her with a fierce hunger. It caused pain in his knee, but he didn't care as he plunged in and out of her hot, wet sheath, and the sounds of her ecstasy were like a balm to his wounds, making him feel invincible. He could endure any manner of torture for her sweet loving and did so with a blind euphoria.

"You are mine," he growled as he moved in and out with sheer determination.

"Yes!" she exclaimed as she thrust her hips forward to meet him stroke for stroke.

He reached under her buttocks, lifted her, increased the depth of his thrusts, and her outcry spurred him on with even greater force. He knew that he was handling her a bit roughly, but she seemed to revel in it as she grabbed his own buttocks in a tight grasp as if she were trying to force him even deeper. Dylan was on the verge of his climax but didn't want to release until she had found her own. He lowered his head and took the tip of her breast into his mouth, laved her nipple with his tongue then gently bit down with his teeth.

"Come for me, Claire," he gritted out and applied a little more pressure with his teeth.

He moved to the other breast and gave it the same attention as he had the other, and she quickly tensed and arched her back, locking her thighs tightly around him and beginning to tremble violently. Dylan's response was immediate, and he followed with a shout and violent tremors of his own. He collapsed on her then and buried his face in her neck and lovingly kissed her on her pulse which was pounding against his lips.

"Naughty minx," he whispered in her ear.

She laughed breathlessly, and he slid off of her to avoid smothering her with his weight.

"I was curious," she said with a pant.

"About?" he asked as he pulled her into his embrace.

She dipped her head and pressed her nose against his nipple, but didn't respond.

"You need not be embarrassed with your husband," he urged her.

"I wanted to see how big it was while you were sleeping," she finally said.

Dylan laughed and squeezed her close.

"Did it meet your expectations?" he asked.

"I really think it has a mind of its own," she said with a giggle.

"To be true; it most certainly does," he told her.

"Every time I touched you, it grew harder and longer, and it flinched when I tickled it," she said with a snicker.

"You tickled it?" he asked incredulously.

"Yes, because it danced around when I did," she said as if in disbelief.

"It wanted you," he told her.

"I confess that I wanted it too," she said, and he could feel the warmth of her blush.

"That's a good thing my love; I only wish my knee didn't hurt so I could show you all the ways that we can pleasure one another. Alas, it will have to wait until I am healed; you don't mind too much do you?" he asked.

"I promise not to throw things at you in my frustration," she teased.

"That's a good thing too, my love," he said kissing the top of her head.

*****

In the week that followed Dylan recovered fairly well, and with the use of a cane he could move around quite freely and was able to have an interview with the magistrate to answer all the questions about the incident with Kenwick. With his interview and Luther's, it was decided that it was a matter of self defense, and no charges would be brought against Dylan for his death. The magistrate looked into Kenwick's background during the week that Dylan was recovering and discovered that he had become something of a bad actor over the last few years and was involved in a number of unsavory business practices, namely human trafficking to fill his depleting family coffers.

Dylan shuddered to imagine what might have become of Claire had the man not been obsessed with having her as his wife but, instead, had tried to sell her into slavery as he had so many others during the course of his unscrupulous career. Dylan offered his financial assistance in trying to recover as many of his victims as he could, but the magistrate told him it would prove next to impossible as most of his victims had been sold to the Barbary Corsairs and would likely never be heard from again. Dylan urged him to try his best and made his fortune available for the task and took his leave of the magistrate's office. He wanted to go home and hold his wife after all he had learned, and he couldn't get to her soon enough.

Though their lovemaking had been limited by Dylan's knee injury, he and Claire had taken every opportunity to relish in their union, and her behavior had improved dramatically. She still seemed sad from time to time about the loss of the child, but her tantrums had become non-existent, much to Dylan's relief. He had decided that a honeymoon trip was in order and planned to take her on a tour of the continent. He had instructed Simmons to book passage on the Rosalynn, which would depart in three days. He hadn't yet told Claire as he was hoping to surprise her with the news tonight at dinner. He would have liked to take her to America so he could see her former home, but the war between their countries was in full scale, and it wouldn't be safe to make an Atlantic crossing at any time in the foreseeable future.

He knew that Claire missed her home in Virginia, but since it had been sold, there really wasn't much reason to return. Perhaps, in time, he could purchase an estate in Virginia as an anniversary gift to her, and they could go there when the peace returned. Claire didn't like to speak of her way of life there as she was raised on a tobacco plantation that was built on the back of slavery, and she told him that she hadn't really seen the cruelty in it until she came to England, where servants were treated fairly and earned a living from their labors. Perhaps, in time, her country would see the wrong in it and make the ratifying steps toward ending it. It was still a young nation, but there was a lot of promise in its greatness, but change like that took time and maturity. After a stop by the florist to purchase a bouquet of roses, he arrived at home just in time for dinner. Claire was waiting for him and met him at the door, throwing her arms around him and weeping.

"What's this?" he asked alarmed as he stroked her back soothingly.

"I thought they were going to take you away from me and hang you," she cried out.

Dylan gasped at the thought that she had been distraught all afternoon as she hadn't shown anything beyond a mild concern when he left.

"I told you it would be fine and that there was

nothing to worry about," he told her.

"I know, but it took so long that I began to get nervous, and then fear set in, and I began to panic," she said with a hiccup.

"I'm sorry that you suffered so, my love," he told her, pulling away and handing her the roses.

Claire took them with a sniff, put them up to her face and breathed in deeply.

"Next time skip the florist and come straight home," she admonished with a pout.

"Had I known that you were wracked with worry, I wouldn't have wasted a single second," he told her.

"It was awful; I probably have gray hair now."

Dylan made a show of looking over her hair with great interest, reached up, plucked a stray hair, and closely examined it.

"Still blonde," he said with a smile.

She playfully swatted his arm, slid her arm beneath his, and guided him to the dining room.

"I have a surprise for you," he told her.

"A surprise?" she asked delightedly.

"Yes, we are going on a honeymoon trip to the continent," he told her with a grin and a twinkle in his blue eyes.

Claire squealed and nearly knocked him over when she began jumping up and down while still holding onto his arm. When his cane fell over, she quickly came to her senses and expressed her joy with more caution. She hugged him, lifted her lips to his, and kissed him sweetly.

"That will be wonderful Dylan. When do we leave?" she asked.

Dylan urged her toward her chair, pulled it out for her, and she sat while he took the seat at the head of the table beside her.

"Three days," he said after he was settled.

"Why Dylan Crenshaw, that hardly gives me any time at all to order new gowns and get my things packed," she complained.

Dylan sighed; he hadn't thought of that in his attempt to surprise his wife.

"You can order new gowns abroad; our first stop will be Paris," he said with a smile.

"Paris?" she said, blinking her eyes.

"You know; in France," he said in jest.

"Yes I know where Paris is Dylan but do you really mean we are going there, and that I will actually get to have gowns made there?" she demanded.

"As many as you like," he said grinning.

"I can't believe it. I will actually have the latest fashion from Paris without having to wait a year for it to reach America," she marveled.

"Believe it," he told her.

"Oh, this is wonderful, Dylan," she said placing her hand over his.

Dylan placed his other hand over hers and lifted it to his lips for a sultry kiss on the palm.

"You are wonderful Claire," he told her.

"And so are you my love," she told him a little breathlessly.

"Now, do you want to hear about the interview with the magistrate?" he asked her.

"Oh yes, please do tell me all about it and leave nothing out, do you hear me?" she commanded.

Dylan told her all that he had learned and Claire was aghast at the news.

"And he said you were a bad man!" she said indignantly.

"He wasn't always like that, but his family fell on hard times, and he had to bring in revenue for his coffers. I suspect he had learned about your dowry and thought to marry a fortune to that end as well," he told her.

"I suppose that two hundred thousand pounds was very attractive to a man like that," she admitted.

"Yes, but I think he was beyond caring about your money and simply wanted you," he said with a tightening of his jaw.

"Well we are rid of him now, and I wish to never think of him again," she told him.

"I agree, we shall never mention him again," he said kissing her hand.

After dinner, Claire and Dylan made passionate love until they were both exhausted and completely sated, and Dylan's last thought before he fell asleep was how wonderful living could really be.

Epilogue

Claire and Dylan returned from their honeymoon trip six months later as traveling had become dangerous for Claire in her condition, and Dylan didn't want to take any chances with her well-being. She was well into her fourth month of pregnancy now and had started to show with a small mound low in her belly. Claire realized that Dylan was happier now than she had ever seen him and that it was a rare occurrence when he was not making jokes and teasing her about something. She loved this side of him and hoped that it was a permanent condition as she was deeply in love with him. She had seen him at his worst and loved him even then, but this man … this man who was her husband was the most beautiful creature she had ever had the pleasure to know, and she felt fortunate to be his duchess.

They had gotten used to their titles now, more or less, and while they were on their trip, they had made plans for the things that they would do to influence society. Claire decided that she would like to help Alyssa with her good works as well as pursue her writing. That would have to wait until the birth of their child, however, as Dylan didn't want anything to jeopardize the health of her or the child. Dylan, on the other hand, had decided to take his seat in the House of Lords, and together with Gabriel would try to use his influence for the betterment of England's working class, which was in keeping with the work his grandfather had done. She was proud of him for it, though she didn't really like the idea of having to reside in London for so much of the year.

They had decided to make Blackstone their permanent home, and were in route, but had to make a quick stop at Pembrook along the way at the behest of Jasper who had completed his flying machine and wanted to give an exhibition of its maiden flight for his friends. Dylan learned upon their return that Jasper had been consumed with his invention and had nearly driven poor Luther crazy as he had been given the task of monitoring Jasper's well-being, which proved to be a rather hectic task.

"I thought you were going to be the pilot," Gabriel teased Luther.

"Jasper wouldn't turn his precious machine over to just anyone; you know that," Luther responded.

Claire stood off to the side with Alyssa as the three men stood there picking at one another while Jasper was preparing to board the craft. The thing looked like the skeleton of some kind of prehistoric monstrous bird made of wood and twisted metal, and Claire shivered with dread.

"I have a bad feeling about this," Alyssa said.

"It does look rather dangerous," Claire agreed.

"The man is a lunatic if you ask me," Alyssa grumbled.

"Are those rockets?" Claire asked.

"Uh huh, two of them," she explained.

"Oh, I don't like the sound of this at all," Claire said.

Jasper called for Luther to come over and instructed him on lighting the rockets on the count of five, then cautioned him to run as quick and as far away as he could, advising everyone else to move farther away from the craft. Claire, Dylan, Alyssa and Gabriel moved about ten yards back, and Jasper gave the signal for Luther to light the rockets. He lit them and did as he was told, running quickly in their direction and reaching them just in time to turn and see the craft shoot forward and quickly speed out of control, flipping end over end until it came to a devastating crashing halt about two hundred yards away.

There was a cloud of smoke; the thing was laying in pieces, and Jasper had been flung out of the machine about seventy five yards away. The men quickly ran in to him, and Claire and Alyssa followed at a much slower pace given that they were both pregnant, Alyssa further along than Claire. By the time they had reached the men, they were all frantic as they were looking over Jasper's wounds. He was unconscious, and he looked broken in many places, but he was still breathing.

Jasper had planned for this eventuality as there was a wagon padded with cushions and blankets and a medical kit inside equipped with a long board, rope bandages, splints and laudanum complete with instructions on their use. Gabriel and Luther lifted Jasper into the back of the wagon, and Dylan jumped up there and started dressing his head wound to stop the bleeding. Then he and Gabriel slid a board under his body and tied him down with the rope, and once they were sure he was secure, Luther hopped on the driver's bench, and they all made their way to Jasper's home. Gabriel and

Dylan carried Jasper to his room, and Luther went to fetch the surgeon. While Luther was away, Jasper regained consciousness with a string of curses such as Claire had never heard.

"The blasted thing wouldn't fly! I couldn't get lift off," he complained.

"No, but it sure shot off quickly; I have never seen anything go so fast," Gabriel told him.

"It was fast wasn't it?" Jasper asked with a laughing grunt.

"You fool; you could have killed yourself," Dylan chided.

"Oh, but what a way to go," Jasper said, then promptly passed out.

The doctor came shortly after and examined Jasper. He quickly went to work setting his many broken bones. Jasper awoke briefly again, but the doctor dosed him up with laudanum and said that he would need to be kept dosed heavily for the next four weeks so his bones could set properly. The surgeon cautioned them all that his wounds were many, and it was conceivable that Jasper may never walk again, that only time would tell the tale. Everyone was devastated by the news, and it was decided that Luther would stay with him for the next few months to help him along. They all made plans to stay for a week to see him through the worst of it, but none of them had a good feeling about his future.

"Whatever will become of him?" Claire asked with a heavy heart as they were readying for bed.

"Don't count him out just yet my love," Dylan told her with a kiss on her forehead.

"He may never walk again," she said on a sob.

"You don't know Jasper like I do; the man has the determination to conquer any obstacle set in his path. Do not despair; it isn't good for the baby," he scolded.

"You're right of course, but it's so distressing," she told him, drying her eyes.

Claire felt a thump in her stomach, gasped, and put her hand on the spot.

"What is it?" Dylan asked in alarm.

"The baby kicked me," she said with a look of complete surprise.

Dylan was relieved and brought her into his arms.

"He was agreeing with his papa," he whispered in her ear.

Claire laughed softly and jumped as he kicked her again. She grabbed Dylan's hand and led it to the spot, and after a moment he kicked again and Dylan threw his head back and roared with laughter. Watching the miracle of Dylan taking pleasure in their child's growth, Claire believed in her heart that if her husband could be resurrected from the depths of his misery, then Jasper too, could survive this devastation and would one day fully recover.

ABOUT THE AUTHOR

My father was a great storyteller and always said that one day he would like to write a novel. My sister is a writer as well, so naturally I'm a dabbler. I thought I'd try my hand at writing romance novels because I love to read them. Romance novels have everything you want, mysteries, villains, wonderful characters, and I easily find myself living in the moment with the story. I hope that readers will find my stories as entertaining as I have found so many. I like to mix tragedy and comedy together with a cast of colorful characters that I create from people that I have met in my life. I will visualize a person that I know as this or that character, and the rest is history.

I hope you enjoy my warped sense of humor and the stories that I tell. If you happened upon this book first, please read Book 1 of the "Brothers In All" series, "My Sweet Alyssa.

Gina Rose is the pseudonym for a very prolific author who spins tales in the Regency Romance genre.

Look for many more of her books to be available soon at most online stores.

Check her website, ginarose-author.com, often for more information and reviews.